The Year We Fell Apart

EMILY MARTIN

SIMON PULSE

NEW YORK   LONDON   TORONTO   SYDNEY   NEW DELHI

This book is a work of fiction. Any references to historical events, real people, or real places are used fictitiously. Other names, characters, places, and events are products of the author's imagination, and any resemblance to actual events or places or persons, living or dead, is entirely coincidental.

SIMON PULSE

An imprint of Simon & Schuster Children's Publishing Division
1230 Avenue of the Americas, New York, New York 10020
First Simon Pulse hardcover edition January 2016
Text copyright © 2016 by Emily Martin
Jacket illustration copyright © 2016 by Sarah Dennis
All rights reserved, including the right of reproduction
in whole or in part in any form.
SIMON PULSE and colophon are registered
trademarks of Simon & Schuster, Inc.
For information about special discounts for bulk purchases, please contact
Simon & Schuster Special Sales at 1-866-506-1949
or business@simonandschuster.com.
The Simon & Schuster Speakers Bureau can bring authors to your live event. For more
information or to book an event contact the Simon & Schuster Speakers Bureau
at 1-866-248-3049 or visit our website at www.simonspeakers.com.
Jacket designed by Karina Granda
Interior designed by Tom Daly
The text of this book was set in Adobe Garamond Pro.
Manufactured in the United States of America
2 4 6 8 10 9 7 5 3 1
Library of Congress Cataloging-in-Publication Data
Martin, Emily, 1987–
The year we fell apart / by Emily Martin. — First Simon Pulse hardcover edition.
p. cm.
Summary: A year ago Harper made the biggest mistake of her life by destroying
her relationship with her best friend and first love, Declan, so now that he is home
from boarding school for the summer, Harper has three months to fix the year of
miscommunications, secrets, and lies or finally let go altogether.
[1. Love—Fiction. 2. Friendship—Fiction.] I. Title.
PZ7.1.M373Ye 2015
[Fic]—dc23
2014048842
ISBN 978-1-4814-3841-4 (hc)
ISBN 978-1-4814-3843-8 (eBook)

To Jim

One

SOMETIMES I THINK THE WHITE OAK TREE WAS listening that night last August. That it knows about the promises we made to each other up in our tree house. That it knows I kept only half of mine.

I circle the oak's trunk—trying to make sense of the bright orange *X* spray-painted across it—and wait for Cory to catch up. The graffiti should come as a relief: Soon the tree will be gone, and another reminder of that night with Declan gone with it.

"Dude." Cory doubles over, resting his palms on his knees. "What is the *matter* with you?"

My fingertips trace the bark. "They're going to cut it down."

"What? Harper, you almost gave me a heart attack. Who jumps out of a moving vehicle?"

Please. We weren't even driving that fast. "The trees up by the road were marked and I couldn't tell how far into the forest it went. I needed to know if ours was tagged too."

"Hey, here's an idea. What if next time you wait for me to pull over before sprinting into the woods like an insane person?"

Light filters through the trees and paints the undergrowth a golden yellow. I've spent countless afternoons in this part of the forest, but today it feels different somehow. Like it's no longer a place of my own.

I close my eyes and listen for the spray of an aerosol can or some sign of the people responsible for marking the area, but all I hear is Cory mouth-breathing and the leaves shuddering on their limbs.

"You don't think it's our fault, do you?" I gaze back up at the tree house, the sanctuary that Cory, Declan, and I built six summers ago when we were eleven. We pooled our allowances for months to buy the supplies and spent most of the school year meticulously planning the design, being extra careful to use supports to take the stress off the tree. The floor still turned out crooked, and there's a hole the size of a quarter in the shingled roof. But it's ours.

Cory points to the matching *X*'s on nearby trees, all the color of Doritos dust. "I don't think it's because of the tree house. They're probably clearing the area for development or something."

"Oh." My palm runs across one of the boards we nailed to the trunk for a makeshift ladder. The wood is splintered along the edge and I pick at it with my fingernail. I try to remember all the stuff we left behind—a deck of playing cards, maybe the binoculars Declan took from his parents' garage. And a blanket. A scratchy wool blanket, also borrowed from Declan's house. Everything neat and organized, waiting for us to come back. I want to climb up now and see if it's all still there, but I won't. Can't. Haven't since last summer. "I assumed it was sick."

Cory scrunches his nose to lift his glasses. He looks at the tree house, finally. Then back at me, wearing a smile that's a little too sympathetic. "We should get going. My mom wants me home for dinner."

Mine does too. But after last night's unsettling family sit-down, I may never eat dinner again.

"Listen, Harper . . ." Cory swats away a mosquito and shuffles his feet. The bed of soggy leaves squishes beneath him. "I'm really sorry . . . you know, about your mom."

My fingers freeze. I haven't told him yet, but I can't say I'm surprised he's already heard. Our moms are best friends, plus Bridget is a doctor.

A lump swells in my throat. I swallow, swallow again, then stuff my hands in my back pockets. "Thanks."

He knuckles his glasses farther up his nose. "You okay?"

My eyes travel up once more, landing on the window on the side of the tree house. A memory surfaces, of me and Declan and Cory armed with water guns, ready to defend our turf.

I shake it off and start walking in the direction of the road. It rained all yesterday, and with each step my sandals fling a few more specks of mud up the backs of my legs.

"Can you just drop me at Sadie's?" I ask.

He doesn't answer until his ancient silver Honda comes into view through the trees. "You sure that's a good idea?"

"Yep. Thanks."

We don't talk on the way back through town. The air conditioner in Cory's car has seen better days, so I lean out the open window and let the sticky breeze tangle my hair. Sunlight glints off the shop windows along Ninth Street and the windshields of cars we pass, and I have to make a visor with my hand to keep my eyes from watering.

When we stop in front of Sadie's town house, I lick my thumb and rub some dirt off my thigh. Cory fidgets with the radio, finally settling on an alt-rock station. But his fingers keep on tapping, and now he's sending me all these sidelong glances.

"Would you stop looking at me like that?"

"Like what?"

"Like I'm a bird with a broken wing."

He squeezes his eyes shut. "Better?"

I flick his shoulder and grab my purse off the floor just as Sadie throws her front door open. She struts over and bends down, draping her forearms across my window. She catches sight of my mud-stained legs and scowls. "It's a good thing we have a few minutes before the guys get here."

I should have cleaned up before coming over. Should be wearing mascara and the lacy black top Sadie bought me for my last birthday. Plus something closer to excitement on my face, because it's the summer before senior year, and that's how we planned it.

The car jolts a few inches forward. Sadie jumps back and Cory stifles a grin. "Sorry. Foot slipped."

Sadie glares at him and I open my door before he can do any more damage. "I'll see you later, okay?"

Cory lifts two fingers off the steering wheel in a lazy goodbye.

"We're still on for the quarry tomorrow?" I ask over my shoulder.

"Yeah, sure."

I step out onto the sidewalk and watch him drive away. Sadie pulls me inside and up to her room. She grabs a pack of makeup-removing wipes off her vanity and hands one over. "So. He asked about you again."

The cloth darkens as I scrub the backs of my calves. "He who?"

"Kyle Marcell. He's coming out tonight, with Will."

"Kyle," I repeat.

I try to focus on this new name, but my head is scattered all across Carson County. My dining room table, where my family is gathered without me. Underwater at the quarry, where I can scream without anyone hearing. And especially the tree house in the middle of the forest, where I still feel the ghost of the girl I used to be.

Sadie's phone vibrates on her vanity. She checks the message and her lips creep into a smile.

She doesn't notice I'm not smiling back.

A beat-up Ford Mustang stops at the curb. Will's Mustang.

Kyle gets out and pulls the passenger's seat forward. His angular face is partially obscured by expensive-looking sunglasses, and his narrow mouth is stretched into a smirk. I cast Sadie a quick glance and crawl into the cramped backseat. Kyle slides in after me.

He moved to Carson a year ago, and although we had two classes together last semester, we've exchanged only a handful of words. One time he borrowed a pen from me and never gave it back. And he plays lacrosse. This is the extent of what I know about Kyle Marcell.

He's wearing a T-shirt with an outline of Michigan on it that says AMERICA'S HIGH FIVE.

I gesture to the logo. "Is that where you're from originally?"

Kyle pulls at the bottom of the shirt and looks down, as if he forgot what he had on. "Oh. No."

The conversation dies on the spot. Meanwhile, Sadie closes

her door and the smell of pot mingled with Kyle's acrid cologne gets trapped inside. And something cloying—a pineapple air freshener dangling from the rearview mirror. A headache brews behind my eyes and I start breathing through my mouth.

Kyle takes off the sunglasses and slouches down beside me, his eyes bloodshot and heavy-lidded. His knee falls out to the side and bumps against mine.

Will puts the car in gear. "What do you ladies feel like doing tonight?"

Somehow I don't feel any less trapped here than at home. But every escape has its catch, and beggars can't be choosers. So as Kyle's arm slides across my bare shoulders, I don't angle away or shrug him off. I sit perfectly still and stare out the window.

"Anything," Sadie drawls in the voice guys always find irresistible. She turns her head toward Will. "We're up for anything."

Will's parents are conveniently out of town until next Tuesday. We go to his house. He swipes a bottle of vodka from the liquor cabinet and Sadie contributes two cans of Boomerang Energy Enhancement.

Boomerang, for the record, tastes mildly of dish detergent and perfume. But Sadie is woefully addicted and at the moment, I'm not overly picky.

I chase a large shot with a small sip of Boomerang. Sadie sidles up to me and uses my phone as a mirror while she reapplies her lip gloss. She dips down and presses her lips lightly onto mine, and I smooth the lip gloss she left behind across my mouth. And just like that, the boys are hooked.

This flirtation comes standard with Sadie, as forced as it might feel to me. Sadie is a lot of things I'm not: glamorous, brazen, and blond, for starters. Add her C-cup to the mix, and it's really not all that surprising she has the effect she does on guys.

Approximately ninety seconds later, Will grabs Sadie's hand and they disappear behind his bedroom door. I take another shot.

Will's kitchen is modern with stainless steel everything. A lighthouse calendar hangs on the wall above the light switch. Mom has the same one. I pour myself a third drink and walk over to the calendar, turn the page from May to June. Then I begin a self-guided tour of the house. I find a small, dimly lit den situated off the far side of the kitchen.

Leaning against the door frame to the den, I down the shot and grip the glass in my fist, then turn back to the kitchen, where Kyle is perched on a bar stool at the island. He's watching me but seems reluctant to come any closer. Probably because aside from that first failed inquiry into Kyle's past, I haven't uttered a single word since the guys picked us up an hour ago.

"Come here," I say, not even trying to sound alluring like Sadie.

He takes his time, like he could think of a dozen other places he'd rather be. Right.

Kyle stops in front of me and squares his shoulders. He's

close to my height, maybe half an inch shorter. I can't recall whether he always has this drowsy look on his face, or if he's just stoned. I nod my head to the couch. "Sit."

"Bossy, aren't you?"

He hesitates a moment longer, then slips past me and sits on the black leather sofa. His eyebrows rise like he's waiting for his next order.

Setting the empty glass down on the coffee table, I edge closer. I guess Kyle is decent-looking, in a preppy-jock-gone-hipster kind of way. His jeans are a bit too tight for my taste, but why sweat the small stuff?

Kyle's sudden interest in hanging out with me probably has more to do with the rumors about what happened after-hours in the school pool this past spring than the fact that I loaned him a pen that one time. And I've been careful since the pool incident, determined not to give my classmates any more ammunition. The problem is, tonight I don't care.

Tonight I need a distraction. So without another word, I slide onto the couch and straddle Kyle. His too-cool-for-school act wears off pretty quickly after that.

He meets me halfway, his mouth moving slowly against mine at first, but building momentum as one hand grips my hair.

Kyle's not a bad kisser, per se. Just not my preferred style. Exhibit A: What is happening with his tongue? Maybe he's trying that thing where you spell out the alphabet? Except he seems to have only awkward letters like *k* and *z* in his arsenal. Or he doesn't know it's supposed to be in cursive?

He pushes against my right hip and turns so that he's half on top of me. I'm short of breath, and Kyle seems to interpret this as a good sign. His legs tangle with mine and his hand starts to roam up my side.

The air-conditioning kicks on. I listen to it blast through the vent in the corner. Then a dog barks outside. I've always wanted a dog, but Dad's allergic. And Mom would never be able to stand the mess and besides, pets just get old and die.

Probably from cancer.

No clock in the room. I sit up a little and move Kyle's hand away from my back pocket so I can grab my phone and check the time. He takes this as an invitation to go after my neck. Which, actually, I like a little better.

But it's later than I thought, well past the dinner I was supposed to be home for, and I decide it's time for me to round up Sadie.

"Gotta go." I spring off the couch.

Kyle freezes with one hand where my hip used to be. "Seriously?"

I knock on Will's door and call to Sadie that it's time to leave, then go wait for her in the kitchen.

Kyle walks in and leans against the counter, looking decidedly less enthusiastic than a moment ago. "What's the hurry?"

"I have a curfew."

He looks out the kitchen window. It's only just getting dark. He slides closer and hooks his finger through my belt loop. "Come on, it's early. I can drive you home in a little while."

I slip out of reach and call Sadie's name again. Kyle crosses his arms and slumps back against the refrigerator door.

Sadie wraps it up in record time, running her fingers through her hair as she walks into the kitchen. Will steps behind her and gropes her waist. She giggles and whines, which seems to be exactly what Will wants to hear.

"Can we go?" I ask.

Will shoots me a dirty look and pushes a fringe of sandy-blond hair off his forehead. The hair stays put, and I imagine his fingers come away greasy. Sadie rolls her eyes at him but follows me out the garage door.

Kyle takes the wheel on the way home, so I ride shotgun while Sadie keeps Will occupied in the backseat. My foot taps out every second that ticks by as we wind our way through town. I've got ten minutes. Then five. Then none and we're still four blocks away.

The car swings into my driveway and I glance over my shoulder. Mistake. I turn quickly back around because there is nothing in the backseat I want to see.

I push the door open.

"Hey." Kyle catches my arm and pulls me into one last thin-lipped kiss I do not close my eyes for. He releases me with a smug smile. "I had a lot of fun tonight," he says, which seems like the kind of thing guys say when they want to leave the option open for repeat performances.

I tuck my hair behind my ears and inch out of my seat. "Yeah. Good times." I jump out and lean down. "Sadie? You coming in?"

She breaks away from Will's face and smiles. "I'm good. Night, love."

"Okay." I hold on to the door a moment longer. I wish she would just come in. "Drive safe."

On my way up to the porch, a jingle of keys a few yards to my right grabs my attention. I squint to make out who they belong to.

My feet stop.

He's strolling down Cory's driveway next door, twirling the key ring around his index finger. He looks taller. I mean, he's always been tall, but definitely over six feet now. Stronger, too. He used to be so lanky. Now broad shoulders give way to muscular arms, and his hair is longer than he's ever worn it— reaching all the way down to his chin. Everything is different. But it's him.

My heart is helicopter-loud, pumping blood through me. But I'm rooted in place, watching the highlight reel of my childhood flash before my eyes.

He holds my gaze as we pass each other. Or rather, as he passes me, since I'm still standing here staring at him like a total freak.

"Night, Harper." His voice is soft. Completely at odds with his rigid posture.

Will backs out of the driveway. I watch the car over my shoulder, and even in the darkness, I can see the front seat clearly from where I stand.

I wonder how much Declan saw.

When I turn back toward him, Declan's gaze is fixed on the ground. He stays that way until he reaches his own car in the street.

"Good night," I call, forcing my heavy limbs into motion.

I peek over my shoulder once more before going inside. Declan is already driving away.

Two

MY PARENTS CALL ME INTO THE LIVING ROOM AS soon as I cross the threshold. They're huddled together on the couch, sharing a blanket. Empty wineglasses and a yellow legal pad covered in writing lie on the table in front of them.

I rest my hip against the bookshelf and wait for Dad to start reaming me out for missing curfew. Even though my new curfew is ridiculous and I'm all of six minutes late.

"You doing okay?" he asks instead.

Mom looks better than yesterday, when she sat my brother and me down to tell us. She has some color back in her cheeks, although that could just be from the wine. She leans forward to look at me and I drop my gaze to the floor. I can see it in her eyes, no matter how hard she tries to hide it. She's scared.

All through dinner last night she kept trying to prove otherwise, telling us they caught it early—just two little lumps— she'll be *finejustfine*. Only, how can she know that?

She wants it to be true. I can feel how much she wants it. But that doesn't mean it will be.

Because the truth is none of us knows for certain she'll be fine, and the more she talks about tumors and treatment plans, the harder it is to believe.

I'm not okay. None of this is okay. But I look at Dad and nod.

"Did you have fun tonight?" Mom asks.

More nodding.

They don't seem to have any more to say than I do, so when a suitable amount of time has passed, I announce I'm going to bed.

"All right, honey."

"Harper." I turn to face my dad. He smiles softly, look-ing like the old him. The version I saw a lot more of before I stopped being his little girl. "We love you."

I shift my weight. "Love you too."

Upstairs, I change out of my clothes, grimacing at the scent of Kyle's cologne clinging to my shirt as I pull it over my head. I sit on the edge of my bed and look around my room, at the swimming medals and team pictures that are all from another lifetime.

Folding my arms around my bare legs, I squeeze my phone between my palms. I scroll through the contacts until I fall on his name. My thumb hovers over the call button. Closing my eyes, I imagine calling him, think through what I would say. My fingers tighten until my knuckles ache.

I open my eyes and loosen my fingers, then scroll back up the alphabet to the *C*'s. Cory answers on the third ring.

"You knew he was coming back?"

"Hello to you, too."

"God, Cory. A little heads-up would have been nice."

"Ah, but would it really have made a difference?"

I scowl and hang up on him, then collapse back onto my mattress. I just want this day to be over, but I know I'll be awake for hours.

Eventually, I wind up on the roof ledge outside my bedroom window, listening to the songs of the cicadas. The sky tonight is more blue than black, and the stars are out in full force. Perfect for making wishes, if I still believed in that sort of thing.

A cool breeze kisses my face and clears my head.

Tracing the infinity pendant on my necklace, I wonder where the invisible line is. The line that determines which parts of our past are still close enough to go back and fix, and which parts we have to live with forever.

My mother is whistling. How can she be bustling around arranging flowers and whistling right now? Chemotherapy starts in three days. She still insists on pretending she's not petrified.

I pad the rest of the way into the kitchen. "Morning. . . ."

"There she is!" Dad says.

Mom smiles and holds out a glass of fresh-squeezed orange juice. I don't take it. I head straight for the coffeepot and pour a cup of the rocket fuel my parents brew.

It's a little past ten and the thermometer outside the kitchen window has already crept above ninety. I pull myself up to sit on the cool granite counter and tap my fingers along the side of my mug. No one says anything about the giant, malignant elephant in the room.

I consider screaming *BREAST CANCER!* just to see how they'd react. But I've rocked the boat enough this year. The least I can do is keep up my end of this charade.

"How are you feeling today, Mom?"

She stops what she's doing and looks out at the backyard, like she's really thinking about it. "I'm great." She tilts her head toward me. "I think it's going to be a good day."

Then she sucks her teeth and taps my thigh, shooing me off the counter. I hop down and stand shoulder to shoulder with her while I sip my coffee. She puts a hand on top of my head and sighs. Mom likes to pretend she's still taller than me, but that ship sailed a while ago. My brother and I get our height from Dad's side, though I do have Mom to thank for the borderline translucent complexion and auburn tint to my hair.

"Is Graham still sleeping?"

"No, he's out playing a round of golf," Dad says. "What are your plans for the day?"

Not that I'm going to win Daughter of the Year anytime soon, but I'm surprised my older brother bailed on Family Time. And a little relieved. If he's not around, I don't have to feel guilty about the plans I made with Cory. Besides, at times like this, Cory is one of the only people who can keep me sane.

"Heading next door in a bit."

Dad folds the corner of his paper over. "Dressed like that?"

I glance down at the gym shorts and sports bra I threw on and roll my eyes. Sure, my parents' concern isn't really that far-fetched—it's been a constant presence, as much a part of me as the freckled nose on my face, this underwater indiscretion of mine. But seriously, a sports bra? *Pick your battles, Dad.*

"It's just Cory."

"And Cory is now a seventeen-year-old boy. Put on real clothes before you go."

"You're right. We're going swimming anyway. I'll change into my bathing suit just as soon as I've finished my coffee."

He grunts and turns back to his paper, a frown pulling at the corners of his mustache. I take the seat across the table from him and scope out the bag of bagels between us.

"So, you two are practicing this morning?" Mom asks as she cuts a grapefruit in half.

I look into my coffee and take another sip before answering. "We're just going to the quarry."

Her face falls a little. "Oh, okay." Then, because she just can't help herself, she puts down the knife and says, "It would be good for you to get back in the pool, though, don't you think?"

I tear off a piece of a salt bagel and take a bite. Mom swoops in, pulling a plate out of the cupboard and handing it to me. Crumbs are the enemy.

"I don't really see the point," I tell her.

"The point is, you're going to have to try out again in the fall. And you can't expect them to let you back on the team if you're not willing to work for it."

Mom's big joke has always been that I swam before I crawled. It's something I've done for as long as I can remember, most recently as captain of the girls' team at Carson High. Right up until I got kicked off.

I'm not sure which part is worse for my parents: the fact that I got caught over spring break, drunk and half-naked in the school pool with a boy they've never met, or that everyone in Carson knows about it. Either way, she's latched on to the idea of me earning my spot back like it's the last piece in the puzzle that will make me whole again.

Too bad I have no plans to do so.

Mom grabs a spoon and starts stabbing apart the sections of her grapefruit. "And I wish you would stop drinking all that coffee."

She says it to me but looks at Dad, who started me on my caffeine addiction a few years back. Unlike Cory, my internal clock never quite got the hang of waking up before the sun.

When we started training with the high school team, I needed the boost for morning practices. Dad shoots me a wink and raises his newspaper a little higher.

"There are worse things," he says from behind the paper. "And it doesn't seem to have stunted her growth."

"Besides, I'm going to need it tomorrow," I say. "Why does this stupid class have to start so early?"

Apparently being grounded for the remainder of junior year wasn't punishment enough, so my parents decided a summer school class at an ungodly hour would be a fitting penalty for the spring break incident. It was either that or get a job. I won't make any money taking a summer elective, but at least this way my punishment is limited to two shifts a week.

Mom's spoon clatters against the counter and she turns to look at me. "If I were you, I'd spend less energy focusing on all the things you're unhappy with and take a moment to appreciate what a great life you have."

My stomach wrings. I stare into my coffee. I'm always saying the wrong thing.

Dad's paper rustles, breaking the silence.

I set my mug down on the table and sit on my hands. Then force myself to look her in the eye.

"I'm sorry," I say for probably the millionth time since getting caught back in March.

Mom straightens and crosses over to me. She wraps me in

a hug I can't help but sink into. "I know, sweetie. Me too." She pulls back and holds my cheeks in her palms. Her eyes search mine as if to reinforce her apology. I nod, and she pats my cheek and drops her hands. "It's a beautiful day out. Go have fun with Cory."

I push aside a pile of clothes and sprawl out on Cory's twin bed.

He pauses his video game and spins around in his desk chair, nudging his glasses up the bridge of his nose. "Rough night?"

Kicking my leg in his general direction is all the response I can muster.

Light trickles in from the crack in the blackout curtains, keeping his room in a sleepy state. School notebooks he hasn't recycled are strewn around the floor, and an even bigger pile of dirty clothes is overflowing from his closet. Cory would call it organized chaos, and I have to admit I love the clutter.

Mom would kill me if I let my room get this messy. I get the stink eye from her if I leave more than one glass of water on my nightstand. "Your room is beginning to look a little lived in," she always says.

But I was there when Cory won the swimming trophies scattered around his desk, and I've read most of the books stacked precariously on the shelf above it. His room feels like home.

Sitting up again, I hug his pillow to my chest. "You ready to go?"

"Go . . ." Cory's dark eyebrows scrunch together for a moment and then he closes his eyes. "Shit, the quarry."

"You forgot?"

"Yeah . . . and I kind of agreed to help Declan paint his dad's house. But I can give him a rain check."

I hug the pillow tighter. "No, that's okay. I'm totally drained today anyway."

He adjusts his glasses again. "Well, why don't you come with me?"

"Pass."

"See, that's a huge mistake. Here's why: It's going to be a ton of fun. Like, way better than the quarry. There may even be pizza involved, I don't know."

"Don't you try to Tom Sawyer me." I pull at a loose thread on his pillowcase. "So, how long is he back for this time?"

"Dunno. You guys talk yet?" he asks. I cut him a look and he sighs. "You know, statistically, the odds of you two working things out would improve if you stopped avoiding him."

"I'm not *avoiding* him."

Now it's Cory's turn to give me a *Yeah, right* look.

Okay, so I may have given Declan a wide berth when he came home from boarding school over Christmas. But it wasn't easy. And now, two days after finding out about Mom, staying away from him all summer seems so much harder. Of course, I have no reason to expect he would want to see me, either. Not anymore.

22

"You two have fun painting." I toss the pillow back into place. "Maybe we can go to the quarry Tuesday?"

"I've got swim practice."

"Oh . . . right. Of course." It's dense, this silence between us. Weighted down by the loss of what made us friends in the first place.

Cory stands and scratches his arm. The chlorine makes our skin chronically dry. Honestly, I don't miss it one bit. "Tomorrow?" he asks.

"Summer school."

"Ah, yeah." He grabs his wallet off his desk. "Which class are you taking again?"

"Photography."

"Right, right. Well, that could be good. Maybe you'll meet someone cool."

"Yeah, I'm sure it's the place to be," I retort.

We head downstairs and out the front door, parting ways on his lawn. Maybe it's for the best he has plans. Because all I really want to do is crawl back into bed and never, ever come out again.

Three

MY PLAN TO HIDE OUT BETWEEN MY JERSEY cotton sheets lasts only until the next morning. Mom bursts into my room at seven thirty, travel mug of coffee in hand.

"Up."

"Don't want to," I mumble. "Personal day."

She takes away my covers. "Up," she says again. "Up or I'll go get a squirt gun."

She will, too. So it begins.

Walking into the art studio at the Carson Community Center is like being back in elementary school. The white cinder-block walls are splashed with pastel chalk portraits, and simple crayon drawings done by younger kids are taped on the cupboard doors. The smell of paint permeates the room. And just like the first day at a new school, I don't recognize a single person. I'm not even sure how that's possible in a place like Carson, but apparently it's only the case for me. In the back corner, students are clustered together, animatedly recounting the first few days of summer. I suppose I could join them, make some effort to be social. . . .

I slide into the chair closest to me and pull a pad of paper and pencil from my bag. I start doodling, trying to look busy while I listen to the chatter. A few minutes later a couple girls take the seats to my left.

". . . grab a salad after, or a gyro," a pretty blonde is saying. Almost doll-like in the symmetry of her features, she immediately reminds me of Betty from the Archie comics. "Ooh, or maybe pizza."

"As long as it's not from that place on Ninth," her friend replies. "They use weird cheese." She's wearing her black hair in a tight knot on the top of her head. Her dark eyes are outlined in darker kohl liner and her lips are stained crimson. She catches me staring at her, and I spin back to the page in front of me.

"True. I think it might be vegan," the blonde says.

I keep my head down, but the scary dark-haired girl is still watching me. I can feel it. "Hey," she leans toward me to say. "I'm Gwen. Do you have any gum?"

"Oh, um . . . yes." I reach into my bag and hold a pack out to her.

"Ugh, bubble gum."

And yet, she takes a piece anyway.

25

The blond girl shakes her head, sending a ripple through her hair. She's dressed head to toe in vintage clothing, and even her ponytail has that original Barbie curl to it. Her small, Cupid's-bow mouth transforms into a warm smile. "Don't mind Gwen, she's just orally fixated. I'm Mackenzie."

"Harper."

They exchange a look. "Do you go to Carson High?" Mackenzie asks.

I swallow and nod. These girls don't even go to my school. I really wish not knowing anybody meant I was safe from them knowing things about me.

It looks like Mackenzie is about to ask a follow-up question, but Gwen jumps in.

"Thanks for the gum. Sorry if I was rude, I just have trouble not blowing bubbles when I chew bubble gum."

She blows a bubble and pops it in her mouth. *All right, then.*

I nod sympathetically, as if I totally know what it's like to be physically unable to control the urge to blow a bubble.

"So, how long have you been into photography?" Mackenzie asks.

"This is my first class, actually."

"Oh!" Mackenzie says. "Me too! I was so nervous everyone was going to be super experienced like Gwen."

"For the millionth time, photography is not genetic," Gwen says. "My mom's a freelance photographer," she adds to me with a roll of her dark eyes.

"Wow, that's really cool."

Gwen shrugs it off, but I'm getting the distinct impression that most of the people in this room really want to be here.

The instructor, Mr. Harrison, stands at the front of the class and asks everyone to please find their seats. I shift mine so that I'm facing him, but Mackenzie leans across the table toward me, twirling the end of her honey-blond hair around her finger.

"Do you happen to know a guy named—"

"Declan!"

I look at Gwen and then follow her gaze over my shoulder. Declan takes the seat next to mine. My Declan.

He scoots his chair closer. So close that if I reach down to get something out of my bag, my head will hit his shoulder.

I turn back to my notebook. Try to write the date in the upper left corner of the page, but the lead snaps off my mechanical pencil. I click the eraser twice and set the pencil down.

Declan doesn't say a word. Just sits there staring at me. And now I'm staring back. Class is already starting by the time I finally remember how to speak. "What are you doing here?"

Declan ignores me. Nods hello to Mackenzie and Gwen.

Besides my confusion over how everyone knows each other, or what exactly these girls know about me, the thing I find most disconcerting is that Declan doesn't seem remotely surprised to see me.

I tear my focus away from his face and turn back to the instructor.

Since it's an introductory lecture, I don't get the chance to talk to Declan again until it wraps up.

"Next week we'll take a field trip to the land conservancy. Please don't forget to charge your camera batteries!" Mr. Harrison calls out while everyone gathers their stuff.

I put away my things slowly, building the nerve to try again. But when I finally turn toward Declan, he's already out of his seat.

With his arms wrapped around Mackenzie.

"Declan! I didn't know you were taking this class!" She gives him an extra squeeze and steps back.

"Kind of a last-minute decision. Someone dropped, so they fit me in."

My eyes narrow. Cory knew we'd have this class together. He may be sick of playing monkey in the middle, but he will pay for keeping that from me.

Gwen and Declan fist-bump and all three of them start talking about some jazz band I've never heard of. Pulling my bag onto my shoulder, I move toward the door.

Declan follows me. "I'll catch up with you guys later, okay?" I hear from behind me.

"Sure!" Mackenzie says. "Nice meeting you, Harper."

"You too." In my attempt to walk backward, I bump into the door frame. I turn around again and grimace, clutching my bag a little tighter. I move through the hall and safely clear the doors to the parking lot, Declan keeping pace with me the whole time.

I scan the rows of cars. Suddenly I can't remember where I parked. And the only thing I can think to say is that our tree might get cut down, which probably isn't the best conversation-starter given what happened the last time we were there together.

"So . . . class was interesting, right? Or, you know, less boring than I thought it would be." I spot my car and take a breath. "What'd you think?"

He turns to me, his face composed. Almost as if we haven't gone nine months without speaking.

Or as if he didn't even miss me.

"Wasn't bad."

I bite the inside of my cheek. "How do you know Mackenzie and Gwen?"

"We took a drawing workshop together." He scratches under the collar of his shirt. "Over winter break."

We reach my car and I lean against the driver's-side door. It's warm to the touch and coated in a fresh layer of the yellow pollen that's everywhere this time of year. "I didn't realize you'd gotten so into art."

"You didn't ask. Believe it or not, there are a few things you don't know about me."

I rock myself upright and open my car door. A burst of

thick, hot air greets me, and I look back at him with as much poise as possible. "I guess there are."

He gives me a small wave with his notebook and steps back.

"Declan, wait." Goddammit.

It's out of my mouth now, and with it comes an expectation. One I don't actually know how to fulfill. I should say something meaningful here, something that will close some measure of the distance between us. The way his hazel eyes are set on mine, it feels like he would wait a lifetime to hear the right thing.

"Welcome home."

If he's disappointed, he's careful not to let it show. But something, maybe curiosity, pulls his mouth to one side. And for that one moment I'm just me and he's just Declan. The boy I grew up with. My best friend.

But too soon the moment passes and he's gone. And all I'm left with is an aching void where all the imaginary reunions I'd carefully planned over the past nine months used to be.

Four

WE WERE FIFTEEN WHEN DECLAN'S MOM DIED. Cory, Declan, and I all had the same biology class, and on that winter day sophomore year, we spent the hour burning peanuts and calculating their calories. I was so wrapped up in the lab assignment, in the novelty of being trusted with matches inside a classroom, I barely noticed when the school counselor came in to get Declan. But then he didn't show up for lunch or the bus ride home, and I started to worry. Cory told me I was over-reacting, that Declan probably just had a doctor appointment.

But we both knew he was wrong once we stepped off the bus onto the slushy curb and found Mom and Bridget waiting for us. Cory and I sat side by side on his living room sofa as Bridget told us how the other driver was drunk and the roads were icy and Natalie's car spun and spun until the guardrail stopped her. My eyes traced the argyle pattern of Cory's wool socks. Watched as he flexed his feet against the floor and pushed his back into the cushion, bracing himself a moment too late. Then I stood, thinking if I could just see Declan, he would tell me they had it wrong. Natalie couldn't be dead.

I took one unsteady step toward the door, and Mom's arms trapped me. Holding me tight against her, she matched me sob for sob. I covered my mouth with my sleeve and my mind spun with thoughts of *Declan-Natalie-Natalie-Declan*. My body forced me to keep breathing even though Natalie couldn't, and with each inhale I choked on the scent of burned peanuts saturating my sweater.

The next time we saw Declan was at the funeral.

From my place next to Cory and our parents, I never took my eyes off him. It was the grayest morning I can remember, the kind of gray that makes your bones cold and your heart brittle. I clutched my winter coat around my waist and listened as one person after another tried to warm up the chapel by sharing stories about Natalie Scott's kindness and humor and the ways she made each of our lives richer. Declan sat stone still until it was Bridget's turn to speak.

His shoulders began to tremble and it was the most terrifying moment of my life, watching helplessly as my best friend was dashed to pieces, knowing that for the first time Cory and I might not be enough to hold him together.

When it was over, I hugged him as hard as I could. Whispered in his ear that we'd be okay, we'd get through it. He grabbed my hand and didn't let go for hours.

Natalie dying, the sight of Declan at her funeral, this is what I think about when Mom leaves for her first chemo session. Because Declan understands how quickly the world can crumble. How everything that used to define you can get choked out. He understands how easy it is to lose someone.

I haven't left my room all morning. I need some fresh air, so I climb out onto the roof ledge and lean back against the house. Graham is right downstairs. I suppose I could try talking to him about Mom, but he's got this attitude, as though all of this is happening for a reason. People around here like to call everything a part of God's Plan. But you can spend years, your whole life, even, waiting for the rest of the dominoes to fall. In the end, good people dying too young will never make sense. And I can't make sense of how this is happening to my mother. I mean, the woman flosses her teeth every single night. It just doesn't compute.

And I refuse to look online for advice on how to deal with Mom. One time I had a black spot on my tongue and the Internet told me I was dying, when really it was the bismuth in the Pepto-Bismol I'd eaten that turned it black. Well played, Internet.

Unfortunately, talking to Declan isn't an option either. Aside from the obvious problem that it's been almost a year since we've had a conversation longer than five minutes, how would I even bring something like this up? It's not as if I can corner him after class and be like, "Hey, Declan, remember when your mom died? Well, pretty soon we might be in the same club!"

God, just thinking that. I'm going straight to hell.

Someone knocks on my bedroom door. Before I can scramble back through my window, Sadie pops her head into the room.

"Graham let me in." She closes the door behind her and then climbs out the window, taking the spot beside me. We both melt back against the siding.

I pick up a pine needle from the gutter and break it into tiny pieces, tossing each little section off the roof. The spotty shade from the trees outside my room is no match for today's mugginess. The heat is coming at us from all angles, carried on the wind and rising up off the black shingles. It gets trapped behind my knees and under the arches of my feet, places I never realized could sweat so much. Sadie watches me tear apart another needle, then sits forward.

"You want to go somewhere?" she asks. "Take your mind off things?"

Sadie isn't big on hugging. Which is fine, since she has zero percent body fat and her hugs are full of ribs and sharp elbows. But she excels in the art of diversion. We've been friends since freshman year, but it was after Natalie passed away that this

34

particular skill started to come in handy. Sadie was there for me in a different way from Declan. There when I needed to be someone else for a little while.

"Like where?"

She grins and crawls back through my bedroom window. Tells me to follow her. And I do. I always do.

Stepping outside of Will's house two hours later, I call Cory.

I can't believe Sadie did this to me. Again. Every Friday it's the same story. We go out together and she disappears with some guy, which inevitably leaves me with another. The only difference is that this time, I'm pissed.

"Hey," Cory says when he picks up.

"Can you come get me?"

He sighs. "Address?"

"Seven eighty-four Beverly Drive."

"You owe me."

The door opens behind me and Kyle saunters out. He lights a cigarette and offers me the pack. I take one, mostly because I need something to do with my hands while I wait for Cory.

He holds the Bic halfway between us. I lean in for him to give me a light and I'm rewarded with another whiff of that god-awful cologne he wears.

I move to the driveway and lean back against the garage door, filling my lungs with carcinogens. I bet my mother has never had a cigarette. She never microwaves food in plastic containers, either. And she hardly ever drinks more than one glass of wine. But this is a world in which beautiful people die ugly deaths all the time. The same world that turned a quick trip to the grocery store one day in January into mangled steel and broken glass and one more kid without a mother. The same world that stole Natalie away from a family that loved her.

I take another drag. My chest burns, but I hold my breath, allow my lungs to smolder, and start counting down the time it will take Cory to get here. I estimate there are twelve minutes to kill and about three to go before I have to remind Kyle that the answer is still no.

It only takes two and a half. Kyle props himself next to me in the forward-leaning, aggressive posture of someone accustomed to getting what he wants. He's having all kinds of trouble grasping the concept of rejection. Though to be fair, lately I haven't been known for saying no any more than he's used to hearing it.

"I'm liking you in this skirt." He flicks the ash off his cigarette and eyes my legs. "Of course, I think I'd like you better out of it."

His fingers graze up my thigh. I shift away. "Fuck off, Kyle."

"Geez, can't you just take a compliment without getting all defensive?"

"I love how I'm supposed to take that as a compliment." I cross one ankle over the other.

He considers this a moment. A car turns onto the street,

but my false hope drains as it drives straight past us.

"I would take it as a compliment if you wanted me to remove my clothes," he reasons.

I take a long drag and blow the smoke in his face. "I'm sure you would."

Kyle squints at me and his smile grows wider. "You're so moody."

"Guess so."

"I like that, too."

My eyes close and I rest my head against the garage door.

"Seriously, you okay?" he asks.

I open my eyes to find something like genuine interest in his. "Like you care?"

"Hey, I'm just saying you look preoccupied. Thought maybe I could help you relax."

"You can't." I look down at my cigarette. "But . . . thanks. I think."

He shrugs and I straighten as not Cory's but Declan's car pulls to a stop in front of us.

"*Shit.*" I toss the cigarette down and yank at the hem of my skirt.

Cory jumps out of the front seat and makes an ushering motion with his arm.

"You didn't have to give up shotgun for me."

"Oh," he says, ducking his head down to give Declan a dirty look, "but I did."

I pull on my seat belt and Cory slams my door shut before getting in the back to sulk.

"Thanks for getting me," I say with a sideways glance to Declan.

"No problem."

He's looking past me, out my window to the top of the driveway where Kyle is. Then he turns his head straight forward, but I catch him taking in my outfit through his peripheral.

Why did I let Sadie talk me into wearing a skirt this short? I must look completely ridiculous. I tug the flimsy cotton a little lower over my thighs and cross my arms.

"So, Harper, who's your friend?" Cory leans forward to look out my window. "Oh, it's Kyle Marcell!" He waves idiotically at him and I slap his hand away from my face. "Nice choice."

I sink against the door and rub my temple. "Shut up, Cory."

"Why don't you lay off her tonight?" Declan asks as he puts the car in gear.

Cory pops back up between us. "Stick around for a while, Declan. You'll see how quickly you get tired of playing chauffeur and carting her drunk ass across town."

It's basically the verbal equivalent of getting pantsed in the middle of a crowded cafeteria. Not terribly surprising given how Cory feels about all the things I've kept from Declan. About the secrets he's had to keep for me. But I'm no stranger to public humiliation and I flat out refuse to let Cory see how much it stings. So I put on my boxing gloves and play along.

"I'm not even drunk. Also, I said shut up."

"Fun fact about Kyle," he goes on, apparently for Declan's benefit. "Last year I was standing behind him in the lunch line and he wondered out loud what an unpickled pickle would taste like. I tried to explain that it would taste a lot like a cucumber, but he said he couldn't picture it."

A small smile tugs at the corners of my mouth. Declan seems to notice the shift in attitude.

"So what you're saying is that Harper's standards have sky-rocketed since I left town?"

My chest constricts. Declan wrinkles his nose and shoots me an apologetic smile, as though he's afraid he's gone too far. I force my grin to stay put, though it takes more work now than before.

"You are both such assholes," I say. "I'm never calling you for a ride again."

"You're an asshole," Cory retorts. "And you better call me every time you need a ride."

Declan turns right out of the neighborhood and looks over at me. "You know what we need?"

I examine my cuticles. "To get the hell out of Carson?"

"Or ice cream."

"Ray's," Cory and I say at the same time.

Declan hands me his phone. "You mind texting Mackenzie and inviting her?"

"Oh." I look down at the phone. My cheeks go hot. "Yeah, sure."

Really, I should have seen this coming. Of course Declan is interested in the cute, bubbly blond girl.

We park down the street and meet up with Mackenzie and Gwen at the back of the line, which reaches all the way out the door. But Ray's is worth it. People come from miles away to try the flavors only we have. Cardamom, praline crunch, peach crumble. Ray's is an institution in Carson, not to mention the only place besides Frank's Diner that's open past nine.

"You know how many flavors they have," Gwen is saying as we approach. "Start thinking about what you want now or we'll be here all night."

Mackenzie loses focus as soon as Declan comes into view. "Hey! Thanks for inviting us! It's, like, the perfect night for ice cream. Such a good idea." She turns back to Gwen. "I think I want something with chocolate."

"That narrows it down to about twenty options," Gwen says.

Declan introduces Cory, and I take the opportunity to slip out of the way.

I squint at the chalkboard menu above the counter—they really do have an insane number of flavors—and don't look down again until I'm near the front of the line. Cory is already ordering, and Declan is ahead of me. He steps to the side to order from someone else, and behind the counter I spot my

epic, what-the-hell-was-I-thinking mistake from the pool over spring break. Jake Thornton.

Jake's back is turned, but the crowd thins as a family makes their way outside to eat, and now there are only a few feet between us.

"Uh-oh," Mackenzie says.

"Don't even tell me they don't have your flavor." Gwen follows Mackenzie's gaze up to the menu board, zeroing in on the handful of flavors they've crossed off. She holds her hand up as Mackenzie turns toward her with her bottom lip stuck out. "Please, no."

"What kind of ice cream place runs out of mint chocolate chip? I thought that was such a good choice. . . ."

Jake hasn't turned around yet. I can still make my escape.

I start to back out of line. "You know, I don't think I want anything. I'm kind of lactose intolerant anyway."

Declan blinks at me. "What? No you're not."

"No . . . I'm not." I tuck my hair behind my ear and my eyes slide back to Jake just as he turns to face me.

"Hey, Sloan." Jake's gaze wavers from my face and I fold my arms across my chest. "Long time no see."

I risk a glance at Declan. With a furrowed brow, he's watching Jake.

"What'll it be?"

"A scoop of java chip. In a cup, please," I say.

"Strawberry milk shake!" A guy in a chocolate-stained apron

holds out Declan's order. He casts me one more glance before walking over to claim it, leaving me without anyone to hide behind. I turn back to Jake just as he holds out my ice cream.

"How much?" I ask.

"It's on me."

"Oh. Thanks."

He grabs a spoon from the canister next to him and hands it to me. "I'm sure you could get creative and figure out a way to repay me."

A familiar tension locks down on my shoulders. Heat builds in my chest and travels up my neck. I keep my eyes on the spoon.

Maybe on a different day, if it wasn't the cherry on top of one of the worst weeks of my life, or if it wasn't right in front of Declan, who after tonight probably thinks I'm a complete skank-wad, maybe then I would let it go.

Instead, I channel Sadie. Twist the spoon around in my ice cream and look up through my lashes. Holding his gaze, I flip it onto my tongue and slowly, teasingly pull it out of my mouth.

"You'd like that, wouldn't you?" I whisper.

He looks over his shoulder, checking that no one can overhear, before resting his elbows on the glass. "Well, I think we should finish what we started in that pool," he says in a hushed voice.

"Right." I stab the spoon into my ice cream and grab a five-dollar bill out of my purse. "But you know what, Jake? I don't owe you a goddamn thing." I toss the money across the

counter at him and move past Mackenzie, who's still sampling flavors, and Gwen, who, judging by the raised eyebrows and stunned smile on her face, witnessed the whole thing.

Declan holds the door open for me and stares over my head. "Everything all right over there?"

I answer without turning around. "Yep. Everything's fine."

After a few more samples, Mackenzie lands on peanut butter and joins us at the picnic table we're occupying.

"It's good." She slides in next to me on the bench. "But not mint-chocolate-chip good."

"We'll get you mint next time," Gwen says.

Mackenzie takes another bite and leans across the table toward Declan. "What'd you get?"

She's propped on her forearms, giving Declan a view of what's under her neckline. Not that her shirt is really that low-cut. In fact, her vintage all-American look is downright wholesome. No wonder Declan likes her.

He holds out his Styrofoam cup and she takes a sip. From his straw.

I drop the spoon back into my melting ice cream.

"Mmm, not bad." She gestures to her cup. "Want to try mine?"

Okay, please tell me she's not about to spoon-feed him.

"No, thanks," Declan says. But he keeps smiling at her, like it's just the nicest thing in the world that she offered.

Cory is staring at her too. Ice cream is dripping down his

cone onto his hand. I wad a napkin up and throw it at his chest. His forehead wrinkles.

"You're welcome," I say sweetly.

Mackenzie looks at my ice cream and frowns. "Do you not like yours?"

"No, it's fine. I just don't have much of an appetite tonight."

"Gotcha. Hey, we should make this a regular thing. Like, after class or something. You too, Cory."

Cory lights up. "Yeah. Definitely."

"Cool. Next round will be on me." She smiles and finally sits back on the bench to finish her ice cream.

God, why does she have to be so nice? It makes it really hard to hate her.

Declan's straw gives that end-of-the-line gurgle, and he sets the empty cup down. Gwen is done too. We wait for Mackenzie to finish—she's seriously the slowest eater ever—before we all toss our cups in the trash. Mackenzie hugs Declan, and then suddenly her arms are around me.

"See you in class!"

I pat her on the back. "Yep. See you then."

She bounces over to Gwen, and after another wave good-bye, the girls head over to an apple-red vintage car.

"Whoa." Cory nudges Declan's shoulder. "She drives a Datsun?"

"Yeah, a 240Z. From 1971, I think. She restored the engine herself."

Beyond how to change a tire, I don't know a thing about cars. "She did?"

Declan nods.

"Amazing," Cory says. He practically needs a drool cup.

Mackenzie revs the engine and pulls out. The boys wait until they can no longer hear the purr of the engine before walking back to Declan's Focus.

Ten minutes later, we're parked in my driveway. Cory ruffles my hair from the backseat, which he knows I hate. I turn around to smack him, and he smirks at me.

"Night, guys." His grin gets bigger, like I'm missing something.

He gets out and crosses over to his house. And then there were two.

And I still have no idea how to talk to Declan.

"So . . ."

"So."

I tug at my seat belt and angle toward him. "My parents are having their Fourth of July party on Sunday."

"Oh yeah?"

"I'm sure they'd like to see you," I say, doing my best to keep from sounding too interested. "You should come by. If you're free."

"Okay."

That's kind of like a yes.

I click my seat belt off and grab my bag but stare at the steering wheel instead of getting out.

He still hasn't asked about Kyle, or Jake, or Cory's asshole comment about my drinking. Which probably means he doesn't care.

Good. It's none of his business, anyway. This is how it's supposed to be now. This is what I wanted.

Right?

"Listen," I say with a nonchalant shake of my head, like this is all a game. A big joke I am totally in on. "I know what you're probably thinking after tonight. But it's not . . . I mean, people say things that aren't . . ."

The rest dissolves on my tongue. Declan's fingers graze my collarbone and grasp the chain of my necklace. He pulls it out from underneath my shirt and slides down to the infinity pendant at the bottom before letting go.

"I know who you are."

Five

WHACK. THE END OF A CARROT FLIES ACROSS the counter.

"Easy!" Mom says. She takes my knife away and hands me a bowl of avocados. "I'll finish slicing the veggies. You can make the guacamole."

She raises her eyebrow at me like she doesn't trust me with a fork, either. She's super on top of her game today, since in addition to celebrating our nation's independence, this year's party is also a sort of last hurrah before the chemo gets bad. In other words, we're staging a portrait of a perfect family because our actual lives are now completely effed.

I get to work, but smashing avocados just doesn't give me the same cathartic release as stabbing crudités.

"Was that a good sigh or a bad sigh?" she asks.

It was an accidental sigh. "Neither. I'm just . . . it's complicated."

Everything was so much simpler when we were kids. When I was just one of the guys. Before Declan's mom got into that accident and everything started to change.

Grief affected all of us differently. Declan's dad became withdrawn, pulling away from Declan when he should have been holding on tight. In turn, Declan got angry—filled with a hurt that simmered just beneath the surface and colored every conversation we had about his father. And grief made me afraid—of the unknown, of fate, if that's what you want to call it. Afraid of losing people I loved. So after Natalie died, I spent the rest of that winter trying not to fall in love with Declan.

This was not a successful endeavor. Because in reality, I'd been falling in love with Declan for years.

He probably won't even come tonight. And I certainly shouldn't care.

I turn a few more avocado slices into mush. Mom watches over my shoulder. She has a history of just knowing things, serious psychic powers, and I'm beginning to feel a bit naked under her steady gaze.

"So you went out with Declan last night?"

See.

"And Cory. And some girls from my photography class."

"Have fun?"

48

I nod and turn my attention back to the task at hand.

She wipes her hands on a dish towel. "Bridget told me he's looking pretty cute these days."

I swear, Mom and Bridget are worse than the girls at school with their gossip. And now she's just standing there, watching for my reaction with crazy hawk-lady eyes.

"Um . . . I haven't really noticed."

"So you don't have a crush on him anymore?"

"Oh my God. Mom."

"You two were so sweet together, is all I'm saying." She stops arranging the veggie tray and looks over the rim of her glasses at me. "You're not still interested in that boy from the spring, are you?"

"No. I told you, I don't talk to him." Unless you count last night. Which I don't.

Dad comes in through the back porch and stops to give Mom a slow, grimace-inducing kiss.

"Do you know where the big ice bucket is?" he asks her.

"Garage."

"Ah." He turns toward me. "Your mother has all the answers, doesn't she?"

With great effort on my part, I manage to pull off a smile instead of rolling my eyes clear across the county. Mom holds out until Dad leaves the room before continuing her investigation. This waiting for privacy is an illusion designed to lull me into the security of our "friendship." The reality is, she will

49

recount this entire conversation word for word to my dad later tonight.

"Well, do you like anyone else?"

The memory of Kyle's lips on mine swarms my mind. Not that making out with Kyle is really worth remembering. His mouth tasted like cigarettes and cheese puffs. It was not awesome.

"No, I don't," I finally say, because she isn't going to wrap this up until I at least acknowledge I've heard her.

"But you would tell me if you were serious about someone, or thinking about becoming sexually active, wouldn't you?"

Sweet lord, this conversation needs to end.

"Yep," I say quickly, "you'll be the first to know."

After arranging the chip-and-dip platter at the speed of light, I make my escape. I find my brother sitting on the porch swing out front.

"I guess we should probably clean ourselves up soon," he says when I plop down beside him.

"Won't take long. Mom has already preselected a few dresses I'm allowed to wear," I tell him.

"She's still doing that? Man, I'm glad I've finally reached the point where she trusts me to clothe myself."

"Must be nice."

"Well, it's a trust that has to be earned, Harper."

"Stop."

"Dressing yourself is a privilege, not a right."

"Jerk."

He grins broadly. "Hey, I'm just teasing. I know you've done your time. Seems like things have returned to normal around here."

My head rolls back and I stare up at the sky. I pick out a cloud shaped like a squirrel and watch as the wind disfigures it. "Normal? Um, no, I wouldn't put it that way, exactly. I'm not grounded anymore, but Mom and Dad still bring up the pool every chance they get."

"They'll get over it."

"Sure. Maybe even before my thirtieth birthday." I pick a cottonwood seed off my shirt and listen to the screeches of little kids playing an epic game of tag down the street.

The closest Graham has ever gotten to anything resembling trouble was the time he pulled a C-minus in trig. And even then, he got his grade up to a B-plus by the end of the year. He simply doesn't have the same bent for bringing shame upon the family that I do.

"Anyway, it's been tense lately," I say. "And now, this whole thing with Mom."

"Yeah, I know." He scratches his cheek. "Hey, if it gets to be too much . . . I mean, when I was home over Christmas, you weren't really in the best of shape. If you ever need to talk to someone . . ."

"Thanks." I wrap my arms around my knees. "I'm better, though. Totally."

We settle into a peaceful quiet broken only by kids laughing and the high-pitched call of a cardinal. I spot its red feathers in a pine tree beside the porch just as Mom comes out to tell me to get changed.

"And, Graham, why don't you put on a nice collared shirt," she adds before stepping back inside.

My lips curl in and press together to keep a laugh from coming out, but I can feel Graham's eyes on me.

"Shut up."

"Didn't say a thing."

Of the three dresses Mom set out, only one of them is tolerable. A simple green sundress with a halter top. I slip it on and go into the bathroom to tame my curls.

After running a flat iron over the same section of hair four times with underwhelming results, I decide to tap the porcelain plate to make sure it's hot enough.

"*Owshitfuck.*" I throw the flat iron into the sink.

I yank the plug out of the wall and move the flat iron to the counter so that I can run cold water over my pointer finger.

Voices travel up from the front of my house and I peek through the window blinds. I can only see Cory from this angle, but I would recognize Declan's voice anywhere.

I look at the mirror again. Somehow, my hair has gotten even bigger in the last few minutes. Clearly the straightened look is out. Fine. It's way too hot to be messing with a flat iron anyway.

Splashing my face with cold water, I try to get rid of the flush on my cheeks. Then I pull my hair into a ponytail that is slightly lopsided but will have to be good enough because I can hear them inside now, and Mom will be calling me down any second.

Doubling back, I apply a dab of floral perfume on each wrist and rub them along my neck.

The boys are standing in the foyer, each holding a bag of ice and listening to Graham recount the glory days of his freshman year. Halfway down the stairs, I lock eyes with Declan. His gaze drifts to my dress. One eyebrow raises and I freeze.

I glance down. This dress has been in the back of my closet for a year. I'd completely forgotten about it. But apparently Declan hasn't. And then it hits me. I wore it the night before he went away to school last August.

Changing now would be absurd. He's already seen me. So I squeeze the banister and move down the last few steps.

Graham sees me coming. He puts his arm around Declan and slouches into his *Boy, have I got a story for you* stance.

"So, either of you still after my little sister?"

I punch him in the shoulder. Then, for a splinter of a second, my eyes meet Declan's again.

Graham rubs his arm and smirks at me, not looking the least bit repentant. "That actually hurt."

"Here, let me take that for you." I grab the bag of ice from Declan and beeline for the back door. Cory follows me outside with the second bag, tossing it down in the cooler next to mine. He tears one open and I hold an ice cube against my burned finger.

"Graham is such a spaz," I say.

"He's just being an older brother, right?"

"I guess. Although it's not like he has anything to worry about with you guys."

Cory is silent for a beat. He tugs at the collar of his T-shirt, which like every shirt he owns is stretched tight across his back and shoulders and hangs loosely around his narrow waist. "You sure about that?"

The ice starts to melt, sending a river down my arm. Abruptly I'm transported back to last summer, a time when Declan and I were inseparable.

For months, I had tried not to get my hopes up every time Declan held my hand in his. Tried not to let my heart break when we were around Cory and he'd put a few extra inches of space between us. Declan was still grieving, and his healing was the most important thing. So I did what any good friend would have done. I kept my mouth shut and my feelings bottled. But we were so much a part of each other already, I couldn't imagine going a day without seeing him. And by that spring, Declan had stopped putting space between us.

Last summer we'd spend entire afternoons at the quarry, and sometimes it was so hot that even swimming wasn't enough to cool us off. Days like that, Declan would fish an ice cube out of the cooler and hold it at the base of my neck, blowing as the water dripped down my back.

I shiver now as Declan slides open the screen door and ambles over to us. I throw what's left of the ice cube at Cory and wipe my hands on my skirt.

"Not interrupting anything, am I?" Declan's eyes flick back and forth between Cory and me, and I shake my head.

Dad swoops in and claps Declan on the shoulder. "Declan! So good to see you, son. How've you been?"

"Can't complain." Declan smiles at Dad and then shifts his gaze down to the patio bricks.

"How's your golf game these days?"

"Not bad. Actually, I just got a job caddying over at Forest Hills. It's only a few days a week, but I get to play some free rounds when it's not busy."

"That's great. And I hear you're really enjoying your new school?"

Declan straightens. "Did my father tell you that?"

Dad nods. "You know if he's coming by tonight?"

"Yeah. He's just out front wrapping up a call for work. I'm sure he'll be done shortly."

"Guess he didn't get the memo about the holiday weekend," I say.

Declan glances at me. His smile is almost imperceptible, but I see it. "No rest for the wicked," he mumbles.

Dad gives him one of those lopsided, sympathetic smiles—

the same one everyone who knew Natalie gives Declan—and pats his shoulder once more. "Well, what can I get you guys to drink?"

I slip back into the house to shuttle the rest of the hors d'oeuvres outside. Mom is in the kitchen having a hushed conversation with Bridget, who is clearly in Dr. Kingston mode. I wonder if she misses Natalie even more now. Because when I look at the two of them, all I can see is her absence. If Mom's diagnosis had come two summers ago, Natalie would be here too, supporting Mom.

They get extra quiet when they notice me. This clearly isn't a conversation they trust me enough to include me in, so I grab the first tray I see and head outside again.

I busy myself lighting tiki torches and citronella candles, and soon the party is in full swing. Dad is in the corner of the patio by the grill, drinking a beer with Declan's dad. Declan isn't anywhere near them. I walk over to see if I can be relieved of my prep duties.

"So, Harper . . ." Declan's dad scrunches his forehead, turning the beer can around in his hand. It's like he can't think of anything safe to say. "How is your summer going?"

"Great, so far."

"Glad to hear it." He smiles, but it's horribly reserved. Like he doesn't remember I'm the same girl he used to lift up to the basketball hoop just so I could score against the boys. The same girl his wife packed extra cookies for in Declan's lunch.

With Declan away at school, both the opportunities and topics for conversation with his father have been limited. But I wonder what he sees when he looks at me now. Whether in his eyes, I'm anything more than a bad influence.

Dad rotates a rack of ribs on the grill, and the smell of barbecue sauce and charcoal wafts over. He closes the lid and dabs his forehead with a paper napkin.

"Anything else you need, Dad?"

Dad scans the yard. Other years, Graham and I have always had to do a round with our parents, saying hello to all the neighbors. I hated it. But I guess now we're past the point of showing me off.

"Why don't you just go have some fun?"

He smiles. We all smile. And then I go looking for Cory.

Unfortunately, Mrs. Malone finds me first.

"Oh, Harper, so good to see you." She appraises my bare legs with one eyebrow cocked.

Mrs. Malone is about a hundred years old and still wears full makeup and heels every day. Her face is caked with powder that has settled into the deep lines in her cheeks, and she wears a vibrant, frosted pink lipstick on her puckered lips.

I sigh quietly. Mrs. Malone has hated me ever since I got caught stealing apples from the tree in her backyard when I was nine. Declan was with me, but for some reason she blamed me entirely, since in her eyes I've never been more than a troubled heathen of a girl. Mrs. Malone is ahead of her time that way.

"Hi, Mrs. Malone. Wonderful to see you too."

She shuffles closer, squinting her watery eyes up at me. "How have you been handling everything with your mother? Poor dear. Lord knows she's been through enough this past year. I do hope you'll let me know if there's anything I can do?"

I clear my throat. Twice. "Of course. We're all doing our best. Keeping faith that it's part of God's plan."

I know how to work it.

She sends me a beatific smile and pats my arm. "Well, that's just wonderful to hear. Because you know . . ."

Uh-oh. She pivots a few inches closer, and I find myself cornered between her and a hanging basket of geraniums. I scan the deck for an exit, and my eyes fall on Declan. He mouths, *Praise Jesus!* and I snort a laugh, covering it with a cough as I turn back to Mrs. Malone.

"Young ladies today just don't seem to have any values," she says pointedly. She fans herself with a folded paper plate. "One hears things, anyway."

Indeed. One does.

The smile melts off my face and I struggle to think of a response. Before I manage to come up with anything remotely appropriate, Declan swoops in and wraps his hand around my arm.

"So sorry to interrupt, but I desperately need you."

I sort of forget where I am for a second and just stare back at him while the words buzz straight down my torso. He cracks

a dimpled smile, probably at my expense, and Mrs. Malone shuffles in her pumps. She pats the bottom of her short white hair, and smiles at Declan.

"It's been nearly a year since I've seen you, young man!"

"I hope you don't mind my butting in," he says with boat-loads of charm. "But I'm afraid I need to steal Harper away."

"No problem at all! You come by my house anytime to catch up, all right?"

"Absolutely. Take care, now."

He leads me by the elbow across the deck. Once we've cleared the masses, his hand slips off my arm.

I tuck a few loose strands of hair behind my ear. "Thanks for that."

He shrugs. "Looked like you needed an out."

"I still don't know why she likes you so much. You stole more apples than I did."

"Only because you coerced me. See, in Mrs. Malone's eyes, I'm a good Christian boy who knows right from wrong. Plus last summer I stopped by now and then to mow her lawn."

Okay, that . . . I did not know.

"Guess that explains why she looked at you like you're her hero."

"Don't worry. The fact that I still hang out with you speaks highly in your favor."

My forehead wrinkles and immediately all of the things I haven't told him—the things I can't tell him—push to the front

59

of my mind. Because he's right. He's too good for me.

And why is he being so nice, anyway? Ever since he got back into town he's been acting like everything is totally fine between us. Like breaking up and going an entire school year without speaking didn't even bother him.

Maybe he really is over it. And me.

Which would totally be a good thing. We could go back to sophomore year, to the way things were before. Just friends. I mean, it's not like I'm still interested in something more.

Blowing out a breath, I smile and gesture to the back of the deck. We pass the cooler and I grab two sodas. "You seen Cory?" I ask as I hand him one of the cans.

"Thanks. He's over with his parents." We settle into a couple of Adirondack chairs and he starts picking at the wooden armrest. "Hey, what do you think of Mackenzie?"

I flick the tab on the can I'm holding, back and forth until it breaks off. "Um, I don't know, really. I just met her."

"But she's pretty, right?"

Staring down at my lap, I scrape the metal tab down my thigh. This is what friends do; they talk about the people they like. So I nod. "She's very pretty." I take a sip of Coke. "Did you want to invite her?"

"Nah, I spoke to her earlier. Her family has their own thing going on today."

"Oh. That's too bad." My gaze slips back to him. His eyes have so much green in them tonight.

Cory collapses into the seat next to mine, balancing a plate full of ribs on his lap. "Have you tried these? So good."

He licks the barbecue sauce off his thumb and I pilfer a cookie from his plate and crumble it into bite-size pieces. I can't stop fidgeting.

"Fireworks will start soon," Declan says. "We should go somewhere and watch them."

Cory shakes his head. "I've got an early practice tomorrow."

I'm about to get on his case, because it's not even nine o'clock and besides, since when does a morning practice keep Cory from hanging out? But then Declan turns his attention toward me.

"Harp? You game?"

"Sure." I try to keep a poker face, but I accidentally smile instead. "I know a place."

Six

THE CARSON WATER TOWER IS A LOT HIGHER up than I remembered.

Halfway to the top, my brain kicks on and starts yammering about how this might be the worst idea I've ever had, and how dead I'll be if I get caught. But I'm already halfway up and all . . . so I press on.

I reach the narrow platform and sit down, wrapping both hands around the railing in front of me and letting my legs dangle over the side. Declan collapses beside me a moment later. He closes his eyes and pulls his knees into his chest.

Wiping my damp palms on the denim shorts I changed into, I rest my head against the cool steel tank and try to catch my breath. From up here, you can see all of downtown Carson.

The shops on Ninth and the blinking yellow traffic light at the corner of Broad Street. The park two blocks over, where families are packed together on checkered blankets to watch the fireworks. Street lamps dot the neighborhoods that sprawl from the center of town, the soft glow fading farther west, where the forest grows thick. Somewhere in the mass of trees, the quarry is hidden from sight.

"Should have known hanging out with you would involve trespassing."

He doesn't say it unkindly. But deep inside, I ache for the before. Before Declan knew this about me.

"So you heard." I lick my lips and try to smile. Can't do it. "About the pool incident."

"I was referring to Mrs. Malone's yard," he jokes. He shrugs his shoulders and comes close to looking indifferent. But not quite. "Cory mentioned something about you getting caught sneaking in. Guess you've had a rough couple of months, huh?"

A couple. Or nine. But who's counting?

"You might say that." I wipe my palms again. The judgmental look on Mrs. Malone's face earlier worms its way into my mind, along with the worry Declan has somehow heard more about what happened with Jake this past spring—or worse, the truth about last fall—than he's letting on. "So, did he tell you anything else about that night?"

Declan turns toward me. "What do you mean?"

"Just curious which version of the story you heard."

"Oh." He scratches his ear. "No, that was pretty much it."

I almost always know when Declan is lying. He only has about thirty-seven tells. But before I can get a good read on him, he looks out over the horizon and changes the subject.

"I really missed this place."

The buildings below are getting more difficult to distinguish. It's almost dark now.

"Really? I can't wait to leave Carson behind," I say. "And North Carolina, for that matter."

"You used to love it here. When did that change?"

When you left.

I don't say it out loud. But he hears it.

"But you're still—well, aside from this week . . ." He smooths his hands over his jeans and looks out at the lush treetops below. "Are you good? I mean . . . happy?"

The thing is, Declan already knows the answer. He knows about the incident at the pool in March. Plus whatever else Cory told him. And happy people don't do that kind of shit; they don't go looking for trouble. But that's not the answer someone wants to hear when they politely ask how you are.

A mosquito bite prickles my arm. Right in the crook of my elbow. It itches ten times more now that I'm staring at it. Everything itches. I pull on the elastic hair tie I wear around my wrist and let it snap onto my skin.

"Did you know that three sparklers burning together generate the same level of heat as a blowtorch?" I ask.

He drags his fingers across his eyebrow, back and forth like he's getting a headache, then rests his forearms over his knees again. "I did not."

"True story," I say, because it is, and because I can't tell him I'm happy, or unhappy, or anything, really.

The wind kicks up and Declan pushes his hair away from his face. I slip the elastic off my arm and hand it to him. He ties his hair into a cute little knot and a few pieces that are too short promptly fall down around his face.

"That climb was easier when we were thirteen," he says.

A blister is forming on my palm. I press my thumb against it. "Well, you didn't have all that hair throwing off your balance back then."

He smiles and leans back. His shoulder grazes mine. "That was a good night."

"It was my birthday," I say.

I'm not going to think about his last birthday back in February. When I tried to find a way to start talking to him again. Or the fact that he never responded. That three weeks later my birthday came and went, and I didn't hear a word.

Coming here was a terrible idea.

From a hundred feet below there's a whistle. A bright pink chrysanthemum firework patterns the sky, and a split second later is the boom. Then the sky is bursting with comets and peonies that shower down on us in vibrant shades of blue and orange.

I stand and lean against the railing, getting as close to the sky as I can. Declan climbs to his feet as well, inching up to the edge of the platform and gripping the rail so hard, blood drains from his knuckles.

His hand slides closer. Our pinkie fingers touch.

I don't mean to say it.

"Has it gotten any easier? Living without her, I mean."

He hesitates. His jaw clenches and I regret asking.

"In some ways I'm used to it. It has gotten a little easier with time, I guess. But I still miss her."

Of course he does. He lost his mother and his home in the same year. And sometimes, I hate his father for it.

Sure, his dad had his reasons for sending him away. He would be gone for work at least twice a month, and didn't think Declan should be spending that much time alone. Cory's parents offered to let Declan stay with them when he traveled, but he argued it would be too much of an imposition.

Every time a solution was offered, his dad came up with another justification. He was just trying to find a shortcut to the end of the grief. I guess we've all been guilty of that at some point. And I do believe he wanted what was best for Declan. I just don't see how he could possibly have thought getting pushed out of his own house was best.

My fingers choke the metal railing as a fresh blanket of remorse settles over my shoulders. Declan lost so much last year. He was hurting when he went away to school, over both his parents. And I was his girlfriend; it was my job to support him, to make sure he got through it. But instead, I made sure he lost me, too.

"You know you don't have to worry about that, though," he suddenly says. "Your mom is going to beat this."

The green and blue and red sparks of light start to swim together and I have to look away, so I settle on my mosquito bite.

"Oh, I know." I nod, too quickly for it to be convincing, and push my thumbnail into the bite, making an *X* in my skin.

He shifts his weight. I keep nodding like a Harper bobble-head, digging my nail in harder. The *X* turns purple.

"Harp . . ."

My leg is bouncing, using up every ounce of space available to keep the panic inside, but the first tear slips out anyway. His hand touches the back of my head.

Distance between us. That's what I need. Otherwise, the whole last year of avoiding Declan—of forcing myself to let him go—was pointless. Calls and texts I never returned, months of silence. He's undoing it all. And after everything we've been through and everything I've done, I don't deserve to find solace in him.

But I am selfish enough to take it.

My fingers connect with his shirt, turning into a fist around the fabric. He pulls me closer. My cheek rests against his shoulder and he smells the same, like citrus detergent and something spicy that is just Declan.

"Hey, *shh* . . . it's okay, Harp. You and me, we can get through this. I promise."

How many times have we rested our foreheads together and said those words? *You and me.*

It's always been him and me. And I can't deny how good it feels to have him here now. Only Declan understands this feeling of being tied to the rails, helpless against the train barreling toward you. Nothing I do will make any difference. I can't change the outcome of my mom's cancer any more than I can bring Natalie back from the dead.

"It's going to be okay," he says again.

Hearing it in his voice brings me so much closer to believing it.

The world continues to explode around us. And all I hear are the words of comfort he whispers into my hair.

Seven

ONE HOUR. I HAVE ONE FREAKING HOUR LEFT TO finish my photography assignment by the time I make it to the river.

What are we even supposed to be taking pictures of out here? National Geographic's website did not prepare me for this. Unless a sea otter miraculously makes its way upstream and strikes a pose for me, I'm completely screwed.

The river is already suffering from the recent lack of rain, and I halfheartedly take a few pictures of the lazy stream. A few yards up the bank, I spot a coiled black snake sunning itself. It doesn't seem particularly photogenic, so I keep my distance.

Some of my classmates catch up to my spot. Gwen scans the area and lies flat on her stomach at the edge of the stream.

Declan is across the water from her. He lowers his camera, standing with one hand in his front pocket and the other cupping the lens. The sun hits him at just the right angle to show the lightness in his hair, and I can't resist taking a quick snapshot of his profile.

Five days have passed since we climbed up the water tower together, and aside from a brief and stilted conversation before Monday's photography class, we haven't spoken since.

Not that I expected that night to change anything. Not really. He was just being a good guy, being there for me when I needed him. Because that's what we do for each other.

Or what he's always done for me, anyway.

With a mental groan, I hike farther down the trail until I'm alone again. Mr. Harrison said not to pay attention to what anyone else was doing today. And anyway I only have . . . Jesus, forty minutes left.

A tree trunk splotched with bright pink and green lichen catches my attention. I take a close shot and move to another tree off the path. A heart is carved into the bark. Inside are the initials *MJ+TK*. All I can think is, *People actually do this?*

They probably aren't even together anymore. MJ probably broke TK's heart. Or vice versa. But seeing it makes me realize how much I want to leave a mark like that behind when I'm gone. Proof that I made someone's life better just by being in it.

After his mom passed, Declan used to go days without smiling. But sometimes I could coax one out of him, and it was the best feeling in the world, seeing him smile because of me.

But that was a long time ago.

Trailing my fingers on the rough bark, I move around the trunk and am surprised to find similar marks on the other side. This is a promiscuous sort of tree.

"Want to walk back with me?"

I jump at the sound of Gwen's voice. "Is it time to go?" I check my phone. *Crap.*

A sucker puffs out one of her cheeks. She wipes her forehead with the bandanna around her wrist and nods. Over her shoulder, I see Declan hopping from boulder to boulder to get back to our side of the river. Gwen notices me noticing.

She pulls the sucker out of her mouth with a pop and jerks her head toward him. "What's the deal with you two?"

"You mean Declan?"

"No, you and Mr. Harrison." She flashes a smile that vanishes just as quickly. "Seriously, though. Unfinished business?"

"We're just . . . We used to be good friends."

She stops to take a picture of a plastic water bottle nestled in a bed of wildflowers, then scoops it up. "Huh. I just thought there might be some history there."

The camera strap is so hot around my neck. I shift it and wipe the sweat off my skin. Gwen and I both examine Declan, who is waiting for us up the trail.

First, ten years of friendship. The kind of friendship that means knowing everything there is to know about each other.

Where every one of our scars is, and how we got them. The pitch of his laugh when he's had a lot of sugar, or exactly what kind of coffee I need after a bad day. Friends who could spend twelve straight hours doing absolutely nothing and still want it to last twelve more. Who listen, even when the other is wrong; even when they're not making sense. Friends who could be mad at the whole universe, but never angry with each other for long. Who love each other unconditionally.

Then, six months of everything. A spring of skipped heart-beats every time he called me his girlfriend, then a summer of learning what being part of someone really meant. Six months of discovering the sound his heart makes with my head against his chest, and the taste of his tongue after he eats something salty. Or how his breath catches when I kiss his throat, and the way it tickles when he traces my collarbone. Two seasons of feeling more connected to a person than I ever thought possible.

Then October up until now. Nine hollow months of being nothing at all.

"What about you?" I ask. "Do you have a boyfriend?"

She smiles. "Jason. He lives in Charleston."

"Long distance, huh? That's rough."

"It's not so bad. I have some family down there—my cousin was actually the one who introduced us. So I get to visit a few times a year, and he drives up on the weekends sometimes."

Mackenzie skips right past us, all the way to Declan's side. We catch up a moment later.

72

"That was so fun, wasn't it? It's, like, the perfect day for a photo shoot." Mackenzie takes a snapshot of Gwen, who glares back at her. She turns to me next. "What are you up to this weekend?"

"Nothing really," I say. "Just lying low."

"What about you?" she asks Declan. "Any plans tonight?"

He nods to me. "Cory told me about a party off Route Two. That old campsite?"

Effing Cory. He almost never wants to come to parties. Suddenly he's interested now that Declan is back?

Everyone from school will be there. Including Kyle. And probably a small handful of other guys I messed around with last year. These are two worlds I do not want colliding.

"That's perfect! So, we'll all go." Mackenzie looks back and forth between us.

Gwen nudges her toe against my foot. "You in?"

Declan looks at me through his viewfinder and I shift my weight. The problem is, I already told Sadie I would go. Now I'm trapped. "Um . . . sure."

"Yay!" Mackenzie actually claps her hands together and I can't help but laugh. "First things first, I'm hungry. I think I want Thai food. Or maybe just a sandwich. Harper, are you coming to lunch?"

"Oh, I—"

"Yeah, she's not going to take no for an answer," Gwen says.

"You make me sound bossy or something."

"Nooo." Gwen shakes her head at Mackenzie, then nods to me.

We all head back to the community center parking lot. Mackenzie and Declan are joined at the hip, nudging each other and whispering as they plan their evening. Gwen hangs back to walk beside me, and I resolutely stare at the bumpers of each car we pass. I barely even notice when Declan rubs his neck and glances over his shoulder at us.

When we reach his car, he taps Mackenzie's arm and says something in her ear. She smiles and bounds over to her Datsun.

Declan leans against the trunk of his Focus and nods at us. "Bye, Gwen."

"Later."

I slow to a crawl. "You're not coming to lunch?"

"I'm going to sit this round out. But I'll see you tonight."

"Awesome," I say. Then I hate myself because I shouldn't have said anything and now I sound all eager. "I mean, cool. See you later."

Nope. Not an improvement.

He gets in his car and I wave because apparently I'm just as incapable of keeping my hands still as I am of keeping my mouth shut.

Gwen eyes me, running her tongue over her top lip, looking like she's trying really hard not to laugh.

"What?" I ask a little too defensively.

She shakes her head. "Let's hit it. I'm starving."

We decide on the Broad Street Deli for lunch. Mackenzie and Gwen pop in to use the bathroom, and I stay outside to guard our table. Less than a minute later, it's already under attack.

"Hey, homewrecker."

I glance up and scowl. Lindsay Sullivan. She crosses her arms and glares back. Behind her I spot Mel Hendrickson, wearing dark sunglasses and a sinister smile. And then I see Jenny.

I lick my lips. "Hi, Jen."

She looks me in the eye. Which is the most direct contact we've had since it happened. Her face is beet red. She gathers her stuff and pulls Mel's arm like she can't get out of my breathing space fast enough.

"Guys, let's go," she says.

Lindsay ignores her. "Throw yourself at anyone's boyfriend lately?"

A rusty pickup roars past, stirring the oppressive afternoon air. I wonder if pretending I didn't hear her is a viable option.

Throw myself at. See, that's the kind of thing that gets me all worked up. Because Jake lied to me just as much as he lied to Jenny. And probably nothing would have even happened if Sadie hadn't snuck off with his friend and totally sexiled me.

If she were here now, Sadie would know how to handle this. She'd stand up for me. And she certainly wouldn't back down from the confrontation.

But she isn't here. And I'm not her.

"I'm sorry," I say in an inaudible whisper. Maybe Jenny can read lips. Apparently Lindsay can.

"Like an apology coming from a skank like you is worth anything."

Through the café window I see Mackenzie and Gwen making their way back outside. *Shit.*

"I'm leaving," Jenny says in a firm voice. Mel is close on her heels. But Lindsay lingers.

This isn't an argument I can have right now. It's none of Lindsay's business, anyway.

"Look, just tell Jenny I'm—"

With a flick of her bangle-wrapped wrist, Lindsay tosses the rest of her iced tea in my face.

"Slut," she hisses, backing away just as Gwen comes through the door. "I hope you get chlamydia."

Gwen rushes over in time to hear Lindsay's closing statement. "What the hell was that?"

"Nothing. Just . . ." With a shaking hand, I tug at my soaked T-shirt. It's stuck to me like a second skin. *"Fuck."*

Each inhale comes faster and louder than the one before. People are staring. Slowing down as they pass by like I'm a car accident they can't help but watch. Blood rushes in my ears and I squeeze my eyes shut.

Mackenzie takes my hand and leads me inside to the restroom. We weave through the line in front of the counter and pass a dozen or so tables, but I focus on Mackenzie's back the whole time, too mortified to meet anyone's gaze. She locks the door once we're all inside.

"Give me your shirt."

I pull it over my head and sit down on the toilet. Try again to breathe normally.

Gwen crouches down next to me. "You okay?" She rips off a wad of toilet paper and hands it over.

The concerned crease between her brows pushes me over the edge. These girls aren't supposed to know this about me. They're supposed to be separate from my school life. So is Declan. But it's all running together, and I can't stand the look of sympathy she's giving me now. I don't deserve it.

"I hooked up with her boyfriend," I blurt out. "Not the girl who threw the drink at me. The other girl, Jenny. They were on the swim team with me."

Mackenzie finishes rinsing my shirt and turns on the hand dryer. I try to explain.

"I got into some trouble a couple months back. I was with him when I got caught. I didn't even like him, but he told me they'd broken up." I wince and wring the tissue between my hands. "And they hadn't. Not yet, anyway."

We're quiet, listening to the buzz and whirring of the dryer.

"I really hate myself for doing that to her. I never meant to hurt anyone."

The dryer shuts off and Mackenzie brings me my top. It's

still damp but less sticky than before. "We all have things we wish we could change," she says.

I look up at her and the realization is a semi truck through my chest. Mackenzie is a girl who deserves Declan.

"And Mackenzie and I have your back," Gwen adds.

"Thank you." I pull my shirt on and no one says anything for a few beats. My skin feels both clammy and flushed. "Do you think . . . Could you guys just not tell Declan about this?"

They exchange a glance before Gwen jumps in.

"Of course not. None of his business."

After getting myself under control, I don't have much of an appetite left. The girls walk me back to my car.

"So . . . we'll see you tonight?" Mackenzie asks.

"Oh." I look over my shoulder at a bed of daffodils, all of them wilting under the midafternoon sun. "Yeah, maybe. I'm not sure if I'm up for that scene."

She bites her lip and nods. "I understand. But I do hope you'll come. Feel better, okay?"

"Thanks," I say. She gives me another fast hug, and I smile at Gwen before opening my door.

I drive home in silence. When I turn onto my street, I pull over and crank the radio up loud. I reach for the spare towel I keep in the backseat, roll it into a ball, and cover my mouth.

Scream until my voice goes hoarse.

Eight

THE HOUSE HAS A DELICATE BALANCE THESE DAYS.
Bloodshot eyes and a tea-stained shirt will throw everything
off-kilter. I sneak up to the bathroom as quietly as humanly
possible.

Hot water helps. Scalding my skin even though it's humid
as shit outside. But I need to feel clean, and ever since what I
did in October, this is the only way.

Besides, I like sitting in the shower. It's become the only
place I ever feel really, truly alone. The only place I can break
down and immediately wash away all the evidence.

At least until the hot water runs out.

After I get dressed, I call Sadie.

"What do you mean you're not coming?"

I'm in the kitchen, which is the farthest from my parents I could get. "This afternoon I sort of had a run-in with Lindsay and Jenny. It wasn't pretty. And look, Declan's going to be there and things are already kind of weird between us. . . ."

"Come on, who gives a shit about Lindsay Sullivan? That girl is the worst. And things are probably weird with Declan because you *act* weird around Declan. Anyway, I'm already on my way to your house."

I rub my temple. "I still have to ask my parents."

"So go ask. I'll see you in ten."

I can't say I really expected that conversation to go any differently. Sadie always gets her way. Anyway, she's right. I shouldn't let people like Lindsay get to me.

My parents are lounging in their bedroom, Dad reading while Mom dozes. More than a week after her first chemo treatment, the side effects finally seem to have taken hold. She stretches herself awake when I come through the door.

"Hi, honey."

"Hey." My arms cross. "So, I wanted to ask you guys . . . There's this party tonight . . ."

Dad puts his book down. "Oh?"

Mom tries to sit up. "Who are you going with?"

"Well, I'm driving over with Sadie. But everyone will be there. Cory and Declan. Those girls—my friends, from Photography."

Mom groans. She shifts over the side of the bed and blows

out a deep breath. Dad walks around and crouches beside her.

"Need to get up?"

She nods and he locks his hands around her elbows, guiding her by both arms over to the bathroom. I stumble out of the way.

"Mom? Are you okay?"

She mumbles that she's fine.

Dad looks over his shoulder. "We'll talk about that party later, Harper."

"But . . . okay. Just, I'm supposed to leave in a few minutes. . . ." He doesn't answer. Mom bends over the sink, her head falling into her hands. She takes deep breaths through her mouth. "Dad? Can I help?"

"I've got this. See you later tonight."

He shuts the bathroom door.

Sadie talks the whole way over to her town house. I roll down the window and watch as we drive past kids running through sprinklers and playing soccer on their front lawns. We pull out of the subdivision and pass Mom's favorite flower shop and the produce stand that she says has the freshest strawberries. I catch bits and pieces from Sadie—Will called her to ask about the party, she bought a new top to wear—but I'm not really listening.

I'm replaying that moment back at my house. Over and over, I see Mom in pain. And I've never felt so helpless. I knew

Mom would have bad days on the chemo, and that it would make her feel sick. I thought I was ready for that. But I wasn't ready for this, for every last thing in my life to be completely out of my control.

We pull to the curb and I follow Sadie inside. She kicks off her shoes and I line my sandals up next to them, walking barefoot into her living room.

"Hey, you're home!" Mr. Walker says from his desk in the corner.

Sadie blows past him and into the kitchen, grabbing a diet Boomerang from the fridge before thundering up the stairs and slamming her bedroom door behind her.

She's been this way with her dad for as long as I've known her. They moved here at the start of freshman year, as soon as her parents' divorce was finalized. That year, both Cory and Declan had a different lunch period than me. The swim season hadn't started yet, and after spending all my free time with Cory and Declan since elementary school, I wasn't exactly flush with other friends. Sadie's first day of school, she walked into the cafeteria like she owned it, spotted me sitting alone, and sat down across from me. She was the most self-assured and, frankly, gorgeous girl I'd ever met. Model-thin, with a mane of golden hair reaching all the way to her waist and ridiculously perfect skin. She was a force to be reckoned with. The only boys immune to her charms were Declan and Cory, who made it clear they thought she was shallow and stuck-up and a few other choice S-words. But despite their antagonism, I certainly wasn't going to argue when Sadie inexplicably chose me to be her friend.

She never talks much about her mom, or the reason her parents split up. And I try to respect her privacy. Unlike most people in Carson, I know when something is none of my business.

Her dad raises his eyebrows at me, eager like he hasn't had a conversation with anyone in days.

"Hi, Mr. Walker."

"Harper! Haven't seen you around much lately. How have you been?"

"All right."

"How are your parents?"

My finger slips under the elastic band around my wrist. It snaps against my skin. "They're good. Thanks."

"Well, tell them I said hello."

"Will do." I make an awkward gesture toward the stairs and take them two at a time, slipping into Sadie's room without knocking.

Her walls are covered floor to ceiling with concert posters and cutouts from fashion magazines, with a few pictures of us scattered into the mix. Sadie grabs a bottle out of a shoe box in her closet and I practically lunge for it. Because if I can't get out of this party, I'm at least going to need some help getting through it.

"Go for it," she says. "I'll drive tonight."

Two shots and half a can of Boomerang later, I manage to repress the memory of my mother doubled over and dry heaving, and arrive in my happy place.

Sadie comes over with a flat iron. She actually has the patience for straightening my curls, so I let her have at it.

"Beautiful," she says when she's finished.

For some reason, I always believe her when she calls me that. Partly because she's beautiful, so she really ought to know. And maybe also because she was the first person besides my mother to use that word to describe me.

"Thanks." I absentmindedly take another sip of Boomerang and immediately regret it. Blech.

She circles back with eyeliner and puts the finishing touches on my makeup.

"You look so hot tonight. Kyle's gonna be all over you."

"Which is precisely why we should go to the movies instead."

Back when we first started hanging out freshman year, I didn't have much interest in all the parties Sadie got invited to. I was perfectly content dragging her out for ice cream or getting dragged through the mall in Raleigh. It wasn't until sophomore year that she wore me down and I finally accepted one of her invitations.

It's comical, looking back at how intimidated I was by everyone Sadie hung around with. I used to beg Declan and Cory to come with me, though I couldn't blame them for refusing 99 percent of the time. At these parties, we were on Sadie's turf, and they still wanted nothing to do with her. Sadie didn't exactly set out a welcome mat for my other best friends, either. But I kept tagging along because other boys I'd never even spoken to were suddenly paying me an awful lot of attention. Being in Sadie's company made me desirable by extension. And at first, I liked the way it felt to finally step out of my bubble and into a foreign social life. Like I was better than the freakishly tall tomboy who swam under everyone's radar.

Sophomore Harper was downright hilarious.

Sadie raises an eyebrow and dabs a fresh layer of gloss onto my lips with the pad of her ring finger. "Well, what else do you expect from Kyle? He tasted the honey and now he wants the whole pot."

"Gross, now I keep picturing him dressed as Pooh Bear."

"Ha, Pooh Bear. That's gonna stick."

Pooh Bear is going to be disappointed if he thinks he's getting any honey from this pot. Anyway, if I'm being honest, he's not even the real problem here. He's like a fruit fly: annoying, but harmless. With most of Carson's underage population planning to attend this shindig, I can think of several graver threats. Including Mackenzie.

I'm not even sure if I trust her or Gwen yet, and they certainly don't owe me any favors. What's to stop them from telling Declan what happened this afternoon? Hell, half the kids from my own school would leap at the opportunity to talk shit about me. Sooner or later, Declan is going to hear the rumors. He thinks sneaking into the pool is bad? If he knew the real reason I stopped speaking to him in October, or that Jake wasn't even close to the only guy I had a lapse in judgment with this past spring, he would never see me the same way again.

Sadie finishes my makeup and touches up her own, then turns to her closet. I sit down on her bed and wipe some of my lip gloss off on the back of my hand.

"So who's it going to be?" she asks.

"Huh?"

"If Kyle's done, who's next?" She slips out of her shorts and steps into a spandex skirt. "No, wait, let me guess. Could it be . . . Declan?"

My fingers find my necklace. "Nothing is going to happen between Declan and me."

"Mm-hmm. I've heard that one before."

She pulls out a different skirt and tosses it in my direction. She's always offering up her closet to me. But if the clothes are tight on Sadie, they're catastrophic around my hips.

"Anyway, I'd hope not," she goes on. "Because we both know how much better you could do."

Summer after eighth grade was the first time I caught Declan looking at me differently. I'd tagged along on one of his numerous trips to the driving range, and by the time he finished hitting a bucket, we were both starving. I found a vending machine and bought us each a bag of pretzels. Then

I put the rest of my change into the machine and turned to leave. Declan reached for the coin release, but I tugged his hand away.

"Leave it," I said. "Might make someone's day better."

He left it, but not before giving me that split-second glance—one so intense it seemed like he wanted to memorize every atom of me. I turned that moment over in my mind for weeks afterward.

But by the time summer wound down and high school started up, I'd decided I must have imagined that look in his eye. And for the next two years, we remained firmly planted in the friend zone. That's the real irony here. Declan and I may never have gotten together if it wasn't for Sadie.

She's the one who gave us the final push during April of sophomore year: a game of Truth or Dare at Leah Gilmore's sweet sixteen party. It was a few months after Natalie's funeral, and at that point Declan and I still hadn't gotten any further than holding hands when we watched a movie alone in the dark, or when we went for walks in the woods. He had this way of smoothing his thumb over the back of my wrist. Sometimes the memory of his touch is so vivid, I can almost feel it.

Declan's dad had already started to throw himself into his work, and Cory was busy with afternoon swim practices, while mine were usually first thing in the morning. So Declan and I began spending more and more time alone together. We spent hours doing homework in the tree house, or playing I Spy at the edge of the quarry. But sometimes our shared history felt like a roadblock. Like it was the fear of losing anything more that kept us from making the leap.

Part of me sensed Sadie was going to do it all along, but I still flushed a deep red when she dared me to kiss Declan. It would be my first kiss. Sadie knew that.

I managed to mumble that it was no big deal, mostly to settle my own nerves, but Declan wouldn't look at me. He was too busy glaring at Sadie.

"What's the matter, Declan?" Sadie asked, a smile playing on her lips. "Can't handle a stupid game?"

Declan finally looked away from her, shaking his head. He stood up, and might have looked down at me, but I couldn't bring myself to meet his gaze.

"It's not a game for me," he said gruffly.

I found him on the front porch. The street lamps cast a puddle of cool light up the lawn. I crossed my arms against the chill and hesitated on the welcome mat outside the door. Declan stared straight ahead when I sat down next to him, and when I shivered he took off his jacket and put it around my shoulders without a word. When he finally spoke, he spoke quickly, telling me that he was sorry, but he just didn't want to kiss me like that—with everyone watching and on Sadie's terms. He paused, taking a long breath before looking at me and smiling shyly. "But I do want to kiss you."

"What's so bad about Declan?" I ask now. Sadie turns to

face me and I look down at the pleated skirt in my lap. "I mean, he's gotten kind of cute, don't you think?"

She stares at me for another beat, her lips pursed, then turns back to her closet. "You're really considering going down that road again? After all those weeks you spent whining about how much you missed him?"

She doesn't mean to be harsh. This is just how Sadie looks out for me. Same as when the rumors about me first started. She defended me to anyone who dared open their mouth in front of her. But when it's just the two of us, she's never been afraid to dish a serving of cold, hard truth.

"Okay, I get it. You have never liked Declan."

"Like that feeling isn't mutual. He practically begged you to stop hanging out with me, as I recall. And whatever, it's not even about that. Do you seriously not remember how long it took you to get over him last time?"

My eyes drift to her windowsill and land on the orchid her ex-boyfriend Christopher gave her last summer. Christopher, the boy she still has pictures of on her phone. She would never admit she holds on to a flower and a few blurry photographs because she never really let go of Christopher.

I fold the skirt neatly and put it on the bed. "I remember."

"Be careful how close you let him get."

A sequined top lands next to me.

"Try that," she tells me, already stepping out of the skirt she just put on and kicking it aside. "Ugh. My thighs are getting so fat. I need to do some serious lunges before I wear that again."

"Sadie, you're a twig. Knock it off."

She wrinkles her nose at her reflection. Turning to look at her profile, she sighs. "With no muscle definition. I'm going to start running tomorrow, I swear."

This is beginning to feel a lot like when someone complains about how disappointed they are in their terrible SAT score, and yours is significantly worse. Whenever Sadie criticizes her chest-stomach-hips-thighs, I automatically compare them to mine. And believe me, my score is definitely lower. Sadie always tells me otherwise, that she wishes she had my legs, or would kill for my butt. But in reality, going from two-a-day swim practices to hardly exercising at all is beginning to change my body. It's hard, though, because my stomach hasn't gotten the memo and I'm still hungry. All. The. Time.

I swap my shirt for hers. "Well, what do you think?"

Sadie yanks on my forearms to uncross them. She looks me over and nods her approval. "Wear it tonight."

I look at myself in the mirror. Despite the couple pounds I've gained, I don't look too bad. It's a cute top. A bit tight, but less revealing than I thought it would be, with just the right amount of cleavage.

Sadie's now wrapped in an even shorter skirt than the last one. "Ready?"

"Yeah." I grab my purse and hand her the to-go bottle, taking one last look at her orchid before following her out the door.

Her dad jumps up from the kitchen table when we get downstairs.

"We're going out," Sadie calls to him as she slips into a pair of wedges and tosses me my flip-flops.

He rocks onto his heels and smiles at us. "Not too late!"

"Mmkaybye," she says, already halfway out the door.

I screw my face up until the taste of lukewarm vodka passes. Blowing out a fiery breath, I eye the far corner of the campsite, where Cory, Gwen, and Mackenzie are standing in a loose circle near the keg.

"Who are these girls, anyway?" Sadie grumbles. She nods in their direction.

She's giving them The Look. The one where she clenches her teeth and wrinkles her nose, and her top lip curls up just slightly. It almost makes her ugly. Almost.

When she gives someone that look, I know the next ten to fifteen minutes will be spent discussing their numerous flaws as well as the various, unforgivable ways they've offended her.

"Gwen is the one with dark hair who looks pissed off most of the time. The blonde is Mackenzie. They're in my photography class."

"Is Mackenzie from 1955?" She squints in distaste at the full, tea-length skirt Mackenzie has on.

"At least she knows who she is."

I scan the party again. A few people are relaying wood over

to the bonfire pit in the middle of the clearing, where another team of guys is alternating between chugging from red plastic cups and trying to get the fire going. All that results is a funnel of white smoke. They haven't realized the kindling is too damp, and at this rate they'll be lit well before the fire. Cory and the girls move off to the side as a group gathers around the keg. Declan has to be around somewhere if Cory is here.

I'm really not as worked up about him as Sadie thinks. I know that one night isn't going to change anything; that there's no bridge back to who we were before. And I was being honest when I told Gwen we were just friends.

But I did feel *something* shift between us up on that water tower. It's not completely crazy to think he might have felt it too.

"Well, she looks ridiculous," Sadie says. She rests her foot on the front bumper and leans back against the hood. "Who invited her?"

I take another sip of vodka and grimace. "Declan did. Kind of."

"Mm, that figures. Your charity case is taking on one of his own," she says. My jaw tightens. Sadie either doesn't notice or doesn't care. "Anyway, all I meant was you're way hotter."

I know Sadie is just trying to be nice. But I don't need to be prettier than Mackenzie, or anyone else for that matter.

A couple yards to my left, Declan strides back to the thick of the party.

"Hey, Declan!" I hop off the car and take a step toward him.

He must not have heard me. He keeps walking, and in one violent swing, he snaps the twig in his hand against a tree trunk. The open aggression of the gesture unnerves me.

Sadie nudges my arm with the bottle. "One more and then let's go."

I take another quick sip and Sadie stashes the vodka back in her purse. She grabs some bug repellent out of her trunk and we take turns spraying the backs of each other's legs and arms. The chemicals coat my tongue, and I cough and back out of the cloud of DEET.

We walk up the row of cars into a clearing where forty or so people are split into small groups. The site is about a mile into the forest, and people are already taking full advantage of the fact that we can be as loud as we want.

Cheers erupt as the bonfire finally catches, and it takes a few moments for the series of congratulatory back-pats and fist-pumps to subside. I love a good campfire—the sound of logs hissing and crackling as they heat up, the smell of burned leaves left on my clothes and in my hair. But I try to keep Sadie away from open flames if I can help it, so I steer us toward the far side where Will and a few other guys from school have set up to play beer pong.

This new location also happens to have a view of Declan, who's rejoined the circle next to Cory. I know I need to stop looking at him. But the thing is, he's wearing this green golf shirt that I've seen a thousand times. The soft cotton one that always smells like his citrus detergent. Only it fits him differently now. Like if he flexed it might burst open and reveal a giant S across his chest.

God. I seriously need to stop looking at him.

Gwen catches my eye and waves. I try to gesture that I'll be over in a minute. Her nose wrinkles and she shakes her head. I guess I'm not that good at sign language.

I turn back to Sadie, who hands me a beer. Before I can ask where she even got it, she raises both arms over her head and opens her mouth at something over my shoulder.

"Pooh Bear!"

Oh boy.

Kyle snakes his arm around my waist and pulls me into a side hug. "Hey, Sloan, having a good time?"

"Yeah!" Sadie says. She sends me a wink. "Harper was just telling me what a great time she's having."

"Glad to hear it."

Kyle's hand is lingering. I step away and sneak a glance at my friends. Declan's back is to me. Gwen nods distractedly to something he's saying, but she's watching me.

I have to get away from Kyle.

No sooner do I think this than he once again shuffles closer. His hand slides around my hip and his fingers find their way into my back pocket. His toxic cologne smothers me. Honestly, what is he thinking with that stuff?

"Nice night for a walk. If you're interested later."

Putting my hand firmly on his shoulder to keep him in place, I take a stride backward. "I'm going to go catch up with some friends now."

"Cool," he says with eyes that travel farther south by the second.

Sadie is already snuggled up to Will, so I wander over to Declan and that group by myself. As I slide between two people, I glance up and catch a rigid look on Declan's face. I hesitate for a moment before pushing the rest of the way through.

He's standing alone when I reach him. "Hey."

"Hi."

"That was a fun class this morning, huh?"

He nods and looks over my head. Looks everywhere but at me.

"You okay tonight, Dec?"

Finally, he meets my gaze. "Why wouldn't I be?"

When Declan first went away last August, we spoke every night after dinner. Even on the nights we had nothing to say, the nights when all we could do was lie in bed with our phones pressed against our ears and listen to each other breathe. We were in love; we were *finally* together. And we were determined not to let the distance undermine our relationship. But after a few weeks, he started to slip. The calls became every other night. And before long, our conversations were even more painful than the silence.

I tried not to let it show how lonely I was without him. I didn't tell him about crying myself to sleep or about how I couldn't bear to go to the tree house anymore. Never told him how much it hurt when he'd forget to call me back. Because I wasn't going to be that kind of girlfriend, the kind so dependent on her boyfriend that she can't manage to be happy without him. Or the kind who would turn his time of need into something all about myself. I just tried to cope with it as best I could. Which, as it turns out, was not very well at all.

I dig my toe into pine needles and sand. "I don't know," I say in a small voice.

Gwen is over by the keg now, with Mackenzie and Cory. Everyone except Mackenzie is filling a red plastic cup. My own drink weighs down my hand. I lower it to hip level.

All of us drinking . . . that would explain why Declan is so out of sorts. Not that he hasn't tried it himself, but that was before a drunk driver killed his mother. As far as I know, Declan hasn't touched alcohol since.

Still, I don't know what else he expected from a kegger in the woods.

Someone throws a bunch of pine needles onto the bonfire, sending sparks up toward the sky. The needles smoke out and the party suddenly smells like Christmas. Like a thousand afternoons spent playing hide-and-seek in the forest with Declan.

"So." I tuck my hair behind my ear. Then I can't keep my

hand still, so I do it again. "Your dad must be happy to have you home."

"Don't know about that. You remember what he's like."

I remember hearing him yell at Declan for leaving dirty dishes in the sink, or for forgetting his basketball in the driveway. He'd holler over the smallest of infractions, with little regard for how much it upset his family.

And then I remember the way he hugged Declan the day he left for boarding school. Holding on so hard I thought he'd never let go.

"I know he's tough . . . but you haven't seen him since Christmas, right?"

"Yeah, well. I think he's gotten used to being on his own. But he's out of town on business half the time and I'll be caddying most weekends, so I doubt we'll cross paths much these next couple months. Then I'll go back to school. Problem solved."

"Oh . . . school is still good, then?"

"Yeah, great. Really great. Thanks for asking."

The wind picks up, funneling smoke straight at us. We both shuffle to the side and Declan leans against the trunk of a pine tree, looking away again.

This attitude is what I've expected ever since seeing him in Cory's driveway. I just don't know why he waited until now to show it. And I don't understand what's changed since the Fourth.

Unless I imagined everything about that night. Confused sympathy for affection. And I must have, because if his stiff posture and closed-off demeanor are any indication, I'll be lucky to get another hour out of this trial friendship of ours.

It was unfair to break down in front of him that night. I can't blame him for wanting to set boundaries. He probably wishes he never started speaking to me again in the first place.

Mackenzie comes over with Cory. "You came! Wow, you look different," she says.

Gwen follows behind them. "Smokin'."

Cory purses his lips. He clearly disagrees with her assessment, but he can also kiss my ass.

I manage not to look at Declan for his reaction. "Thanks. You girls look great too. Mackenzie, I love your skirt."

"Oh, thanks!" She looks down and makes the full skirt sway a little side to side. "I work at Second Helpings. That vintage store on Ninth? Most of my paycheck tends to go right back to the owner."

"Mackenzie wants to work in costume design," Declan adds. He turns to her. "Harper isn't really interested in theater."

"No, that's . . ." I frown at Declan. Where did that come from? "I think that's great," I finish.

Gwen clears her throat. "Need a refill, Harper? I do. Let's go." She hooks her arm through mine and leads me to the keg. "So who was that guy you were talking to a minute ago?"

"He's no one." I pump the keg a few times and fill both cups. "Just this guy from school."

"So you two aren't . . ."

"No. Definitely not."

She nods thoughtfully, and I glance over my shoulder. Declan is over by the speakers now, talking to Catherine Daniels. Catherine has been crushing on Declan since the sixth grade. And if he didn't know it before, he does now.

She pulls him toward the dance party and promptly shoves her huge boobs in his face.

Well. Who can compete with that.

With a tight smile I excuse myself from Gwen, following the perimeter of the clearing and sipping my beer. The farther away from the fire I get, the more I notice how much the temperature has dropped since the sun went down. The song changes, but Declan and Catherine keep dancing. I remind myself I have no claim on Declan. None whatsoever.

Especially now that Catherine is ever-so-discreetly grinding her ass into his crotchal region. God, could she be any more aggressive? Not that Declan seems to mind. He is a guy, after all. And they're all the same. Every. Single. One of them.

Not that it's any of my business if Catherine is his type. It's just, I could understand why he would be interested in someone like Mackenzie, with her shiny ponytail and tiny waist. But now all of a sudden he's into this girl who insists on being called *Cat*? And who, for the record, actually had to serve a suspension last year for breaking the dress code eleven days in a row. No joke. *Eleven warnings,* this girl had. Just put on a fucking sweater.

Anyway, it's none of my concern. I just feel sorry for Mackenzie, is all. I'm not sure what her and Declan's deal is, but it's obvious she likes him. She's around here somewhere, and I bet she'll be crushed if she sees them together.

I scowl and spin around, sloshing beer from my cup that narrowly misses Gwen, who hops out of the way.

"What's going on?"

Pretending to be interested in something across the clearing, I say, "Nothing. Just partying. Having a blast."

"Come on."

She drags me back to the bonfire and sits across from me. The fire is really raging now. Even the stones around the pit are warm. Everyone looks different in the orange light, their faces glowing as they sing along to the music. I try to act as happy as they all seem, but a few minutes later, Gwen checks her phone. "It's time for my phone date with Jason. You all right here for a bit?"

"Of course," I tell her. But once she's gone I change my mind and want to make her come back, because I don't like sitting alone in a crowded party. I need something to do and oh look, my cup is empty again. So I head for the keg.

I stand and step over the log I was sitting on, only I miscalculate how high I have to lift my leg to clear it, and I trip. Right into Declan.

He catches me by the waist and I grab his shoulder to steady myself.

And we stay like that.

Heat blossoms under his touch, spreading from my ribs down to my toes. "Have fun dancing?"

Okay, so . . . not my strongest opener. But I'm pretty confident I kept the stalker-level jealousy out of my voice.

"I guess. Cat's a nice girl."

I want to choke her.

I go to take another drink but my cup is still empty, so I just stare at it instead.

We both stand completely still, and why hasn't he moved his hand off my waist yet? A guy carrying a cooler tries to squeeze past us and I wind up even closer to Declan. Neither of us has said anything for a million years. Someone needs to say something.

"Did you get my card?" I blurt out.

The postcard was an ugly picture of the Carson water tower that I found last winter at the drugstore downtown and saved for three months before finally getting up the nerve to send it in time for his birthday in February.

He nods slowly. "I got it."

The burn starts in my ears and works its way across my cheekbones. I force myself to look him in the eye.

"Just six words," he continues. "'Happy birthday, Declan. Thinking of you.' Six words after all those months of nothing. What was the point?"

Biting the inside of my cheek, I trace the seam on his shoulder. "Just—I just . . ." I've lost all control over my fingers. They curl around his collar, the ends of his hair. Track down the back of his neck. "I missed you. You have no idea how much I've missed you."

His eyes are dark hazel tonight, smoldering. His lips part and his hand skims another inch up my side.

That same pull from the other night is back between us. And I know he feels it too, because you can't look at someone the way he's looking at me and not feel something.

"You missed me?" he asks. I nod and he dips his head. His mouth lingers by my ear, each of his exhales tingling down my neck. Then he turns, whispers onto my cheek, "Are you this sweet to all your charity cases?"

Frozen. My tongue, my lips. And it doesn't matter, because there are no words.

His hand drops off my side.

"No, that wasn't—Sadie said that. I never said—"

"It's fine." His lips curve but it isn't a real smile. It's painful. "No hard feelings, okay?"

No. I smash my lips together and shake my head. *No.*

He's straightening, not looking at me anymore, and I have to make him see.

Time stands still as my heart races faster. I lift onto my toes until we're almost the same height. My eyes are on his mouth. Then my lips are.

And then he pulls away.

I tumble down onto flat feet and in my head I take it all back.

His hand covers my wrist. "Harp . . ."

I yank my hand down to my side. I can't speak. Don't dare breathe. I am paralyzed and I cannot believe I convinced myself I deserve him.

"You've been drinking."

My eyes flash back to his. "I know, but . . ."

His teeth rake over his bottom lip and he looks away. I follow his gaze to Mackenzie. She's standing next to Cory, and her back is to us. And the way he's watching her, the longing and frustration etched on his face, it feels like swallowing acid. My insides burn. "I just don't want you to do something you're going to regret," he finally says.

The air is crushed out of me. Not only does Declan not want to kiss me, he wants so badly not to kiss me that he feels sorry I would even fathom the idea. And he's right. What the hell is wrong with me? Why would I do something like that to Mackenzie? She has only ever been perfectly nice to me. What kind of person am I, that I can't keep my hands to myself even when I know she has feelings for Declan?

My eyes fill with hot tears that I cannot let him see. I stumble back and everything around me—the deafening medley of voices and heavy bass, the chaos of people drinking and flailing—all of it collapses in.

"Too late."

Nine

TIME IS STUCK IN SLOW MOTION. I'M STUCK IN
front of Declan, searching the crowd for a way out. My eyes
fall on the fire, follow the smoke floating up, gray against the
near-black sky. I step back just as Sadie throws her arms around
me from behind.

"Found you!"

She shoves the bottle of vodka at me and glides over to
Declan. She smiles at him, and I know that smile. Why is she
giving it to Declan?

I take a sip from the bottle. She puts her hand on his shoulder, right where mine was. His eyes drift to meet hers. I take a
longer drink.

"Long time no see," she says with a seductive lilt.

"Hello, Sadie."

"Know what, Harper? You might've been right," she says without taking her eyes off him. "He has gotten cuter."

She smiles wickedly. I blink. Or maybe flinch. What the fuck did she say that for?

Her gaze lingers on my arms, which are crossed in front of me. I shift and let them slip down to my sides.

"So, guys, what've I missed?"

My hand presses against my sternum. My chest is so tight. No room to breathe.

Sadie wants an answer.

"We were just . . . catching up."

"Ah. Just like old times, right, Ducklan?"

Sadie's nickname for Declan is more obnoxious than it is offensive. Still, he straightens and her hand slips down to his elbow.

"Just like," Declan says.

And it is. It's exactly like old times the way Sadie is provoking Declan, doing everything she can to get under his skin. Even though she knows, has to know, that it means getting under mine. It isn't cute anymore, not that it ever was to begin with. If this is Sadie's idea of keeping me from getting hurt, I might be better off without her protection.

"Oh. You're here," Cory says, walking up. Mackenzie and Gwen are still talking a few yards away. "Hey, weren't you puking in Harper's bushes last time I saw you?"

I close my eyes and when I open them, Sadie's smile is

gone. She isn't touching Declan anymore either.

"Who can remember?"

"Not you, probably."

Sadie glares at him.

He's undeterred. "Because you were blackout. Get it?"

Declan smirks at Cory's joke and I shift forward to say . . .
I don't know. Something. But I'm not fast enough. Sadie spins
around and yanks the vodka out of my hands.

She tosses her hair over her shoulder and casts me a cool
smile just as the other girls join us.

"Mm, yes, well. You all have fun playing catch-up. And
speaking of old friends . . ." She glances over her shoulder.
"I know I saw Jake Thornton around here somewhere. Oh,
and there's Jenny." She turns back to me with combative eyes.
"Better look alive, Harper."

She storms off and even though I'm trying not to look at
anyone, I catch Gwen's eyebrows rise.

Cory rolls his eyes and moves back toward Mackenzie.
Gwen hesitates before turning away.

And I have nowhere to go—can't stay here, and it's like the
bonfire sucked all of the oxygen out of the forest. How did I let
this happen? Let myself think he could still want me after all
I've done, what I've become, I am nothing.

"I see you two are still BFFs," Declan says.

The ground is swimming and I try to nod, but my head
feels heavy.

He nods too, then cocks his head to the side. "Guess some habits are hard to break."

My arms are crossed again. I hug my ribs tighter and back away, knocking into someone and turning and pushing through bodies.

I make it halfway back to the cars, past a guy peeing on a tree and a girl puking behind another, and press the heels of my palms under my eyes to keep my eyeliner from running because there is almost nothing more embarrassing than being That Girl Who Cried at That Party. And I've already reached my limit for humiliation tonight.

Gwen catches up with me. "What happened back there?"

I shake my head.

"Okay . . . um, I think we're all taking off in a few minutes."

Over her shoulder, I see Kyle. He's propped against a card table, smoking a cigarette. He isn't going to fix anything. But he can distract me for tonight.

I hold eye contact with him. Three. Four. Five seconds. Long enough. He flashes a cocky grin.

"You need a ride?" Gwen asks.

"No. Thanks." I watch as Kyle ditches the girls around him and makes his way over to the sure bet. "I'm staying."

"Oh . . . okay. But if you need a ride later, you can call me. Here, give me your phone." She takes it and saves her number in my contacts. "Call anytime."

I thank her again, even though I know I'll never call. I'll tell my parents I'm sleeping at Sadie's. When we're sober, we'll drive back to her house. That's our routine.

Kyle stops in front of me a moment later. "Walk?"

His arm wraps around my shoulders, guiding me down the trail to his Ford Escape. Behind the barrier of trees and outside the ring of people, the music is quieter. Distant. I can hear my own footsteps and Kyle exhaling smoke from his cigarette. Suddenly all of his friends hovering near his car get real interested in tossing around a football, leaving us in relative privacy.

He pops the trunk and flips open a cooler.

"You know . . ." He twists the cap off a beer and hands it to me. "A few of us are planning on camping out here. You should stay."

"I'm just waiting for Sadie."

He takes a sip of his beer and cocks one eyebrow, and I know he's thinking the same thing I am: I'll be waiting for a while.

He sits down in the open trunk and pulls my hand along so I'll sit next to him. I let him.

"No problem. We can still have a good time while we wait."

His arm falls back into place around my shoulders, and he holds his cigarette up for me. Heavy-lidded eyes watch me lean forward and take a drag. I blow the smoke straight up at the stars.

Rolling the beer bottle between my palms, I wait as he takes one last puff and stubs the cigarette out. His hand slips under my hair and curls around the back of my neck. Straight out of the playbook. His thumb traces my jaw and he leans closer and I know what his next move will be. I know. And despite the fact that he isn't Declan, isn't anyone to me, I also know what I'm going to do.

I'm going to let Kyle kiss me.

Ten

FIVE WEEKS INTO HER TREATMENT, MOM STILL hasn't let me see her cry. But I can't pretend not to hear it today.

I'm sitting on my bed, reviewing the files from last week's photography class, but about a half hour ago my attention was hijacked by the shot I took of Declan out on the rocks. At the sound of her shower shutting off, I stow my laptop away. Mom's sobs travel through our shared wall and vibrate right through me, shaking loose any lingering thoughts of Declan or the disastrous bonfire last weekend.

I wait a moment for Mom to get dressed before I go to check on her.

"Mom?" I call from outside her bathroom door. "Everything okay? Do you need Dad?"

"No, honey," she says in a high-pitched voice. She clears her throat. "No, I'm fine."

I hesitate on the other side, half turning away before reaching back for the doorknob. "I'm coming in, okay?"

No answer. I push open the door. She's sitting on the edge of her bathtub, wrapped in a towel. Her hands are in loose fists on her lap, clutching thick clumps of her own hair. More of it is spread across the damp bathtub behind her. She's still crying, but silently now. Trying to hide it.

It's not like we didn't know this was coming. She started waking up with strands of auburn hair on her pillowcase a week ago. We even went to pick out a couple of wigs. We were prepared. But the nausea and the fatigue following each chemo treatment are one thing. Actually seeing all this hair—an impossible amount, considering there's still some left on her head—is something different. I can tell by the way she stares down at her palms that she feels the same way. Seeing it makes the cancer real.

I grab the waste bin from under the sink and hold it out for her. She cleans her hands over it and I help her get into bed, towel and all. She pulls the covers up to her chin and I go back to rinse the bathtub.

My hands shake and I want so badly to run and hide in the forest until this is all over, because that's what I do best. Flee from the problems I can't fix. But this is my mother, and I can't just leave her all alone right now, so I focus on the one mess I can clean up.

When I finish, I curl up beside her. She strokes the side of my face like she used to when I was little. It's unnerving, how quickly this cancer has become the center of her whole identity. It's present in the hair left on her head and the deep cracks on her lips. I can see it written on her cheekbones that seem to become more defined with each passing week, and in the sores in her mouth that keep her from eating any real food.

Everyone says I'm the spitting image of my mother—same wide eyes and full lips. It's terrifying how little I recognize the woman beside me now.

I prop myself up on one elbow. "Want me to shave my head in solidarity?"

"Don't you dare." She twists a curl around her finger.

I try to return her smile, but it doesn't feel right. "Sure I can't get you anything?"

"No, thanks." She sinks into her goose-down pillow. "I'm just fine."

I'm late for class. I left the house as soon as Dad came upstairs to check on Mom, but the next forty-five minutes were devoted to driving aimlessly around town. Now all the parking spots near the front entrance to the community center are taken, so I have to park all the way around the building. I go in through a side door, which is right near the indoor pool. I slow as I pass by the window. Only one person is taking advantage of the quiet lanes, and I wish I could join him. If I had a suit with me, I probably would ditch Photography.

It's been four months since I swam in a pool. And fine, I'll admit it: Every time Cory heads off to a practice or I see my team swimsuit in the closet, I start to miss everything about it. The burn in my lungs on the last lap, the smell of chlorine. And cheering on my teammates. Those friends, being a part of something bigger than myself, that's what I miss most of all.

Mr. Harrison is halfway through a critique of another student's photograph when I slip into the room. In our usual spot, Mackenzie is sandwiched between Gwen and Declan. A seat is open on Declan's other side. Maybe he saved it for me.

Probably not.

I walk past them and sit on the opposite side of the room. After I've settled in, I try to focus on what Mr. Harrison is saying about lighting and aperture, but my eyes keep sliding back over to Declan. I still can't believe I tried to kiss him.

I remember every kiss we ever shared. I always considered our second kiss to be the worst. It was two weeks after Leah Gilmore's party, and in the days between, we'd barely spoken. And we were quiet then, too, sitting on damp grass in his backyard, watching fireflies spark between the pines. We were scared. Or I was, at least. Terrified that our first kiss had ruined everything. Terrified it would never be repeated.

Most of all, terrified that Declan wanted me only because I was a relic of the life he'd lost when Natalie died.

But then he leaned closer, stopping half an inch away. He whispered my name, and I closed the distance.

I wanted to be excited, but all I could feel was Declan's anguish. He was overflowing with it, and with his lips pressing hard against mine, his hand clutching my hair, the doubts started to drown me.

Every nerve ending in my body rioted when I pulled away. "What is it? Did I . . . Was that okay?"

I nodded, but didn't say anything until he gently tucked a curl behind my ear. "What am I to you?"

He recoiled from my question. "What are you? Harper, you're everything."

"I can't be everything." I shook my head and picked at the blades of dewy grass.

"Well . . ." He frowned. "Then what do you want to be?"

"I want . . ."

"I mean, what am I to you?"

I let out a shaky laugh and dried my palms on my jeans. My answer was barely more than a whisper. "Everything."

He grinned and took my hand in his. "So are we really doing this? Are we together?"

My smile slipped as I traced his fingers. I wanted to be there for him, in every way he needed me. But I wasn't sure I could give this much of myself away, not if these kisses meant something different to him than they did to me. "Would you have wanted this if things were different? I mean . . . how long have you . . . ?"

"You're kidding me, right?" Declan shifted to face me. "Sixth grade, when you went as Alice in Wonderland for Halloween, why do you think I went as the Mad Hatter? Why do you think I walk over to your house every morning so we can spend an extra four minutes on the bus together? Harper, I've been falling for you for as long as I can remember."

As perfect as that night turned out, that second kiss was still the worst, most desperate one we ever had. Up until the kiss I stole at the bonfire last week.

We are never going to be able to have a normal conversation again. What was left of our friendship is definitely ruined. And anything more than that . . . well. It doesn't matter what I was stupid enough to think could happen. If deep down I'm starving for Declan. The hunger pangs are there for a reason. They're a necessary reminder that I had my chance. And it's gone now.

Too much has happened since he left, and anyway, he has Mackenzie. Which I probably should have considered *before* attacking his mouth.

God, the look on his face when he pulled away. Pity. That's what it was. And there is actually nothing worse than someone you love looking embarrassed for you. Not that I *love* Declan. That way. Anymore. I was just drunk, and it's just some kind of residual crush. The kiss meant nothing.

He grabs Mackenzie's spiral notebook and scribbles something in the margin before giving it back. She smiles and starts writing a response.

The page in front of me is still blank. I start shading every other line, pressing the pen harder and harder until the white page turns black.

I should be happy for him. Besides, Kyle isn't all bad, now that I know him a little better. He's exactly what I'm looking for. Just a casual summer fling.

Mackenzie giggles on the other side of the room. I glance up again, only this time I lock eyes with Declan. He isn't laughing with her. A crease forms between his eyebrows, and it's like he's seeing straight through me, like I have no control over what sides of myself I let him see.

His lips part, as if he wants to mouth something to me.

"Miss Sloan, what would you call this one?"

I drop my pen. Mr. Harrison is looking up at the projected image of some flowers I took for today's assignment.

"Call it?" I ask.

"Yes, give it a name."

"Oh, um . . ." I push myself to sit up a little straighter. It's just a stupid picture. Taken on a day that I thought Mom's garden looked nice. "I really don't know."

"That might be the whole problem."

Funny, I wasn't aware I had a problem.

"Try to figure out what you want to say before you take the shot. See if that helps, next time."

"Sure. Thanks."

Sinking back down into my chair, I resume turning everything light to dark until class is over. I don't take my eyes off the page again.

Eleven

ALL-AGES NIGHT AT THE BOURBON LOUNGE only comes once a month, and attendance is pretty much mandatory. My group hasn't actually made it inside yet, but the pregame drinks are running low, so it's only a matter of time. Kyle is sitting in the open trunk of his car. He takes a swig from a water bottle and holds it out to me. I shake my head.

Kyle passes the bottle off to Sadie and then snags his finger through my belt loop. He's always doing that now. He pulls me closer, so I'm standing between his legs, and runs his hands up my hips. "You sure you don't want anything to drink?"

"Yep." As much as I'd love a little help outrunning the racing thoughts of Mom's hair smeared all over the tub this morning, one of us needs to stay sober enough to drive. I look away again and Kyle lets go of me.

He stands and slams the trunk door down before drawing his arm over my shoulder. "Guys, we're heading in, okay?"

Sadie is already deep into not-so-deep conversation with Mike Sanders. Her latest victim.

I mean infatuation.

She tucks the half-empty water bottle into the bottom of her purse and follows us to the entrance. None of us says another word until we're past the bouncer, but once we're inside, Sadie lets out a squeal and pulls Mike out onto the dance floor.

"You want to dance?" Kyle asks.

"Not really."

He shoves his hands in his front pockets and looks around the room. Bourbon is part of an old tobacco warehouse that was converted into a series of restaurants and shops. Wood support beams are scattered throughout the main room, and the exposed brick walls are covered in vibrant paintings of jazz and rock musicians.

The stage is a small platform outlined in red velvet curtains. At the front, huge burlap bags of rice hang from the ceiling to help with acoustics. The band is already playing, filling the space with rich brass notes and a palpable energy.

I step away from Kyle and head to the bar. Sliding onto a stool, I catch the bartender's attention and order a Coke. Kyle takes the seat next to mine, sending me a sidelong glance.

"Hey." He swivels toward me and taps my wrist. It's too

familiar a gesture, and I pull my hand out from under his. His smile tightens, and I wonder if I've actually managed to hurt his feelings. He clears his throat. "You look nice tonight. I don't remember if I told you that earlier but . . . yeah."

I take a sip of my drink, then press the pad of each finger onto the bar top one at a time. "Thanks."

I realize I'm bracing, waiting for him to touch my neck or lean closer. But he just clears his throat again and sits back in his bar stool.

"You know, the Bulls are having a really great season."

"Oh . . . cool."

"Yeah, ever been to a game?"

Across the bar, Declan is standing at a high-top table next to Mackenzie. Cory and Gwen are across from them. A guy I've never seen before has his arm around Gwen's waist. I watch as Mackenzie lifts onto her tiptoes and whispers something to Declan, who tilts his head back in laughter.

I stab my straw into the ice in my glass. Kyle is watching me, waiting for me to respond. "Sorry, what?"

"A game. A Durham Bulls game. Ever been?"

"Oh. I think so. When I was a kid."

"Maybe we could go together sometime."

It must be Gwen's boyfriend. And he's probably only in town for the weekend. It would be rude not to say hello.

"Maybe. Um, I'll be right back." I slip off my stool and head over to them.

By the time I reach their table, Declan is gone. I turn around, scanning the crowd.

"Looking for someone?" Mackenzie asks.

"No." I shift my weight and stand up straighter. "Nopers."

She turns to Gwen. "Hey, did you see where Declan went?"

Gwen shrugs. "Harper, this is my boyfriend, Jason." She winds her arm around his waist and beams up at him.

Jason isn't exactly who I pictured Gwen with. I guess I figured he'd be a wacky musician covered in tattoos. Or at least have a piercing. But with his blond buzz cut and military posture, Jason is more boy-next-door than Cory.

I step forward and shake his hand. "It's really nice to meet you."

"You too. Guinevere has told me a lot about you."

My eyes widen and I smash my lips together, barely able to contain my excitement. Guinevere already has a warning finger raised.

"Don't. Don't even try it. One hundred percent you are not allowed to call me Guinevere."

My laugh catches in my throat when I see Sadie sandwiched between Mike and Kyle on the dance floor. Not that it's a big deal, but I'm just not sure why she feels the need to dance with both of them.

Kyle whispers something in her ear. She pulls the water bottle out of her purse and hands it to him. He looks around, and then chugs from the bottle. *Super.*

The tempo of the music picks up, and Jason drags Gwen out

121

to dance. Mackenzie watches them go, then turns back to us with a hopeful expression. "Come on, guys! This song is so good!"

I wave my hand to decline, but Cory steps forward. "Okay."

Mackenzie smiles broadly and skips after them with Cory in tow. I tuck my hair behind my ear and glance around again. Kyle is back at the bar, looking sloppier than ever.

I go outside for some fresh air.

Food trucks are lined up on the far end of the Bourbon parking lot—Korean barbecue, gourmet grilled cheeses, fried chicken and waffles. The scent of baked rosemary and warm maple syrup waft toward me. Suddenly I'm starving.

I pull one of the cigarettes Kyle gave me out of the mint tin in my purse and fumble with my lighter.

"Harper?"

Declan pushes off the brick wall a few yards down from me. He slides his phone into his back pocket and flips his keys around his finger. I look down at the unlit cigarette in my hand and quickly hide it away.

"Hey," I say when he's closer.

"Wasn't sure if it was you for a second. Don't know if I'll ever get used to that straight hair."

I comb my fingers through it and smile weakly.

He holds his keys a little higher. "I was just about to head out."

"So early?"

"Yeah, my dad wants me home. You know how he is. . . ."

"Right." I cross my arms and look at my feet. And since this moment isn't awkward enough already, my stomach rumbles. It is ridiculously loud.

"Are you hungry? I can stay a couple more minutes if you want some company."

A group of guys from school are standing around the pizza truck. Pete Carpenter is one of them. He and I made out for a while on New Year's Eve. I also fooled around a bit with Jared Barlow after a swim meet in February. And in the parking lot after a school baseball game this spring, Connor Wates got all the way to third. Basically, I've hooked up with three of the four people waiting in line. Not a great ratio.

"No, that's okay," I say.

"All right." He nods and looks over at his car. Maybe I should have said I was ravenous. "Listen, before I go, I wanted to ask if everything is okay. In class this morning you looked a little shaken up."

"Oh." I pick at a hangnail, keeping my eyes off him. "My mom started losing her hair today," I say with a shrug.

"Oh, wow. Are you . . . well, no, of course you're not okay."

"Comes with the territory, right?" I try to smile, but I'm sure it comes off as more of a grimace. Declan still looks concerned. "It was just *so much* hair. I was cleaning handfuls of it out of her bathtub. I don't know how that happens in one day."

Declan hesitates with his hand over my shoulder. I think for a second he's going to hug me, that tonight will be like it was up on the water tower, but he just gives my upper arm a squeeze and drops his hand. "Might get worse before it gets better. But it will get better."

"Yeah. Thanks." I hook my thumbs in my back pockets and rock onto my heels. "Well, I don't want to keep you."

Declan doesn't move. He doesn't react at all, actually, just keeps chewing his bottom lip. I start to wonder whether he heard me.

"Harper, I've been thinking a lot about that party the other night."

Dang. This was going so well.

"You really don't have to say anything. We can forget it ever happened."

"Just let me get this out." He drags his hands down his face, looking like he doesn't actually know what to say at all. "With everything that's been going on with you lately, I can understand you needing someone."

I cross my arms a little tighter. "I see."

Declan rubs his forehead. "That came out wrong. What I meant was . . . I didn't want to take advantage of the situation, because I know you've been upset about your mom."

"Look, I already apologized. Like you said, it was a mistake."

He exhales sharply and shakes his head at the ground. "You know . . . you were right before. Let's just forget it." He lifts his gaze and his eyes shift to something over my shoulder.

"*Heyyy,* was wonderin' where you went," a voice behind me says.

Before I can turn around, Kyle leans against me, propping his chin on my shoulder. His arms wrap around my waist and he stumbles sideways, pulling me with him.

"C'mon, gorgeous." Kyle tugs my arm. "We're goin' to get some food."

"Um . . ." My face is burning up. I slip out of Kyle's grasp and look up at Declan. He's glowering at Kyle.

Kyle finally notices him. "Who's this?"

"Why don't you just give me your keys," I say to him. "I'll meet you over by your car."

Declan's eyes go wide. "Are you kidding me? He drove you here?"

"Dude, this really isn't any of your business. Why don't you back off?"

He does the opposite, stepping into Kyle's personal space. "Why don't you let Harper speak for herself?"

"Declan, don't."

He turns to me and I can't make myself look any higher than his chest.

I put one hand on Kyle's shoulder and push him away from Declan. "Just give me your keys, okay?"

Glaring over my head, Kyle reaches into his pocket and hands me the car keys. Then he turns and stumbles his way across the lot. It takes me another moment to face Declan.

"He wasn't like that earlier. When he drove, I mean."

His jaw shifts to one side. "You know . . . I kind of thought Cory was joking. But are you actually seeing that guy?"

My insides squirm. "No. I mean, kind of . . . but not—"

"Smoking, drinking, hanging out with jerk-off guys. Guess that's your thing now, huh?"

"You don't even know him."

"I know enough." He wipes his hand across his mouth. "So what, you're going to drive him home and then . . ."

I don't know what he wants to hear, or whether I'm actually supposed to fill in the blank. I'm not even sure what he's mad about anymore. But before I can get an answer out, Declan scowls again.

"Whatever. Do what you want. I just don't like the way he looks at you."

"Oh, okay, and how's that?"

His eyes sink down to my necklace and he steps off the sidewalk. "Like you're replaceable."

I grip Kyle's keys tighter. "Declan . . ."

He keeps walking.

"You might want to say good-bye to Mackenzie before you leave," I call out. "She was looking for you."

Twelve

CORY HANGS ON MY REFRIGERATOR DOOR, CON-
templating the pathetic selection in front of him. He picks up a
half-empty jar of questionable pickles, reads the expiration date,
and puts it back.

"There's cereal in the pantry," I offer. "Other than that, you're
pretty much out of luck."

He dives in and returns with a box of Cinnamon Toast
Crunch tucked firmly under one arm. He shoves a handful of it
into his mouth and moves into the living room.

Cory and I would always binge eat like this after practice. It
was kind of our ritual. So despite the chlorine-laced BO wafting
off him right now, it's nice having him here.

Mom comes down from her bedroom and relaxes into the

armchair across from us. She eyes Cory's swim trunks. "That better not be a wet suit on my sofa."

"Dry as a bone. We were just about to head over to the quarry."

She lights up like a kid at Christmas. "That's wonderful. I keep telling Harper she's got a lot of work to do before the fall."

"Mom, please. . . ."

"No kidding," Cory says. "I heard she can barely float anymore."

I take his cereal away. "Shall we?"

"Now, wait a second." Mom licks her cracked lips and adjusts the scarf masking her hairline. "I haven't had a chance to hear how Cory's summer practices are going."

"Yeah, and I would hate to eat and run," he says. Then he ruffles my goddamn hair.

I palm his face and take the cereal box back to the pantry. Cory starts telling Mom how his 200 meter freestyle still isn't improving from last year, but overall his times are looking good. He's been competitive about swimming since the kiddie pool, but right now I can't handle hearing him go on about it. I empty the dishwasher in an attempt to drown them out, but I still catch Mom mention something about tryouts.

". . . just hate to see her throw away all those years of hard work."

I'm back in the doorway in a flash. "We should really go now. It could start raining."

Cory and Mom both squint at the window. Not a cloud in the sky. Still, Cory nods and gets off the couch.

"Mom, you need anything before we head out? I think there's some fruit in the freezer. Want me to make you a smoothie?"

She gestures at the glass of water by her side. "I'm all set. Could you just hand me that book?"

She reaches for the shelf behind her and I pick up a paperback travel guide on Western Europe. "Going on a trip?"

Mom takes the book and opens to a dog-eared page. "Someday."

I kiss her cheek and then Cory and I head over to his house. He stops in the driveway and digs in his pocket for the keys to his Honda.

"Did she seem okay to you?"

He unlocks his door and gets in, then leans across to unlock mine. I slide into the passenger's seat.

"You mean, aside from the cancer?" he asks. "Yeah. Seems like she's doing well."

"Like maybe too well?"

His forehead wrinkles. "Is there such a thing?"

"I just mean . . ." I sigh. "Like that travel book. And the way she's always laughing it off, like it's the most normal thing that she's practically dying."

Cory is quiet. He puts the keys in the ignition but sits back without turning them. "You don't really think that, do you?"

The lump is back in my throat. I can't swallow it down this

time. The waterworks threaten to start up, and I press my fingers under my eyes and growl. "I don't know. Just . . . never mind."

"I think it's a good thing. If making plans means she's fighting this."

"Yeah." I click my seat belt on. "No, you're right."

He starts the car and backs down the driveway. "Oh, and if she asks, I gave you the hard sell about getting back on the team."

"Noted."

He hesitates. "It *does* seem like a shame to give up the joy of six a.m. practices. Not to mention goggle marks and itchy skin. Sore muscles and a chronic chlorine cough."

"Do you not understand the concept of a hard sell?"

"I'm just saying, it's senior year."

"And?"

"Maybe it's time to turn over a new leaf."

Cory knows as well as anyone, it's not a simple matter of trying out again. The girls don't want me back.

He slows before pulling out of our neighborhood. "Senior year," he repeats. "We're almost out of here!" He smacks the dashboard to emphasize his point, and he's so full of conviction, it's borderline contagious.

"Did you mean for that to rhyme?"

He scoffs. "Obviously."

"Right. Do me a favor?" I smile and turn the radio up. "Save the sentiment for my yearbook."

* * *

Cory and I have been at the quarry all of ten minutes when the rest of the crew shows up. Mackenzie emerges from the mouth of trees and comes bouncing down the dirt path, followed by Declan and Gwen.

How she has that much spring in her step is beyond me. It's the kind of afternoon where I begin to doubt the sun is really ninety-three million miles from Carson. It feels much closer. And with the sky set to broil and the scattered pines providing little shade, my skin is craving some relief. I was just about to jump into the water, but I smack Cory's arm instead. He lifts his head and pulls out his earbuds, squinting at me in the sunlight.

"What's your problem?"

I gesture toward Mackenzie, who hops over a tree root and begins her descent to the stone ledge where Cory and I are sitting. "Why didn't you tell me you invited them?"

"Oh, hey, I invited Declan."

"Yeah, thanks. That's super helpful."

Cory props himself up on one elbow. "Are you going to make this weird all summer?"

He's wearing contacts today, and sans glasses his stare is all the more cutting. It says everything he never does—that this is hard for him, too. That he missed having his best friend around just as much as I did. It's the same look he gave me on Christmas Eve, the last time I pressed him about Declan.

"My mom and I ran into Declan's dad at the store this morning," I had told him. He dribbled his basketball once, twice, and took a shot. "He said Dec was doing really well at school. Adjusting, and all that."

Dribble. Dribble. Shot. "Yeah, he seems good."

I stuffed my hands deep inside the pockets of my coat. "Do you think . . . Is he dating anyone?"

Cory hugged the ball under one arm and huffed out a breath that turned to fog between us. "C'mon, Harper. Back in October we agreed not to do this. Your idea, as I recall."

"I know. . . ."

"I don't talk to him about you—"

"Sure you don't."

Cory took one last shot. Neither of us went for the rebound. "Look, what do you want me to say? You made it really clear you'd moved on. So he did too."

And there it was, the answer I'd been searching for. Declan had moved on. Just like I'd pushed him to do, and just like I'd pretended to do. It didn't matter that I'd been holding out this ridiculous hope that I could somehow figure out a way to make things right with Declan. What mattered was why we broke up in the first place. And that could never be undone. We were both better off this way.

I nodded, already backtracking toward my driveway. "Sure, of course."

"Harper . . ."

"No, it's fine. I'm fine. Merry Christmas, Cory."

It wasn't fair of me to involve him back then, and it isn't now.

So I smile and shake my head. "No. No weirdness. Sorry."

"Hey, guys!" Mackenzie lays her beach towel down beside mine. Behind her, Declan sets a bag of food by the fire pit and makes his way over.

"Hey, Mackenzie."

Gwen sets her beach bag next to Mackenzie. "Damn, it's hot."

Declan stops at the edge of my towel. "No kidding," he says. Then he takes his shirt off.

And my eyes become glued to his abs. Those are new.

He pulls his hair back with an elastic band and I wonder if it's the same one I gave him the night we climbed the water tower. His Ray-Ban-covered eyes turn toward me and I swivel back to the quarry, dipping my hand in and bringing some water up to my forehead.

Mackenzie stands up and pulls her sundress over her head. Her bathing suit is vintage-inspired, of course. The high-waisted bottoms and halter top give her all the right kinds of curves. "I'm going in."

"Me too," Cory says. He jumps in after her, followed by Gwen.

Declan is still standing behind me. I feel his eyes on the back of my head, but I stare straight ahead until finally he sits down on Cory's towel. The only sounds come from our friends splashing their way out to the middle of the quarry and waves gently lapping against the stone edge.

"Declan," Mackenzie calls out. "You coming in?"

"In a bit," he calls back. Without looking at me, he says, "Never known you to stay out of the water."

"Just getting some sun first."

He nods and holds his forearm up to mine. "Good call."

Suddenly I'm a lot more self-conscious about my paleness. "Wow, you are ridiculously tan already."

He smirks. "Perk of spending my mornings caddying. It's just my arms, though. I'll have an awesome farmer's tan going by August."

I lean forward, cupping some water in my palm and dripping it over my legs. "Well, at least you won't be covered in freckles like me."

"Nothing wrong with freckles."

Methodically I push my finger into each droplet of water on my thigh. Heat creeps up my neck, and it has nothing to do with the beating sun. It's because I'm thinking about things I shouldn't. Like the way Declan used to kiss his way across the freckles on my shoulder. Or the way he'd trace the bridge of my nose with his pinkie. Sweet touches that belonged to him and me.

I hate the thought of him touching other girls that way.

I never pushed Cory for details again, and honestly I don't really want to know the particulars of Declan's sex life at school. And I'm certainly in no position to judge, given the roster of guys I fooled around with. But none of them meant anything to me.

As much as it hurts to picture Declan hooking up with random girls, it's so much worse to think about him actually *liking* someone else. Even if it's currently someone as nice as Mackenzie.

I'm out of water drops to focus on. And now I don't know what to do with my hands. I take the hair tie off my wrist and start fiddling with it. Then I look over at Declan.

He's already studying me. My shoulder, to be more precise. He swallows and then slowly lifts his gaze to meet mine.

Water crests over both of us and my breath catches in my throat. I snap around to find Cory treading water with a shit-eating grin on his face.

"Let's race," he says.

A shiver runs up my spine from the cold. I kick some water at him. "Asshole."

Declan stands. He runs a hand over his now-wet hair and mumbles something about getting lunch ready. Then he walks back to the forest, not stopping until he's reached the fire pit.

What the hell just happened?

Cory climbs up the boulder and nudges my arm. "Count of three," he says.

Nothing. Nothing happened. My imagination was running wild, and I let it get the best of me. Let myself slip back into that dangerous pocket of my memory.

I tie my hair into a ponytail and shove Cory back. "One."

"Two." He takes his stance. "Three!"

His dive is longer than mine. I keep a fairly close distance all the way across the quarry, but I know I'm going to lose before we even turn around.

Cory smacks his hand against the boulder. "Oh man, I smoked you."

"I don't know if you've gotten faster, but man, I am out of shape."

"Whose fault is that, Captain?"

I dip my chin under water to hide my flinch. "Thanks."

"Oh, come on, you know I didn't mean anything by it."

"I know." I keep treading water as he pulls himself onto the rocks. "No big deal."

The girls get out of the water then too. I spend a few more minutes floating on my back, staring up at the sky until it's impossible to tell whether the clouds are moving or I am. Then Cory calls my name.

"Food is ready," he says when I swim back to the edge.

I climb out and hug my towel around my shoulders, then make my way over to the picnic table next to the fire pit.

"Admittedly, he was a rather poor choice," Mackenzie says.

"Epic understatement. Mack, that guy was a total and complete bastard."

"Hindsight!"

Gwen makes room for me at the end of the bench.

"What are we talking about?" I ask.

"Mack's ex-boyfriend. A.k.a. the Douchenozzle."

"I see."

Mackenzie elaborates. "He broke up with me approximately five minutes after we slept together for the first time. Via text message."

"Whoa."

Gwen holds her palms up. "Right?"

Mackenzie sighs. "I'm over it. Mostly. Anyway, lesson learned. Better to be friends with a guy first."

"Yeah." I pull my towel tighter over my shoulders. "That's probably true."

"Ready to eat?" Cory calls out.

The boys come over with grilled hot dogs and start passing them around. My stomach is too upset to really eat, so I opt for some of the baby carrots in the middle of the table. Cory takes the seat next to Mackenzie, which leaves only one spot open.

Declan drops his plate across from me and slides onto the bench. I finish my carrot and twist the chain of my necklace around my finger.

He's staring again. Only this time he looks . . . crushed. At first, I think it's the necklace. That he's remembering his last night in town, when he gave it to me. Remembering what the infinity pendant is supposed to mean. But it's the side of my neck he's focused on, and suddenly I know exactly what he sees.

My hand flies up to my jawline, covering the evidence. Declan's eyes snap to mine, then down at his food.

"Holy shit, girl." Gwen yanks my hand away. "Can't use the curling-iron excuse for that one, can you?"

Mortification simmers beneath my skin, and I'm pretty sure I've never blushed this hard before. Even when it was just going to be Cory and me today, I'd been so careful to cover the hickey up. The makeup must have washed off in the water.

Declan picks a potato chip up off his plate, holding it in mid-air for a moment before dropping it again. Mackenzie glances at him and the moment becomes infinitely more painful. She leans forward and smiles sweetly at me.

"I heard you have a new boyfriend," she says. "Kyle, right?"

"He's not my boyfriend."

"Oh, well, you should invite him to hang out next time! We could do a group thing!"

"Um, sure. Maybe."

Declan pushes his plate away and moves over to the quarry. Mackenzie winces before excusing herself and following him. Cory tucks back into his food.

Gwen shifts toward me, bringing her foot up to the bench. "I'm really sorry; I didn't mean to embarrass you. It just . . . came out."

"No, it's okay," I say. The damage was already done.

Declan is standing with his arms crossed, looking at the water. Mackenzie puts her hand on his shoulder, and his arms unfold. He nods, and his hand finds its way to the small of her back.

I look away. That touch belongs to them.

Thirteen

SINCE CORY PRETTY MUCH DECIMATED THE LAST OF our food supply the other day and our house has a particularly claustrophobic vibe this morning, I volunteer for errand duty, starting with a list of post-chemo fare we're running low on. Mom has another round of treatment coming up in a few days, and we want to be fully stocked.

I drop off her newest prescription at the pharmacy counter and gather some groceries while I wait for them to fill it. Once I collect her favorites—ginger ale, ginger tea, and ginger snaps—I get in line to check out. Right when I go to pay, I catch a glimpse of Jenny walking into the drugstore with her mother. Just what today needs.

I dip my head and hand the woman at the register a twenty.

Go talk to her.

But I can't, not when she's standing with her mom. That would be beyond uncomfortable. What I need to do is get out of here without her seeing me. I'll try again a different day, I tell myself. Just like I've been telling myself ever since it happened.

It's not like she makes it easy for me. Technically she wasn't a part of the confrontation that last day with the swim team, when I went to get my things out of my locker. But she didn't put a stop to it either.

I tried to sneak in after practice had started, but they were all waiting for me, blocking my path. They knew if they yelled, they'd get caught. So they were eerily silent, allowing the looks on their faces to do the shouting. I had to push my way in, all of them throwing their shoulders at me and shoving me around like a rag doll. Then, when I got close, they all cleared away. They wanted to watch my reaction when I saw it, the four-letter word scrawled across my locker in bright red lipstick.

My hands were shaking so hard, it took three tries before I got my combination right. When the door finally swung open, they all went back to their own business and I gathered my things as quickly as possible. When I slammed it shut and turned to leave, I saw Jenny standing in the corner. She wasn't glaring at me. She didn't lay a finger on me. She just opened the door for me and I was free to go.

Only I wasn't really free. Because I never really left that room behind. We carry our past with us everywhere we go.

Stupid, anyway. What am I supposed to say to Jenny? What could I possibly tell her about that night that would make up for what I did? *I swear, Jenny, it isn't my fault I took so many shots that it became impossible to tell your boyfriend's lies from the truth! Now, how about we forgive and forget?*

Right.

God, why is this woman taking so long to count my change? My foot taps out syncopated beats and I am this close to telling her to keep it and bolting out the door when finally, she hands me back a few bills.

"Thanks." I grab my bag and take one last peek at Jenny. Her head snaps up and I spin around, hopefully before she recognizes me.

Once I'm safe inside my car, I turn the music up loud. Louder. Loud enough that I can't hear my own breathing.

It's already late afternoon by the time I get home and finish unpacking the groceries. The sky is turning grayer by the minute, and the wind picks up as I climb onto the roof to treat myself to the cigarette I've been craving. The first clap of thunder sounds in the distance and I shiver despite the heat clinging to the shingles beneath me.

I stub out my cigarette and immediately detect the scent of a different kind of smoke. One that I've smelled every day for the last week. The first time, I went straight to my window and looked out at the backyard. I figured if Graham was smoking pot that blatantly, I was going to have to call him out for being a complete dumbass. Only, it wasn't Graham. The wafts of pot-laced air came from Mom's bathroom window. Blowing right back into the house through mine.

That first time, I burst out laughing. My mother, Miss Proper, a total stoner. She probably thought she was being so stealth about it too.

Then I took two seconds to think about why she was smoking and it stopped being funny.

Now, a text from Kyle pulls me back in through my window. *You up for a party at Cat's?*

I'm not sure I have it in me to put on a happy face for Cat or anyone else. But knowing Kyle, he'll have a bottle of the antidote ready and waiting. And there's no way I can stay cooped up in this house all night, so I tell him yes. But when I go downstairs, I'm intercepted.

"Harper! Come sit down and have dinner with us."

My dad carries a plate of barbecued chicken in from the back patio. He slides the screen door shut behind him while Graham pulls cornbread from the oven.

"Actually, I was just on my way out."

"Nonsense. I've barely seen you all week."

I put my purse on the counter and slump into a chair. "I can stay for, like, ten minutes, but then I have to go."

Dad serves up the chicken and I help myself to some salad, skipping the cornbread. He takes his seat and skewers his first bite.

"I don't want you going out tonight," he says without even looking up from his plate.

I put my fork down and cross my arms. "Why not?"

"Because," he says, "school starts soon. You need to get back into a regular sleep pattern. And it won't kill you to stay in for one night with your family."

I roll my eyes and shoot a look at Graham like, *Can you believe this?* Graham just raises his eyebrows and busies himself with his dinner.

Thanks for having my back.

"Okay, well, I already made plans, and it's still summer and Friday night, and it's not like anything will be going on here anyway."

Dad's hands pause over his plate, and I watch his mustache curve as he frowns. Finally, he looks up at me. "Be home by eleven."

I stab a piece of lettuce and mouth, *Fine.*

"Did you pick up that prescription I asked you to get today?"

Sitting up a little bit straighter, I chew the lettuce slowly. *Shit.* I knew I forgot something at the store.

"Um, no, I dropped it off but they were busy and then . . . I forgot. I'll get it first thing in the morning."

Dad puts down his knife and fork and tilts his head back. "Come on, Harper. I asked you to do this one thing."

"I know; I'm sorry." I twist my fork into the chicken breast, tearing the meat off the bone.

"Your mother might need those meds tonight. You've got to work on being more responsible, you can't just—"

"I know. I said I was sorry." I throw my fork down onto the table. "I'll go right now."

Pushing my chair back, I grab my purse and car keys off the counter and storm out to the driveway, hesitating once I reach my car. I kick my tire and spin around to sit on the hood, dragging the keys down my leg.

My dad calls after me, but it's Graham who walks out the front door a few seconds later. He stands on the porch for a moment before strolling over to me.

"I figured you could use some company." He holds out his hand for the keys, automatically expecting to drive just because he's older.

Wordlessly, I get behind the wheel. Graham retreats to the passenger side and we drive to the drugstore in silence. Well, silent not counting the series of sighs Graham exhales.

"Why don't you just say whatever it is you want to say?" I ask when I'm one sigh away from steering us into a tree.

"I know all of this hasn't been easy on you, Harper. But do you think it's been easy on any of us? On Dad?" He stares me down and I hate him. Hate that he thinks he has any right to lecture me. "None of us asked for this. And it isn't exactly how I wanted to spend my summer either. But you don't see me acting like a total brat."

My teeth grind together. "No, instead you act like everything at home is normal."

"Excuse me?"

"All of you, even Mom—you keep pretending like the cancer is just some blip in our regularly scheduled programming, like she's just going to get through it, no questions asked. So yeah, maybe I do think it's been a little bit easier on you, because you've been faking a happy family this whole time."

Graham shakes his head. "You know, that's an awfully bold statement coming from someone who has barely been home for the past three weeks. You're crazy if you think the rest of us aren't freaked out. You'd rather hit the self-destruct button and party with your friends than spend time with Mom? Fine. But you are in no position to judge the rest of us for how we're coping."

Heat sparks inside of me, a potent mixture of fury and shame. I grip the wheel tighter and ignore the way my knuckles throb. "You done?"

He shuts up and I pull into a spot outside the drugstore, and I go inside to get Mom's prescription. When I get back to the car I find him waiting in the driver's seat. Jackass.

"Seriously?"

He shrugs behind the window. I scowl and go around, then toss the keys at Graham. He doesn't start the car.

"Harper, I meant what I said before. . . ."

"About me being a brat? Got it the first time. Loud and clear."

He gives me a hard look. "That I'm here if you need someone to talk to."

"I told you, I'm fine. Can we please just go?"

The first drop of rain falls on the windshield. The storm clouds have taken the sky hostage, and the downpour finally starts when we're halfway home. We pull into the neighborhood the back way, which goes right past Declan's house. Through the sheet of rain, I study his driveway, where we made entire worlds out of colored sidewalk chalk. The basketball hoop above the garage door doesn't have a net anymore. There must be a thousand other changes I haven't noticed.

And then I do notice another difference in the landscape—a red Datsun parked at the curb. The only light in the house is coming from Declan's second-story bedroom. My chest constricts and my throat burns and then we're past his street and I force myself to think about Kyle instead.

We park in the driveway and I sprint to the porch swing. Graham holds the front door open for me.

"I'll wait out here." I pull out my phone and text Kyle to come pick me up. Graham is still standing there. I hold out my hand. "You can give me my house keys back now."

He walks over, holding them just above my palm. "Eleven o'clock curfew, Harp."

"Thanks, *Dad*." I yank the keys out of his grip.

Thankfully, Graham doesn't wait with me. Kyle pulls into the driveway ten minutes later.

Fourteen

THE THING ABOUT PARTIES IN CARSON IS THAT they're all the same. The players or venue may change, but not much else. And not enough to make a difference.

We spend the first hour in the kitchen with everyone else, hovering over the cooler. I'm already drunk by the time Kyle grabs my wrist and pulls me toward the living room.

We move through a hallway where a girl is having a total meltdown with her boyfriend. The guy backs up against the wall and throws his hands in the air, sloshing half his beer onto the carpet. "I'm not dealing with this right now!"

"Fine, so do whatever you want! See if I care," she yells back.

I hold my breath and squeeze past her, lifting my drink over our heads.

The whole house is dim, the only light coming from accent lamps on side tables, and outside of the kitchen it smells strongly of incense. Loud music plays from a speaker in the corner of the room. Cat and a few other girls from school are swaying to the beat in the middle of the floor, no doubt hoping to catch the attention of the guys across the room. Haley Smith is among them. She hands her drink to Cat and peels off her shirt, revealing a cropped tank top underneath. It works. One of the guys gets off the couch and makes his way over.

Kyle sits on another couch and I slide onto his lap. His hand settles on my hip, and he leans in. I turn back to my red plastic cup. I hate making out in front of people.

Kyle's friend Aaron or Alex or something that starts with *A* sits down next to us.

"That girl Mandy is so hot," he says.

Mandy Philips. Another one of the dancing girls.

Kyle's hand slips down to my thigh. "So go talk to her."

The friend doesn't move. "You think I have a chance?" he asks.

"For sure. Andy, look at what she's wearing. You know she's easy."

Andy. I was close.

Then I play back the rest of what Kyle said. My palm starts to sweat, mixing with the condensation on my cup. I can feel my pulse everywhere—my ears, my stomach. "What did you just say?"

He pretends he didn't hear me. I stand up, gripping the arm of the couch to keep myself steady.

"Where are you going?" Kyle asks.

I pretend I didn't hear him.

I stumble my way back to the kitchen and pour another drink. Something to wash down the sour taste in my mouth.

He said it like it was nothing. That's what always gets me— how everyone can act like that kind of slut-shaming is no big deal. An internal timer goes off, and I have to get out of here as fast as possible. But Sadie left with Mike twenty minutes in. I missed my chance for a ride. Not that she really would have wanted me tagging along.

Kyle finds me in the kitchen; he hooks his finger through my belt loop and runs his other hand down my neck.

"Fuck off, Kyle."

He grins. "You're always so mean to me, Sloan."

"Well, maybe that's because you're an asshole."

He stops grinning. "Why am I an asshole?"

"You know they say that kind of shit about me, too, right? Is that why you're interested in me?"

I can't believe I just asked that. Because (a) of course that's why he's interested in me. And (b) what do I want him to say? That he's madly in love with me?

We don't mean anything to each other. That's why it works.

"Oh, come on, I was just trying to help Andy out."

"Don't ever call a girl easy in front of me again. Don't call girls easy, period."

"Okay, okay." Kyle reaches for me again. I pull back. "Hey, I'm sorry."

I shrug and take another gulp of my rum and Coke.

"Harper." Kyle steps closer and reaches for my hair. He tucks it behind my ear, almost shyly. "I mean it. I'm sorry."

Kyle looks me straight in the eye and I notice for the first time they're a nice shade of blue. Not spectacular or anything. But nice.

"Fine."

He blows out a long, relieved breath. "Do you want to get out of here?"

I set my cup on the counter. "Let's go."

He grins again. His teeth are perfectly straight and super white, and when he smiles it makes him look older. Kind of handsome, even.

But he doesn't have dimples.

He takes my hand and we weave back through the party, saying good-bye to anyone who cares that he's leaving. He does a weird handshake thing with a few guys from the lacrosse team, and all of them give him this smug look. Like they're congratulating him on leaving with me. Like they know exactly what we're about to go do.

Outside the storm has passed without putting so much as a dent in the humidity. The smell of soil hangs heavy in the muggy air, and we cross the soggy lawn to the sidewalk. Kyle stops twice on the way back to his car to kiss me. Not his usual sloppy kisses. I mean, he still tastes like sour beer and cigarettes. A mint would seriously improve the situation. But his lips are soft, and the tongue is minimal, and if I didn't know better I might think Kyle actually did like me.

We reach his car and he opens the door for me. But it isn't the front door. I look back at the house we came from. It's only a block away, and other cars are parked nearby. Not an ideal amount of privacy. But at least his windows are tinted.

I get in the backseat. Kyle climbs in after me and locks the doors. Only our knees are touching. Just like that first drive in Will's Mustang.

He slides closer. From here, we can't hear the music from the party. Inside the car it's silent.

"Do you know how sexy you are?" he whispers.

It's a yes-or-no question without any good answer. But he doesn't expect an answer; he expects something else. His lips are by my ear, and all I have to do is turn my head.

I turn my head. Kyle's mouth hovers over mine a second longer, then he's kissing me. His fingernails graze up my thigh. His palm folds over my hip, then slides between my legs. I push his hand back down to my knee and look out the side window.

My heart starts to race. Not in a happy, swept-off-my-feet kind of way. Anxious. Like when I let Sadie copy answers from my math quiz last semester. Like I shouldn't be doing this.

152

But I just need to calm down. Let go and drown those voices out. Because being here is still better than facing what's waiting at home.

Kyle starts kissing my neck. The same way that gave me that hickey. I don't want another hickey.

My lips crush against his again, and I squeeze my eyes shut because I'm not sure what it says about me that I keep my eyes open when I kiss him.

But with my eyes closed, it only makes it easier to think about other things. To remember other moments in time. Like Declan's final night in Carson last August.

He'd spent the whole day with Cory, and the three of us went out for an early dinner. Once the last slice of pizza was gone, we dropped Cory off at home, but Declan and I kept driving.

I'd tried to savor that summer, tried to appreciate every moment of time I had left with my boyfriend. But that night the clock had run out and we were desperate to escape. Someplace better than the backseat of a car.

We'd both grown too tall to stand up inside the tree house we built five years earlier in the woods near the quarry, so Declan spread a blanket across the floor. The space was just big enough for us to lie down diagonally.

It was pouring out, and every now and then a raindrop would slip through the cracks in the wooden ceiling. One landed on my cheek, and Declan wiped it away with his thumb.

He kept his hand there, wrapped around my jaw, until I turned and planted a kiss in his open palm.

I watched Declan's breath become heavier, his eyes darker, and his smile dissolve into something hungrier. His hold on me shifted, his thumb grazing across my bottom lip. Then our mouths were melting together.

The best kiss of my life.

My hands skated down his back, then pulled on his belt buckle. His hands were tangled in my hair and then skimming all the way down my thigh and back up again, taking my skirt with it.

Everything he did felt so good, and I wanted more of it.

"Do you—" My lips were covered by Declan's again, then he moved his kiss under my jaw. "Condom?"

He paused with his mouth on my neck. He pulled back and blinked down at me. Blood rushed to my cheeks, and he kissed me again, slower than before.

"Yes."

Of course, I already knew that would be his answer because come on. He'd even tidied up the freaking tree house. But once I'd said it that meant it was expected, and I didn't want to think anymore so I sat up and pulled my dress over my head.

Declan's gaze trailed over me. With trembling fingers, I started to unbutton his shirt. Before I could finish, he pulled it over his head and tossed it next to my dress. When he kissed me again, all of the urgency from earlier had dissolved.

His skin was hot against my torso and I could feel his heartbeat orchestrating with mine. His fingers grazed all the way up from my knee, and then he was making me feel like only he could.

A moan escaped, and I gripped the back of his neck tightly, pulling his mouth harder onto mine. Doubts drifted away as his hand moved faster and the world caught fire and I carved his initials onto every tree on the planet.

But I was still so nervous. I couldn't catch my breath. And Declan could tell.

"We don't have to do this."

"I want to. I've always wanted it to be you."

I reached for him again and he pulled back, catching my hand and kissing my knuckles.

"We'll wait. Until we're both ready."

That was the first promise we made each other. And I've kept it. Because I don't know if I'll ever belong with anyone the way I belonged with him.

But it's Kyle's hand pushing my skirt up now. I grab his wrist again. "Don't."

"What's the matter?"

I'm not sure what else to say. I don't know why I'm even stopping him.

He isn't Declan.

It's a ridiculous thought. Declan isn't available. And what happened between us is so far in the past, it's like it happened between two completely different people. We've been broken up longer than we were even together. I have to let it go.

"Is it that time of the month?"

I jump at the out Kyle's given me. "Yeah. Sorry."

He looks mildly disappointed, but recovers quickly. "No problem."

His hand moves up to my waist, pulling me closer. He kisses me again, and I try to feel something. Anything that will keep me in this moment and out of my head.

Kyle leans back until I'm half on top of him. He twirls my hair around his hand, then he's touching the crown of my head. No, not touching.

Pushing.

Applying pressure the way no guy who respected me ever would. Trying to take things the way Declan never, ever did.

I look up, and his expression catches me by surprise. He looks nervous.

I've already put him off for weeks. Kept making him wait, giving him hope every time I whispered, *Not yet*. I've gone that far a couple of times before with guys from school; it wouldn't have to be a big deal. I should just get it over with.

Except I don't want to. I never really did. I slide back across the seat and straighten my clothes, then open the car door.

"Where are you going?"

"Away."

I'm standing on the sidewalk, trying to get my bearings. It's

Fifteen

IT'S THAT TIME OF NIGHT THAT'S TOO LATE FOR dinner and too early for the after-hours crowd. Frank's Diner is empty.

Frank's is an old car garage that was rehabbed into a diner. It has a fifties-era vibe to it, and a menu that spans six pages. The huge carport doors are raised tonight, allowing the humid air to waft in.

I slide into a booth near the front and order a coffee.

I set my phone on the table and stare at the screen, sending Cory a telepathic message that he needs to call me back. I'm still two miles from my house. I would just walk, but it's really dark out now. And I'm wearing a skirt. And that voice in my head is screaming at me not to be an idiot.

dark out and my head is still spinning and I want to go home, but I don't know anyone else at the party well enough to ask for a ride.

Kyle climbs out of the backseat. "Sloan, come on. Don't be like this."

I think Main Street is a few blocks north of here. I can walk to Frank's Diner and figure things out from there.

Kyle grabs my arm. "Okay, I'm sorry—"

I yank out of his grip. "Leave me alone."

"Jesus, you're so melodramatic. Get back in the car."

"No."

"Just get in. I'll take you home."

"I'm not going anywhere with you."

He smirks and looks back at the party. "Whatever. Your call." He starts walking toward the house. For a split second, I start to panic. Wondering whether I should just follow him. But I don't need him. I never did.

I pull out my phone and call Cory. No answer. With a sigh, I dial Graham's number next. *This will be a fun ride home.*

I listen to it ring. Six, seven, eight times. Then voice mail. And Sadie is who knows where, no doubt too drunk to drive. As a last resort, I try Gwen. She doesn't pick up either. I'm out of friends.

Except maybe one. But there is absolutely no way I can call him for help.

So I start walking.

More of an idiot.

I was kidding myself with Kyle. I keep ending up with these guys who don't give a shit about me, who just use me to get what they want. And I guess I was using Kyle, too. It just didn't work.

I think Graham might have been right before. He basically called me a coward and, given how the rest of tonight has played out, I'm finding it real hard to build my case against the idea. For so long, I've been fixated on all the things I can't control. Mom's cancer, her hair falling out, the days she's too sick to get out of bed. Natalie dying, Declan leaving, the rumors people whisper behind my back.

What I need to focus on are the things I can change. I didn't let it get too out of hand with Kyle tonight; that's a start. Earlier this year, it might have been a different story. All spring long, I made carbon copies of the same mistake.

But that's over with. And all I have to do now is figure out how I'm getting home. The way I see it, I could wait for someone to call me back (unlikely), or I could call my parents (even less likely), or . . . I could bite the bullet and try that last number.

I take a sip of coffee and eye my phone. I can't call. He might still be with Mackenzie. My eyes screw shut and I rub my temples and try very hard to erase the image of them alone in his bedroom.

It's not like he would actually answer if she were over. And besides, I'm pretty sure he already hates me. So, what have I got to lose?

It starts ringing before I even fully commit to calling him. Then I start praying he won't pick up. Then he does.

"Harper?"

"Hey." I squeeze my coffee mug. "Are you busy?"

Declan hesitates. "Not really."

"You're not with anyone?"

"No . . . why?"

My eyes close again. "I was wondering if you could meet me at Frank's? I kind of . . . need a ride."

"Oh. Uh, yeah, I guess I could do that. Just give me a few minutes?"

"Sure. Take your time."

We hang up, and I set my phone back down where it was before. I pick it up again, and check my reflection in the screen. Grabbing a napkin, I try to wipe some of the eyeliner from under my eyes, and then run my fingers through my hair, untangling it.

A little while later, my waitress comes by to refill my coffee. When she moves away, Declan is standing in the doorway.

He spots me and slowly makes his way over. He slides into the seat across from me and studies my face. I look away first.

I can't stop tapping my nails against the edge of my mug. I sit on my hands. "Thank you for coming."

"No problem." He checks the time on his phone.

"Are you in a hurry? We can go." I take a gulp of my coffee and reach for my bag.

160

"No, it's okay. Actually, I'm kind of hungry. Mind if we stay for a bit?"

"Oh. No, that's better, actually. I could use a few more minutes before going home." I grab a couple of menus and hand one to him. "Get whatever you want. It's on me."

"You don't have to do that."

"I want to."

He takes the menu and flips it open. I set mine down again. I know Frank's menu backward and forward.

Our waitress, a stocky middle-aged woman with a frizzed-out beehive, waddles back over. "What can I get for you two?"

Declan gestures for me to go first. The waitress scribbles down my order, then Declan's, giving him a wink before she leaves. And then our table gets too quiet.

Declan tucks his menu behind the napkin dispenser and leans forward. "Are you okay? Did something happen tonight?"

"Fine." I lick my lips and look back down at my coffee. "I'm fine. Thanks."

He watches me a few more seconds before relaxing back into his seat.

"So, did you have work today?"

Declan nods. "Yeah. Early shift. Caddying tomorrow, too."

"Nice. Keeping busy . . ."

We fall back into silence, but thankfully our food arrives, lightning-fast since we're about the only customers. Declan smirks at me.

"Solid choices," he says.

"Shut up. Sweet potato pancakes totally go with fried pickles."

"Uh-huh." He dabs hot sauce over his eggs. "Forgive me for not taking your word for it, but I have seen you dip one of those pickles in peanut butter, so."

This ease is what I miss most. Moments like this, I can close my eyes and almost convince myself nothing has changed. That it's still him and me.

"That was delicious," I say. "You don't know what you're missing."

He cracks a smile and I take a bite of my food. Another lull settles in while we both eat.

I'm having trouble looking at him again. Because I keep seeing him the way he was a year ago. Up in that tree house. The more I want to stop thinking about it, the fresher the memory of us holding each other becomes.

The necklace originally belonged to his mother.

He'd held it above me, sending the pendant spinning around and around. "Something to remember me by."

"Like I need a piece of jewelry to remember you." I smiled and traced the infinity symbol. "But thank you. It's beautiful."

Color crept over his cheeks. "I figured it was at least better than one of those cheesy broken heart, best-friends-forever necklaces."

"Much better."

He helped me put it on, and then his face grew serious. "You and me."

"Forever."

Across the table, he checks his phone again. Probably waiting for a text from someone he actually wants to be spending time with.

I don't know how I'll ever get over him. For Christ's sake, I was thinking about him while I was with another guy. Nine months is too long to still be thinking about him that way.

Of course, the only other thing I can think about is Kyle's hand on my head. I can just imagine what he told people when he went back into that party. And they'll all believe anything he says. Because it's me, and because that's how it always goes. Someone will say they walked right by the car, saw it happen. By tomorrow, everyone will have heard the new scandal.

I stab my pancakes with my fork.

"Were you with him earlier? The not-boyfriend?" Declan taps the end of his spoon against the table. Over and over.

I hate the idea of discussing what happened tonight with Declan. But I also hate lying to him. "Yes."

He nods slowly. But it abruptly changes to a shake of his head. "I really don't get what you see in that guy."

I really don't get how it's any of Declan's business. It's no secret he doesn't like Kyle. But Declan's the one who rejected me this time around. Now he's simply throwing salt on the wound.

"Could we not talk about him?"

Declan drops the spoon. "I just thought you'd want to know your friends are wondering about you."

"My friends."

"Yeah. Cory, the girls. The people who care about you."

"Wow." I pick up my coffee and set it down again. "That's great."

Declan sighs at my sarcasm, clenching his jaw like he regrets saying anything.

"No, really. Your concern means so much." I push my plate away. Suddenly this booth feels too cramped. "So, what, you guys all just sit around like some Sunday-afternoon book club and talk about me behind my back?"

"No, it's not like that—"

"Sure sounds like that."

"Hey, maybe Mackenzie was right. Maybe we should all hang out together, get to know him better."

"Like a double date?" I ask. Declan crosses his arms. "How is Miss Pinup tonight?"

"Do you have a problem with Mackenzie or something?"

The air is thick—difficult to breathe. And it's so hot, my thighs are sticking to the vinyl seat. I wipe my palms on my skirt.

"No." Under the table, I snap the elastic band around my wrist to keep myself calm. "You brought her up."

Declan rubs his eyebrow and sighs. "All I'm saying is I don't like seeing you this way."

"Then I guess it's a good thing you're leaving in a month."

I regret it before it's even past my lips. A pathetic, self-serving remark. But somehow it slips out anyway.

His expression shifts from angry to hurt and then he isn't wearing any emotion at all. He's closed off and quiet for too long. I clutch the infinity pendant until my nails dig into my palm, and I try to focus on that pain as ten seconds drag by. Eleven. Twelve, now.

He pulls his hand through his hair and shakes his head.

"Nice, Harp." He takes his wallet out and throws a few bills on the table. "I'll be in the car."

The drive home is awful. We don't speak, don't even turn on the radio, and the silence roars in my ears. I hold on to opposite elbows so tightly that my knuckles cramp, trying to make myself as small as I feel. Trying to figure out a way to undo this night.

Declan pulls up to my house before I'm ready. He leaves the car running.

"Thank you," I say.

He adjusts the rearview mirror. "Sure thing."

I open the car door. Hesitate. Shut it again. "I'm sorry about what I said before."

"Okay."

"Okay"? Does that mean he accepts my apology? He's still staring out the windshield, brushing his thumb across his bottom lip. It doesn't look like he forgives me.

I can't leave it like this.

"No, I got overly defensive, and I don't know where that comment even came from. I was having a terrible night and it really meant a lot that you came to get me, and I guess I've just been tense lately because of my mom—"

"Don't do that." Declan shakes his head and turns toward me.

"What?"

"Don't use her as an excuse. You make your own choices. And you've been selfish a lot longer than she's had cancer."

In the hushed moment that follows, my thoughts all blur together. Declan thinks I'm selfish. I am selfish. I knew that already so it shouldn't hurt, but it does because it's Declan who said it.

Declan has never said anything like that to me before.

My hand is shaking. I miss the door handle once and then pull it open. "Good night, Declan."

Sixteen

"COME OVER. IMMEDIATELY. I NEED FEMININE INPUT."

I check the time. It feels too early for Cory to be in crisis mode. And to be honest, I'm not sure I have the patience for it today. I was up all night, replaying my drive home with Declan. So in addition to being sleep deprived, I'm in a foul mood.

"What's the problem?"

"JUST COME OVER."

Yikes. "Okay, fine, I'm on my way."

I cross the lawn and let myself in. The downstairs is quiet, and I head straight up to Cory's room.

"They both look pretty similar to me," a familiar voice says.

Pausing on the top step, I close my eyes for a moment. This is just so typical. I can't go a single day in this town without running into someone I don't want to see.

"Not to worry, the feminine input has arrived." I cross the threshold and send Declan a chaste, totally friendly, not at all resentful smile.

"Great, which shirt?" Cory is holding a blue button-down in each hand. They are literally the exact same shirt.

"The one on the right. Definitely." Out of the corner of my eye I catch Declan grin surreptitiously. "So are you going to tell me what's got your panties in a bunch?"

"I have a date," he says with a dopey smile.

"Aww."

He points a finger at me. "Don't get all girlie on me."

"Isn't that why you invited me over?"

"Oh. Right."

"So who is this mystery girl?"

He pushes his glasses up and grins. "Mackenzie."

Before I can stop myself, I look at Declan. He leans forward, resting his elbows on his knees.

"You've got a date with Mackenzie?" I ask.

"Yeah. Declan set us up. You're sure about this shirt?" He holds the hanger in front of him, inspecting the collar.

Cory is going out with Mackenzie. Which means Declan isn't.

"Uh-huh," I say. "It's perfect."

"Good. Great." Cory darts out of the room. The faucet turns on in the adjacent bathroom.

I'm still processing. This doesn't make any sense.

"I thought . . ." From the way Declan's avoiding eye contact, it's clear he knows exactly what I thought.

He's the one who let me think it.

"Should I put gel in my hair?" Cory asks from the bathroom.

"No!" Declan and I chorus.

We hold each other's stares for a beat. Then we both turn away again.

I don't understand why Declan wouldn't have said something to me about this. Did he ever like Mackenzie? Or was this his intention all along?

Cory comes back in the room before I can ask any of these questions. He keeps shaking the loose change in his pocket, pacing around his room like he's lost.

"Where are you taking her?" I ask.

"She wants to go bowling," he says. Then his eyebrows shoot up. "You guys have to come with me."

Declan straightens. "Dude, I don't think you want us crashing your date."

"Right," I say. "This is your chance to spend some time alone with her."

Cory shakes his head. "She's always talking about hanging out as a group."

Neither of us says anything. Declan rolls his neck and fixes his gaze on the ceiling. I turn to face the window.

"Guys, come on." Cory looks from Declan to me. "Whatever is going on between you, I need you to drop it for one night and just do this for me. Please."

"Yeah. Of course," I say. Last year, when Declan and I first became more-than-friends, Cory never let it get weird. And, I mean, it must have been weird for him. But even when he joked about being a third wheel, I could tell he was just happy we were happy.

After all the support Cory's given me, I can hardly say no to bowling.

I'm not that selfish.

The smell of stale popcorn and cigarettes hits me the moment we walk into Regal Lanes later that evening. Pins crash together and bad eighties jams blare from the bar. I kind of love it. I pick up a pair of size nine shoes and slide onto the plastic bench across from Cory to lace up.

Declan sits beside me. We drove here together, so Cory could pick up Mackenzie. We're getting really good at sharing stone-silent car rides.

Cheers erupt from lane three. Jake Thornton and his crew. Perfect. They're exchanging high fives and taunting one another after every frame, impossible to ignore. I yank my shoelaces tighter and tie a knot.

"This town is too small," I mumble to Cory. He shrugs, not taking his eyes off Mackenzie.

She bowls like such a girl. Her full skirt swishes like a bell as she rolls the ball granny-style between her legs. She spins around and claps after she knocks down five pins.

Declan turns to me. Of course we're on the same team. "Would you like to go first?"

"No, you go ahead."

He bowls a strike. Then Cory gets a spare. And I follow their act with two gutter balls. Awesome.

My score remains in the double digits until the last frame, when I finally break the pathetic one hundred mark. Cory resets the scoreboard for our second game and Mackenzie slides closer to him, whispering something in his ear.

They both start laughing. Meanwhile, I think I'm getting frostbite from Declan. And I hate this awful silence between us. I just want things to be civil.

"I think I was using the wrong ball," I say to him. "Yep. That was my problem."

He gets up and stands in front of me. "I'm sure that was it." He gives me a tight smile and moves toward the restrooms.

I watch him go, then turn back to Cory. Mackenzie is practically glowing beside him. And I have no idea how I never noticed before. Their affection is beyond obvious now that I'm looking for it.

Behind them, the group from lane three start to pack it in. Jake leers in my direction.

"I'm going to get a soda," I say to Cory and Mackenzie. "You guys want anything?"

"No, thanks," Mackenzie says.

The bar is way in the back. Practically in a different building. I figure there's no way Jake would follow me. But maybe hiding in the ladies' room until he left would have been safer.

"Hey, Sloan."

His tone implies no response is expected, but rather that I should wait on the edge of my seat because he's about to say the most amusing thing anyone has ever heard. He stops beside me. My fingers curl over the back of a wooden barstool.

"You were awfully rude to me last time I saw you. Want to kiss and make up?"

The bartender, a burly guy with a bald head and a reddish-brown beard, ambles over to us. He gives me a skeptical, *You better not be ordering a cocktail* kind of look.

"Can I have a Coke, please?"

"Make that two."

My jaw knots and I pull a few singles out of my pocket. The bartender fills two glasses at the fountain and puts them down in front of us.

"Two fifty."

Jake knocks my hand out of the way and pays with a five. "Keep the change."

I'm still clutching my money. "I don't want you paying for me."

"Don't worry. No strings." He takes a long drink and I shove the bills into my front pocket. "You're welcome, by the way."

Whatever his endgame is, walking away isn't going to change it. If Jake has something he needs to prove to himself, I'd rather he do it here, in private.

I look over my shoulder. No sign of Declan. "What do you want, Jake?"

"Heard about a party tonight. Thought you might be interested."

"I'm not." I shoot daggers at him, but he doesn't move. "So you can fuck off now."

The bartender lets out a long whistle, and wipes down the counter with a grin. I decide he's an okay guy.

Jake ignores me. Walks his fingertips up my arm. The same way he touched me in the shallow end of the pool.

I bring the Coke to my lips but it splashes onto the back of my hand, dripping down my arm. I wipe it off on my shorts.

"What's the matter, Sloan? Don't you like me anymore?"

"I never liked you." I shrug him off. "And don't touch me. I don't know where your hands have been."

Jake's eyes sink to my nether regions and his smirk grows wider. "Sure you do."

Leaving my Coke behind, I head for the bathroom. Jake manages to get a stride ahead and block my path.

"Aren't you late for your circle-jerk?" I ask, looking at his friends instead of him.

He keeps smiling. He knows his burn was better.

And I don't even care. I just want it to be over. But it isn't. Jake won't let me have the last word twice in a row.

Silently I tell myself to ignore him, it doesn't matter, nothing he says matters. But then the restroom door behind him opens.

"So, you and Kyle Marcell, huh?" His smirk deepens and I start to panic. "You always have had a thing for public places, but I gotta give the guy credit. Was his car really right in the driveway of that party?"

Declan doesn't look at me. He glares at the back of Jake's head. "Apologize."

Jake turns slowly around. Declan's eyes are flat, moss-colored steel. He steps closer to Jake.

I cast a nervous glance over to Cory, who's still at our lane. He stands up but keeps his distance.

Jake tries to maneuver around Declan, stepping toward the exit. Declan catches his sleeve. "You're not going to make me ask twice, are you?"

With no room left between them, Jake suddenly seems to notice Declan has about four inches on him. He shifts his weight. "Sorry, Harper," he says without turning around.

Declan drops his hand and watches him leave. He turns to me, his face still flushed. I shrink back a step and stare at my bowling shoes.

"You okay?" he asks.

I nod, but it's a lie. Humiliation simmers in the pit of my stomach. Somewhere in the back of my mind, the pieces start to come together.

Let it go, Harper. "Why did you do that?"

His forehead wrinkles and he kind of smiles, like he thinks I'm joking. "Because that guy owed you an apology?"

I nod again and he follows me back to our group. Mackenzie fitfully examines the hem of her skirt and Cory does his best to act like nothing happened. But I catch Declan lock eyes with him. Seeing their silent exchange, that prickling awareness from a moment ago becomes a devastating certainty.

Declan already knows what they say about me.

I heard she hooked up with three guys at once.

I fucked her freshman year.

Slut.

He's heard it all. Everything I never wanted him to find out.

Seventeen

I CHOKE OUT A LAUGH. IT SOUNDS A LOT LIKE a cat coughing up a fur ball. "Whose turn is it?"

Mackenzie pulls at the ends of her hair. "New game . . ."

I grab the pink ball I've been using and step up to the edge of our lane. "I'll go."

I throw it as hard as I can and with completely the wrong form, practically shot-putting it down the lane. It lands with a heavy thud and swerves directly into the gutter, trickling the rest of the way down.

My hand doesn't feel right. It doesn't feel like my own. I wipe my palm on my shorts and turn around. Keeping my eyes on the hideous gray carpet with neon squiggles, I start moving, grabbing my purse from underneath the plastic bench.

"Harp, hold on." Declan sets his ball down and reaches his arm out to stop me.

Pushing his hand away, I slip past him. "Please don't."

He trails after me for a few feet, but Cory is quicker. He's already kicked off his bowling shoes and slipped on his Vans.

"She just needs a minute to calm down," I hear him say to the others. "Wait here. I'll talk to her."

I pace the parking lot in my bowling shoes, stopping when Cory comes out. "How much does he know? Did you tell him about October?"

He sighs, rubbing his eyes tiredly.

I shove him. "Did you fucking tell him?"

"Slow your roll, okay? I didn't tell him anything."

"But he's heard other stuff about me, right? I can tell; I could see it in the way he looked at you in there." I stop in my tracks. "You swear he doesn't know?"

"I swear. He doesn't know what happened that night."

Crouching down against the brick wall, I dig through my purse. "Okay. I'm sorry."

Heat radiates off the blacktop, making it difficult to take full breaths. I think I might throw up.

I find what I'm looking for and pop open the mint tin, pulling out my Bic lighter and a cigarette.

"What do you think you're doing?" Cory asks.

I light it and stand up, closing my eyes as I exhale.

The cigarette is ripped from my fingers. My eyes fly open

in time to see Cory pitch it across the parking lot.

We stare at each other.

"I wasn't finished with that."

"Actually, you were."

He doesn't back down and I think about lighting another, just to piss him off, but really I don't even want one anymore. I just want Cory to stop frowning at me that way. Like he's disappointed in me again. Same as the night he carried me out of that party last fall, the night I had to beg him not to say something to Declan. *Please don't tell, please don't tell, I'll handle it myself.*

I blink back the tears that are suddenly trying to surface.

Cory puts his arm around my shoulder and sighs. "You're such a pain in my ass, you know that?"

"Cory, what about the other rumors, what else has he—"

Declan comes out the door with Mackenzie. Cory's arm slips off my shoulders and around Mackenzie's waist, but Declan keeps glancing back and forth between us, and I haven't seen that look on his face since he overheard Cory asking me to homecoming freshman year. He looks like he doesn't know who to trust. Like all this time, he had some version of me memorized, Harper 1.0, and he's finally realized a year has passed and his memory is now obsolete.

Declan looks at his hands, which are holding my sandals. He hands them to me wordlessly.

"Oh." I'm the only one still wearing the red, white, and blue numbers. "Yeah, I'll just . . . be right back."

I go inside and drop the bowling shoes off at the counter, and when I come back out only Mackenzie is smiling.

"Why don't we go get some food?" she suggests.

"Sounds good," Cory says.

Everyone looks at me. I look at my toes. "I'm kind of tired."

Declan scratches the back of his neck and turns to the others. "Why don't you two go ahead? We'll catch up later."

They climb into Cory's car, and we watch them drive away.

"Thanks," I say. "I didn't want to ruin their entire date."

"Are you really okay?"

Elastic snaps against my wrist. Over and over but it isn't helping. "Uh-huh."

He steps closer and reaches for my hand. Stupidly, I let him take it, and a weird tingle shoots up my arm when he runs his thumb over my wrist.

He leads me to the curb and takes a seat. I fold my arms into my stomach and bend over my knees, even though it makes me hotter to sit that way.

"I know . . ." He rubs his eyebrow before continuing. "I know you feel more comfortable sharing some things with Cory. But if you need someone to talk to . . . I'm still here."

Three mosquito bites near my ankle. Three X's.

He's always been there for me. Always. And I wish nothing had changed, that I could still tell him anything and know that he would never judge me. But I saw the look on his face when he noticed my hickey, and I see it now. We can't talk about this.

"Thank you," I say. "But I think it's better if we just . . . leave it alone."

He's quiet for a long time, staring across the lot at something I can't see. He stands up, so I do too. He runs his hands over his face and rests them on top of his head, making his elbows bow out to the sides.

"I can't leave it alone. Not when you're this upset." He drops his hands. "You can't let that guy get to you like this."

He steps closer. Stands so close, I can smell the fabric softener on his clothing and can see his breath move through his chest.

But I'm not really there. I'm back in the pool four months ago, the day after my seventeenth birthday. Downing the contents of Jake's flask because Declan never answered my birthday postcard and I had nothing left to look forward to, except becoming numb.

Jake waited for the vodka to kick in and then his fingers moved up my arm-shoulder-neck, and it felt soft and dull and lovely. The water was soft too. Liquid velvet. I cupped it in my palms and poured it onto Jake's hair and started laughing. Then he pulled me to the side of the pool.

"Wait. What about Jenny?"

He pressed himself against me. Pressed me into the wall. "It's over between us. I only want you."

Then my lips on his lips and his lips on my neck and my legs around him and his hand between them until the locker room door swung open and the flashlight found us.

What about Jenny? I asked only once. And only after we were already in the pool. As if I didn't know what would happen if someone like me was left alone with someone like him.

"Harper, are you listening to me?"

I refocus and start toward Declan's car. "Really, I'm fine."

He drives us through town and pulls up to a stop sign in our neighborhood. After a few seconds, he's still stopped. I look over at him.

"My dad's working late," he says. "Do you want to come over?"

Eighteen

REPAINTING DECLAN'S HOUSE APPEARS TO BE A work in progress. He and Cory have only gotten as far as scraping off old paint, and now gray wood is exposed in patches along the white siding, like zebra print.

Declan unlocks the front door and his dog, Lula, bounds over to greet us. I crouch down to give her a proper hello.

She seems determined to cover every inch of me in kisses, and her tail wags so hard that the whole back half of her body is swaying.

I scratch behind her ears. "She remembers me."

"Of course she does. You were her favorite." Declan moves through the kitchen and lets her out to do her business in the backyard.

Walking into the living room, it hits me how long it's been since I came over here. Certain things are the same as ever. Along the mantel, Declan's old school pictures are still lined up chronologically. But there's something lesser about this house now. The floral-print throw pillows are threadbare and full of lumps. The silver cross on the wall has lost its luster. Over time, the crimson curtains were sun-bleached into a milky red. In all the details, Declan's mom is fading.

He comes in behind me while I'm looking at a framed picture of her. He starts shuffling magazines and junk mail into a pile on the coffee table. Then looks around the room like there's something more he should be doing.

"Can I get you anything? I could make coffee."

"No, I'm fine."

He goes into the kitchen anyway, and comes back with two glasses of water.

I take one and sip on it. "Thanks."

He lines up the TV remotes and shoves his hands in his pockets. "Why are you suddenly pretending to be that kind of girl?" He says it all in one breath, like he's been holding it in since the bowling alley.

"What kind of girl?"

"Come on, you know what I'm talking about. What that guy was saying . . . what kids from school say about you. You act like all those rumors are true. You don't even defend yourself."

"Yes I do."

"Not today."

He's right, not every piece of gossip about me is true. Not even close. But most of the time I don't bother to deny anything. The rumors are all true enough.

Besides, people believe whatever they want to believe. Take Declan, for example. Right now, his face is a mosaic of disbelief. Scraps of our past, moments he spent with the old me, are clouding his judgment.

"What makes you so sure I'm pretending?"

"Because I know you."

My heart swells, pressing hard against my rib cage. His voice is almost pleading, and it makes me dizzy knowing some part of him still thinks of me as the same girl he used to love. Even if he is wrong. I set my glass down, using the moment to catch my breath. "Everyone pretends something, right? Even you."

"What's that supposed to mean?"

"You could have told me about Mackenzie and Cory. You made me think you liked her."

He stares past me, at the blank TV screen. "I didn't make you think anything. You assumed." His eyes dart back to mine. "You do that a lot."

"Fine. I guess it was all in my head."

"What difference does it make, anyway? You have Kyle. Not like you were jealous, right?"

"Right." I shake my head. "I mean, no." Declan's eyes narrow. "I'm not with Kyle. That's done."

"So he isn't the reason . . ."

"Reason for what?"

He picks up a pillow and turns it over in his hands. Then tosses it back down. "Nothing."

"No, what were you going to say?"

"I thought he might have been the reason why . . . we ended. Before."

I stare out the bay window. A cloud passes over the setting sun and the whole room darkens. "I didn't even know him then."

He waits. Waits some more. A year's worth of unanswered questions and buried pain flash across his face. "Is that really all you have to say?"

I push the hair off my face and take a step back. "What do you want to hear, Declan?"

"I just want you to be honest with me! Tell me what happened, tell me why you did this to us!"

The bookshelf hits my spine and I can't back up any farther. I can't give him what he wants, either.

His last few months in Carson, I tried so hard to help Declan. To be everything he needed. But the fear I'd carried since Natalie's death—the fear of losing people, losing him—that hadn't gone away. It had gotten stronger, growing inside of me like a tumor of my own. I needed Declan just as much as he needed me. On bad days, I needed to feel his hand in mine, feel the pulse on his wrist as a reminder we could survive anything. And on the good days, days his smile would light up his face and my whole world, that was enough to convince me we would make it to the other side.

But then he was gone. And it was so much harder to make him smile over the phone.

I try to swallow. "After you left . . ."

It was more than just state lines dividing us.

I missed you and I missed her and I needed to feel something else. Something less.

That party in October was supposed to be like any other. But things were off to a bad start before I even left the house.

"Are you going out with Sadie again tonight?" Declan had asked.

It was code for "Will you be drinking?" and I had the wrong answer.

"I wish you'd get to know her better. She's been really supportive."

Declan coughed a laugh. "Yeah, she supports you when you can barely stand."

I took a deep breath and gripped my necklace. It was the first time we'd spoken all week, and I couldn't handle another fight with him. "What are your plans this weekend?" I asked before we could get any further off course.

"Just hanging out with Dave. We might see a movie."

I could hear Dave, his roommate, in the background. I sat on the floor and leaned against my bed. "Anyone else?"

Declan hesitated. Cleared his throat. "Yeah, uh . . . I think a couple girls from my French class. And we might meet up with a few other guys. . . ."

I'd stopped listening. My lungs were lined with lead. They wouldn't expand.

This was ridiculous; I had no reason to be jealous. But I was.

Declan waited for me to say something.

"Sounds fun," I whispered.

The background noise faded, and when he spoke again there was a slight echo, like he'd shut himself inside his bathroom: "Everything okay?"

"Yeah, just . . . It's weird. Not knowing anything about your friends."

"Well, what do you want to know?"

I wanted to know if they were pretty. If they were the reason he kept forgetting to call me back. If they made him smile on the days I couldn't.

But I wouldn't say it. I wouldn't. "Have any become more than friends?"

Declan was quiet for a long time. "How could you even ask me that?"

Every day I woke up missing Declan. And whether we talked or we didn't, by nighttime I always wound up missing him more.

Telling ourselves it was temporary didn't help one bit. He'd been gone only two months and already he was drifting out of reach. We still had the rest of the school year, and then another, and even then we might end up at different colleges and have to start all over again.

We were trapped in this cycle, and each day we spent apart put another fracture in our forever.

"There's just so much of your new life that I'm not a part of and . . . it feels like we're changing."

He let out a long exhale. "I don't know what to say to you right now."

Tell me you love me. Tell me I'm crazy.

Answer the question.

"God, Harper, you make this so much harder than it already is."

An hour later I was wasted.

My memory of that night is spotty, even after Cory helped fill in the blanks. But I remember the important parts, enough to know Declan's best guess about what happened is too close for comfort. And calling him the next morning—that I can remember like it was yesterday.

Telling him the truth would have hurt him. No matter what I did at that point, I was going to hurt him.

So I ended things. Told Declan I couldn't make it work anymore, because it was easier than telling him about drinking until my lips went numb. About ending up alone with an older guy whose name I never learned and using the lips that had only ever kissed Declan to kiss someone else. Touching him and letting him touch me. Easier than telling Declan about Cory finding me there, pulling the guy off of me and stopping things from going any further because I was too far gone to stop it myself.

Or about making Cory swear not to tell. *Please don't tell. I'll handle it.*

And I did handle it. I saved Declan the trouble of ending things himself. And he would have ended it, of that much I'm certain. Because no matter which way you cut it, I cheated on Declan.

It was the right thing to do, sparing him the gory details.

"After you left, I . . . It just got to be too hard."

I hear the defensive tone in my voice and I see his expression tighten. I would have seen it coming with my eyes closed. If there was ever a person who called me on my bullshit, it was Declan.

He leans forward, hovering over me now. He grins incredulously. "Hard. For you."

My arms slip down to my sides and all the air I breathe becomes his breath too. "You don't understand."

"You're right, I don't." He steps back, pulling his hand through his hair. "My mom dies, I get kicked out and sent to a boarding school where I know no one, and then you cut me completely out of your life. Like what we had meant nothing to you."

"Of course it meant something!"

The muscles in his jaw tense and release. It becomes a game of chicken, both of us waiting for the other person to say something. To fix this. And I want to, I just don't know how to explain what it felt like to get left behind. It didn't matter that it wasn't his choice to go away to school. Declan wasn't holding up his end of the deal—he was pulling away faster than I could catch up—and it hurt. So I pushed him harder, I hurt him back. But telling him all of this now will only make things worse.

"Good to know," he finally says. He looks away and rubs his neck. "Listen, I've got a lot to do before my dad gets home. . . ."

Behind my back, the elastic snaps against my skin. "Are you asking me to leave?"

He shoves his hands in his pockets and looks up at me. He nods.

Another small piece of my heart breaks. This isn't how it should be between us. We were best friends; he knew me better than anyone. And now he can't stand to be in the same room as me.

I meant what I said earlier this summer, at that party in the woods. I miss him. Even now, standing in front of him, I miss him so much it aches.

But I do what he asks. I leave, pausing on his porch and trying to get my breathing back to normal. I take one last look at his door, and sprint back to my house.

Nineteen

PHOTOGRAPHY CLASS THE NEXT DAY IS OUT OF
the question. I email Mr. Harrison my shots and include a message citing my mom's health as the reason for my absence.

Yeah, I'm going to hell. What else is new?

Mom left super early for another round of chemo, so I stay in bed and try to catch up on sleep. But before long I'm fully awake, staring at my ceiling and remembering the glow-in-the-dark star stickers Declan has on his. At least, he used to have them. We stood on top of his bed and put them up together, re-creating all the constellations we knew. And every so often, one of us would jump on the mattress, just to make the other lose balance.

Anyway, that was ages ago. We were kids—young enough

that our parents still let us play alone in each other's rooms. He's probably grown out of the stars by now.

My phone buzzes on my nightstand.

"Hey, Sadie."

"I've got the best news. Mike's great-aunt died last night, so his parents are going out of town for the weekend."

"Oh my God, that's so sad."

"Right. I guess. Anyway, he's having a party tonight. And Kyle's older brother offered to supply the drinks. It's going to be epic. So, I was thinking of wearing that pink top I got at the mall the other day? And if you want to come over early, I can straighten your hair, and I have the cutest new skirt you can borrow—"

"Thanks, but . . . I can't go out tonight."

"Why not?"

I focus on my hardwood floors. I don't usually lie to Sadie. But she never takes no for an answer, and I'm so sick of Carson parties, the thought of going to another makes my skin crawl. "Family night. My mom's making a big deal out of it . . . total pain. Sounds like you'll have a lot of fun, though."

"That's so lame."

"Totally, I know."

"Well, I'll let you know how it goes. Maybe you can sneak out after your mom gets her fill of board games or whatever."

"Maybe . . ."

She clears her throat. "So, did I tell you what happened to me at the drugstore the other day?"

192

I cradle the phone against my ear and listen as Sadie recounts how she was innocently shopping for new lip gloss and wound up meeting a college guy who just wouldn't leave without getting her number first. I gasp and laugh at all the right places, kicking my covers off and pulling my laptop onto my bed. I start scanning through pictures, trying to get some ideas for my next assignment. I'm such a multitasker.

She's still talking when the garage door opens below me. I shut my laptop and cut her off.

"Hey, sorry, my mom just got home. Call you later?"

"Okay. And seriously, try to make it out tonight."

"Sure. Bye."

I realize too late I'm still wearing my pajamas. Class is way over by now, and normally this would totally give me away. But Mom's had a pretty bad case of chemo-brain lately, and she doesn't even notice them when I walk into the kitchen.

She's already deep into her routine of acting like everything is perfect as pie—even though her head is wrapped in a scarf and she flutters her fingers self-consciously around her head every thirty seconds, never actually touching her thinning hair, probably out of fear that a gentle breeze will be enough to blow the rest away. But everything is totally normal. Completely fucking fine. At least that's the word Mom keeps using over and over.

But she was barely able to choke down a yogurt at dinner last night, and can't remember half of the things we talk about five minutes later. Never has this situation been anything short of horrendous, and it's getting harder and harder to pretend otherwise.

She looks up from the dirty dishes and smiles at me. "How was class?"

"Class was class," I answer. "How was chemo?"

She gives me a conspiratorial look. "Fun as always. Actually, it's not too bad. Your dad was there to keep me company for most of the time, and I finished a book while he made some work calls. He just headed to the office."

"You know, you don't have to keep putting on a brave face for me. You're allowed to have bad days or be upset or just call this what it is."

"And what is it?"

"It's . . ." I swallow. "It's unfair."

Mom laughs. "Aw, honey. Nothing is ever fair."

With that, she turns back to the pile of dishes in the sink.

"Can't you admit for once that you're scared?"

She stops what she's doing and frowns at the sink. "Yes, sometimes this is all a little scary. But I'm not going to let that keep me from living. There's no sense letting this temporary situation swallow up my whole life, right?"

We're so different, Mom and me. She takes every day as it comes, never runs from the truth or has to trick herself into staying in a moment. The future is wide open for her, because she doesn't dwell on her past. But for me it's become impossible to separate her cancer from the experience of having someone

I cared about taken from me. Every time I get stressed about Mom, I automatically see Natalie.

She must be able to tell how worked up I am, because she wipes her hands on a dish towel and turns to face me. "Hey, I don't want you worrying about me. Everything is going to be okay. I promise."

She offers me a smile and I squeeze my hand into a fist and smile back. "Here, why don't you let me do those?"

"Oh, that's all right, sweetie. I'm almost finished. But you know what would be a big help?" She pulls a glass casserole dish off the drying rack. "Would you mind taking that over to Bridget?"

"Sure."

I slide into a pair of flip-flops and cross the lawn to Cory's house. After knocking quickly, I let myself in the front door.

"Bridget?"

"In the kitchen!"

"Hey, I'm just returning your—"

They're sitting at the kitchen table. Cory, Bridget, and of course, Declan.

Why didn't I change out of my pajama pants before coming over here? And why do they have little yellow ducks on them? Just why.

"Oh, thanks!" Bridget says. "Is your mom back from the hospital already?"

"Yeah, she just got home."

She nods. "You hungry? The boys are helping me get rid of some leftovers."

"No, thank you."

Taking another sip of coffee, she checks her watch. She's wearing scrubs, probably about to leave for a shift. She gets up and stands behind Declan, resting her hand on top of his head. It's the same gesture Natalie always made to Cory and me. From the way Declan's forehead wrinkles and the intense interest he's taken in his placemat, I'd guess I'm not the only one thinking of her now.

"It's so good to see the three of you together again. We sure have missed you, Declan. Haven't we, Harper?"

Bridget loves making us feel awkward. And clearly, she's a pro at it.

I stare at the dish in my hands. "Of course we have."

He sets his fork down on his plate.

"All right, I'm off to work," Bridget says with a second glance at her watch. "Cory, make sure those plates find their way into the dishwasher, please."

He nods and uses his finger to push the last bite of leftover macaroni onto his fork as she swoops down and smooches the top of his head.

Bridget stops in the doorway. "Oh, Harper honey, there's another casserole in the freezer for you to take home. I'll stop by tonight to check in on your mom."

"Thanks, Bridget."

She waves and is out the door.

"Okay," Cory says once she's gone. "I'm going to brush my teeth and then I'm ready."

Declan nods while Cory stacks his plates. He drops them in the sink on his way out of the room.

Suddenly the ratio of people to uncomfortable silence is unbearable. I busy myself putting the casserole dish away in Bridget's cupboard, praying Cory will come down quickly and make this as brief as possible.

I fiddle with my necklace, sliding the pendant back and forth across my bottom lip while I stare at the pictures stuck to the refrigerator door. One in particular catches my eye, and I lift the magnet to get a better look at it.

It's a snapshot of Cory, Declan, and me from a few years back. I remember it being taken, on Cory's fourteenth birthday. The three of us are wearing party hats and enormous smiles. I'm standing in the middle, one arm around each of them, looking into the camera. Declan is on my right, but rather than looking forward, he's looking at me.

Heat creeps up my neck. The evidence is everywhere— Declan has always been a better friend than me. And I took him for granted.

He stopped calling ten days after I broke it off in October. And that was my fault too. Because I hadn't answered a single one of his messages. Instead, I shut down. Barely left my house except to go to school. Barely spoke to anyone, which worked fine with

Cory since he didn't have much to say to me either, but it did not go over well with Sadie.

Then winter break drew closer and I started itching, right down to my skeleton, to see Declan. So on Christmas Eve, I broke my own rule. I asked Cory about him. And my heart shattered all over again. Declan had already moved on. I was too late.

Everything started to fade after that. There would be no going back, no undoing the past. So I committed to the choice I'd made. I started going out with Sadie again, and at the first party I kissed someone. And the list grew from there. With each new guy I buried the moments I'd shared with Declan a little deeper, cementing myself into a life without him. A life where I could do whatever I wanted with whomever I wanted, because it didn't matter anymore; no one was getting hurt. And it did get easier. To fake liking those other boys, to shut my eyes and drift away for an hour. But deep down, the pieces of my past I was trying so hard to bury always mattered. Because I hadn't just lost the Declan I was in love with. I had lost my best friend, too.

I sent him one postcard. Like that was the best I could do, as if that insignificant gesture even merited a response. But Declan deserves so much better, and I can't give up on him that way again. I'm so sick of running from what's difficult. Sick of being scared of everything, of being the coward Graham says I am. I want to be someone worthy of Declan's friendship; I want to earn it back.

I stick the picture onto the fridge again. "Did I miss anything good in class?"

Declan leans back, draping one arm over his chair. "Saw your photograph. The shot of the roses."

My leg won't stop bouncing. "Yeah?"

"Yeah." More silence. "Aren't you going to ask me what I thought?"

"What did you think?"

"Didn't care for it."

I give my pendant one last squeeze and let it go. Guess I should have anticipated that response. "Oh."

"Don't get me wrong, it was pretty and all that. But safe. And therefore completely boring."

"Well, thanks for the feedback."

"Anytime."

I tug at the hem of my shirt, gripping the fabric in tight fists. "Can we start over?"

Declan pushes back from the table and passes by me on his way to the sink. He turns on the faucet and rinses his plate. "How? Shake hands and pretend we've never met?"

"No, I don't mean that. I just . . . Things got kind of intense yesterday. And I was hoping we could all do something fun this afternoon. Maybe mini golf? Give you a chance to show us your awesome caddying skills."

Ugh. So lame.

He shuts the water off. After a pause, he starts loading the dishwasher. "Cory and I were about to meet up with the girls and head over to the fair."

"Oh, cool, I totally forgot that started today."

He dries his hands on a dish towel. And doesn't look at me. Clearly, I'm not going to get an invitation.

"Well," I say. "I should probably head back home anyway."

His thumb moves over his bottom lip. The same gesture he always uses when he's thinking about something.

Cory comes back into the room, twisting his back left to right. "Warming up is the key to avoiding stomach cramps," he says. Then he nods to me. "You ready to eat a deep-fried Twinkie?"

"Um . . ." I glance at Declan. "I mean, if you guys are okay with me tagging along. . . ."

Cory frowns at me. "What are you talking about? Of course it's okay."

Declan takes his keys out of his pocket. "Everyone ready?"

I tug at the extra fabric of my pajama pants. "I just have to run home and change—"

He heads toward the front door before I've even finished my sentence. Cory watches him go, then smirks at me.

"So this'll be fun," he says.

"Maybe I shouldn't come."

"You're probably right. Better off keeping your distance until he leaves. Hey, how's that been working out for you so far?"

I make a face. "Shut up."

"Just go get changed already."

The fair is beyond crowded. I get caught in a swarm of middle schoolers, and then bump into an older couple. I turn to apologize and fall behind my friends. As soon as I've caught up, Mackenzie grabs Cory's hand and sprints toward the Ferris wheel.

They get in line and I feel a twinge of loss. Which isn't at all justified, since it's not like Cory has stopped including me, or that he was ever *mine* to begin with. But without swim practices, I already see less of him. And it's little things, like the way he's always near Mackenzie, looking out for her, that make me wonder whether he's done looking out for me that way.

I shake it off. None of that matters as long as Cory is happy.

Gwen smirks. "You guys up for rides?"

Declan and I always ride the Ferris wheel together. Every year. He shrugs. "Not really."

He's wearing his sunglasses again, and not being able to see his eyes makes me feel like he's terribly far away. It's as if summer is already over; he and I are miles apart.

We keep walking, passing by a deep-fried pickle vendor. I smile at Declan, but he's looking the other way.

I clear my throat and try, for the tenth time today, to engage him in conversation. "Are you guys hungry? I could get us some snacks."

Gwen perks up. "I could go for a frozen banana."

I turn to Declan. "How about you?"

"I'm fine."

"Are you sure? I could—"

"I said I'm fine."

I bite my lip. Nod. "Yeah. Got it."

Gwen wrinkles her nose and looks at her feet. I turn and walk away.

The smell of fried dough and sausage, mildly nauseating yet comfortingly nostalgic, hangs heavy in the air around me. I stop in front of another food stand. Apparently you can deep-fry anything these days. Pecan pie, Oreos, even marshmallows.

I think about getting some to take back to the group, but Declan only likes marshmallows when they're raw. I would know, because we used to have bonfires all the time at the tree house. Cory and I would make s'mores, and Declan would just eat all the ingredients straight out of the packages.

He even brought some that last night we spent together. We'd planned to build a fire, but then the rain started and we went up into the tree house and dessert didn't seem quite as important after that.

"What looks good?"

Gwen stops on my left and checks out the menu board. I straighten and tuck my hair behind my ear. "Oh, hey. Um . . . sorry, what did you say you wanted before?"

"Frozen banana. Ever tried one?"

I shake my head.

"They're addictive. And not as terrible for you as fried cookie dough, so that's a bonus." She taps my arm. "Come on, my treat."

We go over to the stand she saw and order two dipped in chocolate. She hands me mine and we sit down on a nearby bench.

I take my first bite. "Interesting."

"Kind of like banana-flavored ice cream, right?" She wipes one side of her mouth with a napkin. "So, do you want to talk about it?"

"Talk about what?"

"You don't have to. I just couldn't help but notice this is a particularly hostile chapter in the Declan-Harper saga."

"We don't have a saga."

"You do. But that's beside the point."

I wipe my palm on my shorts. "We were together for a while. He hates me now. That about sums it up."

"Please, he doesn't hate you."

"Um, were you not there a minute ago?"

"Yeah, and he was being kind of a jerk. But trust me, Declan only wishes he hated you."

I cough a laugh. "That makes me feel so much better."

She smiles. "Well, it should."

I pick a flake of chocolate off my dessert. "I just feel like there's all this space between us now, and I don't know how to get rid of it. It's like every time he looks at me, he's disappointed that I'm not the person I used to be, you know?"

Gwen crisscrosses her legs. "People change. And sometimes that means drifting apart. But other times it just means working harder to find some common ground."

I think about everything Mom said in the kitchen earlier today, and I try to picture the next year of my life. I try to figure out what it would take for Declan to be a part of it, but I keep getting stuck on last October and every terrible moment between us since. Actually facing Declan's reaction to the truth was the scariest thing imaginable, so I never gave him the chance. Because as much as I wish I could undo the past or change the present, what I'm really afraid of is the future.

"I'm willing to work," I say, almost to myself.

We finish the food and walk back to meet up with the group. We pass a fresh-squeezed lemonade stand—the kind that's really just half a lemon and a bunch of sugar-water. Personally, I think it's disgusting. But Declan loves the stuff.

I order one and follow Gwen back to the group. She pulls a toothpick out of her pocket and gnaws on it, casually angling away when we get close.

"Here." I hold the drink out to Declan. "I ordered this by mistake. Want it?"

"You sure you don't?"

"Yeah, I'm sure."

He takes it from me. "Thanks."

He gives me a small smile. It doesn't show his dimples, and I know he's just being polite. But it's progress. And when it comes to Declan, I'll take whatever I can get.

I cross my arms. "Guess you shouldn't have asked if you didn't want my answer."

"Whatever." She starts walking a little bit faster, turning left onto Ninth.

We pass by Second Helpings, and I pause to see if I can spot Mackenzie working behind the counter. The mannequins in the window are dolled up in floral aprons and skirts with petticoats underneath. Vintage cat-eye sunglasses and sparkly brooches are also scattered around the display, along with a few old postcards that rival the one I sent to Declan in terms of ridiculousness.

"Don't tell me you're going to start dressing like a 1950s housewife too."

"I was just looking for Mack. Don't think she's working today, though."

Sadie keeps walking without comment. "Want to get some food or something?"

"Yeah, I'm starved."

We head to a fast-food Mexican place down the block. I order a burrito with extra guacamole. Sadie orders a salad, hold the dressing. We grab a couple seats and I take my first bite of melty cheese and bean goodness. Sadie keeps her head down, but I catch her raising her eyebrows.

I cover my mouth while I chew. "What?"

She looks up innocently. "Oh, nothing. I just wish I could get away with eating like that."

Twenty

SADIE IS TEXTING AS SHE WALKS AND NEARLY trips over a small child playing on the sidewalk. I yank her elbow, pulling her out of the way. She doesn't even look up.

"Hey, who do you think is cuter, Mike or that sophomore John?"

"You're considering dating a sophomore? How progressive."

We split to walk around a couple of window shoppers and meet back up. She rolls her eyes and pockets her phone. "I'm not dating either of them."

"Well, in that case, John."

"Mm, I knew you'd say that. But then, we both know you don't have the best taste in guys."

My stomach immediately shrinks and I look down at my food. Maybe she's right. Over the past couple weeks I'd just started to lose some of the weight I gained after being off the swim team, and this isn't exactly the healthiest option. I set the burrito down and wipe my mouth with a napkin.

"So you never told me, how was that party the other night?"

"Fine." She looks at her phone.

"Just fine? I thought it was supposed to be epic."

She shrugs and takes a bite of her salad, which without the dressing is really just lettuce topped with cucumbers and shredded carrots. Seriously, how can that be any good? I take another small bite of my burrito and wait for her to elaborate.

"It was. Tons of people were there, and it didn't end until, like, four in the morning. I told my dad I was sleeping at your place and crashed there. But ever since, Mike has been so clingy. I think it's time to move on to someone new."

"Like John?"

She sighs. "Like whoever. Who cares?"

Clearly, she's done talking about this. I pick at the foil around my food. "So things with Declan have reached an all-time high on the awkward meter." Silence. "I think he'd rather I give up trying to be his friend. But I really don't want to; I just want to fix things before he goes back."

Sadie's texting again. I'm not sure whether she's even listening to me. She doesn't react either way.

"Are you mad at me?" I ask. Even though I know I haven't done anything wrong.

She doesn't look up from her phone. "Nope."

"Really? Because you seem pissed about something."

"No, I'm just . . . whatever. Tired."

I take a few more bites of my food, then get up and throw the rest away. I stand at the edge of our table, and don't sit down again. Because all of a sudden, *I'm* a little mad. "Ready to go?"

She doesn't answer until she's finished crafting her text. Then she stands up and follows me to the front door. We step outside and are bathed in humidity. Sadie puts on her sunglasses, and I squint down the street, in the opposite direction of her car.

"Ready?" she asks.

"Actually, I think I'm going to wander around down here for a bit. I'll call Graham for a ride home later."

"Oh." Sadie puts her phone away for the first time all day. "You're sure?"

She's already taken her first step toward her car. And even if I asked her to stay, I really can't handle an entire afternoon of her preset conversation topics. I guess we're both a little *tired*.

"Yeah, I'll just talk to you later, okay?"

She gives me a quick hug and then lets me be. I walk around for another hour, past the park where parents are lathering their kids with sunscreen. Past Frank's, where a line of churchgoers are grabbing brunch. I walk until the heat becomes too much and my shirt clings to the sweat on my back. I call my brother for a ride, and when I turn back onto Ninth Street to wait, I spot a quarter on the sidewalk.

That day at the driving range with Declan pops into my mind, when I left my change in the vending machine for someone else to find. Such a small gesture, but the way he looked at me when I did it, like I was someone special—I'll never forget that look. I hear him tell me he knows who I am, and I want so badly for him to be right.

I pick up the quarter. Along the sidewalk, I scan the row of parked cars until I find one with an expired meter. When I slip the coin in, for that tiny sliver of time, the old me doesn't seem so far off anymore.

By the time the sun starts to rise the next morning, I've already given up on sleep. I pack my camera bag and get in my car. At least I can get a head start on this week's photography assignment.

I drive around on autopilot for a while, trying to brainstorm. We're supposed to capture *life*. Could Mr. Harrison have been any more vague?

As usual I don't really have a clue what I'm doing. Which becomes evident when I pull to a stop at the Carson cemetery.

Natalie's grave is a quarter-mile walk from the gate. I wander slowly up the path, reading names and dates as I go along. I stop and take a few shots of a row of gravestones, silhouetted in the rising sun. A new day, a fresh start.

Mr. Harrison will eat it up.

I pop the lens cap back on and thread my arm through the camera strap so it crosses my body. She's just up ahead.

I kneel down a few feet back from the tombstone and set my camera bag beside me. It always felt a little silly to me, talking to someone who isn't there. I don't know what it was like when Declan visited with his dad, but whenever we came here together, he'd spend the whole time catching Natalie up on his life. The way he spoke to her made me forget to be embarrassed. But once he was gone, and we were over, I lost the courage to speak to her on my own.

"Sorry I haven't visited much lately," I say in a soft voice. "I don't think my mom's been able to come see you for a while either. But you probably already know she's sick." I pick a lone dandelion and twirl it around. I should have brought her flowers. Declan and Mom always do, when they visit. "Bridget has been amazing; she keeps sending over casseroles faster than we can eat them. And she's been helping Mom deal with chemo and stuff." I drop the dandelion. "But I know they both miss you. We all miss you."

I sit back and hug my legs to my chest. Stare at her name. BELOVED WIFE AND MOTHER.

Everything would be so much better if she were here. Declan would be happier. And we might still be together, too.

I tuck my chin and rest my forehead on my knees, closing my eyes and breathing as deeply as I can. It's useless wondering what would have happened if Natalie had survived that accident. I can't be sure Sadie's stupid game of Truth or Dare would have worked, or whether we really would still be together if Natalie were alive today.

All I know is we were never just a couple. We didn't suddenly stop hanging out together with Cory. Our history and friendship was inextricable from what we became. But being friends first didn't make the transition any easier. It didn't settle the butterflies in my stomach when he touched someplace new. Didn't keep me from accidentally biting his lip once when we kissed, or from worrying about saying the wrong thing. But it did mean we knew how to read each other.

We communicated in eye contact and gentle touches as much as with words. And that's what we lost when he left. Neither of us was as good at communicating over the phone. We never had to be before then.

A twig snaps behind me. I spin around and find Declan standing a couple yards back. I turn and wipe quickly under my eyes, and then stand to face him.

"What are you doing here?" he asks. He doesn't have a camera with him, and is instead clutching a bouquet of daisies.

"I'm sorry." I look at the grave again. "I was just taking some pictures and thought I'd say hi."

His forehead wrinkles. He bounces the stems of the flowers against his leg.

"Um . . . I'll leave you alone." I grab my bag and turn to go.

"Hold on," he says. He frowns again and steps toward me. "You don't have to leave."

I get the feeling it's the warmest welcome I'm going to receive. "Okay."

He nods and sets the flowers at the base of his mom's grave. He slumps down, leaning back onto his palms. His T-shirt is wrinkled and his hair is mussed all over his head, like he rolled out of bed and left without combing it. Or maybe he had trouble sleeping too.

After a moment, I sit beside him, folding my arms back around my legs.

"This was nice of you. To visit."

I scratch my arm. "It's nothing."

He sits forward. Wipes his mouth. "It's something to me."

We both look straight ahead. "What should we talk about?" I ask.

"Bridget said your mom had another treatment yesterday?"

"Oh. Yeah, she did."

"How is she?"

"Fine. Well, she says she's fine. But she is getting poisoned on a biweekly basis, so I guess it's all relative." I pause. "She's been losing a lot of weight."

"That's par for the course, though, isn't it?"

"You and your golf metaphors," I say. He grins and rocks into my shoulder. I smile a little too, unwinding now that he seems willing to speak to me again. "Anyway, I think so. But it's stuff like that, and her hair, and the fact that she doesn't have eyelashes anymore." I bite my lip and shake my head. "It's just kind of weird."

He nods thoughtfully. "It's been a weird summer."

"Totally. And fast." Too fast. Three more weeks and it will be over. Declan will be gone. "You must miss your friends from school."

"A few, I guess." He shrugs. "Dave is all right. But I'd rather stay here."

This takes me by surprise. "But earlier this summer you said you really liked it there."

He shrugs again.

"Does your dad know you want to stay?"

"He knows."

"Because maybe if you talked to him—"

"Do you honestly think he would have sent me there in the first place if he cared at all how I feel?"

Declan picks at the grass. He twirls a blade between his fingers, and the words start pouring out of him.

"It's like he's punishing me. Because he never signed up to be a single parent, and now he's stuck with me. And what really pisses me off is how he acts like he's doing me this big favor. Because he's gone so often for work, or he thinks I'd never be able to take care of myself, or . . . whatever his reasons are. He acts like it's best for both of us. And nothing I do or say is ever enough to change his mind."

"Dec, I'm so sorry. I didn't know you still felt that way."

"Right, well, how could you have?"

It isn't that he says it bitterly. Compared to our conversation in Cory's kitchen, it's practically cheerful. But the longer we're quiet, the heavier the weight on my chest becomes. I'm only now realizing how completely alone Declan must have felt this past year, especially when it comes to grieving his mom's death. After I talked with his dad and Cory over winter break, I assumed Declan was content, in a better place in life than he ever was with me. That I really had made the right decision ending things with him and keeping my reasons to myself. But now I don't know what to think. The rationalization I've been using for the past year was based on a lie.

Everything I think to say sounds like another excuse.

I take a deep breath. "Well, I'm glad you told me."

"Yeah, sorry to vent like that. I just get so mad."

"You should vent! It isn't fair that you don't get a say, and . . ." I hesitate. Declan looks over at me. "I wish you were staying too."

He studies me for a long moment. His eyebrows knit together, and he drops his gaze back to his hands. "Thanks."

He leans back, settling in again. We don't talk to Natalie. We don't talk at all, actually. But it's different from all the other stretches of silence this summer. It's comfortable somehow. It feels like us again.

Twenty-One

THE FOLLOWING WEEK, DECLAN SITS NEXT TO ME in photography.

As class is wrapping up, he turns toward me with a hopeful expression. "You doing anything after this?"

"Not that I know of."

He grins. "We're heading to the quarry. You should come."

The obvious answer is *Yes, of course, because I would go anywhere with you, Declan.* But on the flip side, I promised Mom I'd do the laundry when I get home. I tell him so.

"We'll only be gone a couple hours." He checks over his shoulder to make sure the girls are out of earshot. "Besides, Cory has a plan to get Mackenzie to take her clothes off. It's going to backfire beautifully. You don't want to miss it."

Well, I'm not made of resolve. "Okay, it's a date."

I regret my choice of words immediately, see them hover in the air between us like a word bubble that I want so, so badly to be able to erase.

"But not—I didn't mean . . . You know what I mean."

Oh God. Shut up, Harper. Shut. Up.

He tries to hide his smile. "I'll meet you at Cory's, then?"

"Sure."

I gather my stuff and practically sprint out to my car. Why? Why did I say "date"?

After speed-shaving my legs and saying a quick hello to my parents—who have become surprisingly lenient when it comes to plans that involve Cory and Declan—I'm out the door.

The guys are waiting in Cory's driveway. Cory has faint red lines from his goggles under his eyes.

"Practice this morning?"

Cory nods. "Uh-huh."

We have nothing left to say about it, and I'm kind of sorry I even asked. Declan clears his throat. "Looks like we're good to go."

He makes Cory give me the front seat again on the ride over, much to Cory's chagrin. We park alongside Mackenzie's Datsun and Gwen's SUV, then follow the trail through the pines and down to the quarry where the girls are sunbathing at the rocky edge. I drop my beach bag next to Mack's towel, which is Disney princess themed and extremely pink.

She pushes her sunglasses on top of her head and Cory crouches down to say hello.

I strip off my cover-up and stand with my hands on my hips. Under my bare feet, the granite is warm and inviting. I lay my towel down near Gwen's and take note of her fuchsia-framed sunglasses.

She looks up from the book she's reading to respond. "Present from Mack. She's slowly trying to take over my wardrobe, one accessory at a time."

"Crafty, that one."

She grins and sticks her nose back in her novel. Declan has moved down the rocks a ways, testing the water. I take a deep breath and walk over to him.

"Cold?" I ask.

"Not too bad."

He's lying. I can tell by the way his lips are scrunched to one side. Plus he has goose bumps on his arm.

"After you," he says.

I raise an eyebrow and stare him down until he starts to crack. His lips twitch, and he takes a tiny step closer. His hand finds my lower back.

My breath hitches, but now he's really smiling, and I start to get it.

"Wait." I try to step away from the edge, pressing back against his hand. "No. Declan, don't you dare—"

He pushes me in. By the time I resurface, he's already cannonballing in next to me. I push wet hair off my face and splash him.

He's giggling. This silent, shaking laughter that only comes out when he thinks something is really hilarious.

"I'm going to get even, you know."

"Oh yeah?" He dips his head back again. "Something to look forward to."

We tread water, circling around each other. He's still smiling his dimpled smile, and I splash him once more. He reaches for me, and I let out a squeal and sneak out of his grasp. And immediately regret it because all I really want is for him to touch me again.

He grabs my waist, twirling me around. I reach for his shoulders and . . . wait.

Is he flirting?

It feels the same as all those days we spent here last summer, and we were definitely flirting then.

He dives under. I go on treading, waiting for his next move. But when he comes up for air, he keeps his distance.

"It really is kind of cold," he says. "Want to get out for a bit?"

"Okay." I hesitate until he turns away, then follow him slowly back to the edge. We hoist ourselves up onto the boulders.

Cory is lying next to Mack, having a quiet conversation with her. Gwen looks half-asleep, with one arm draped over her eyes. I take my towel out of my bag and wipe down my legs.

"Oh yeah, he *loathes* you."

My head snaps toward Gwen. Her eyes are still closed, but she's smiling.

I check behind me, but Declan's back is turned. He's out of hearing range. "Were you watching us?"

She squints up at me. "Time for a dip." She turns to Mack and Cory. "You guys feel like swimming?"

All three of them splash into the quarry. I shuffle and cross my arms. I want to know what Gwen meant by that. Whether she noticed the way Declan was acting.

Nope, it doesn't matter what she saw. Because I am not going down that path again. Today should be about earning Declan's trust back and rebuilding our friendship. Which does not involve lusting after him.

I rifle through my bag for sunscreen. I find the bottle and spread some over my legs and stomach.

"Mind if I use some of that?" Declan tucks his sunglasses on top of his head. "Forgot mine."

"Oh, sure." I squeeze a healthy amount into his palm, and we both slather our arms and shoulders.

He gestures for the bottle again. "Want me to get your back?"

"No, that's okay."

He rolls his eyes and grabs the bottle. "You're already turning pink."

He moves behind me and I pull my wet hair over one

shoulder. The muscles in my back tense and my breathing becomes weirdly fast and I hope it isn't obvious. I focus on the stone beneath my feet, the way flecks of the granite sparkle in the sunlight. Not on his hands sweeping over me.

He moves efficiently, slowing only when he traces the lines of my bathing suit top. And then it's over.

"Your turn," I say, quickly trading places with him.

I use broad strokes, trying not to even look at what's in front of me. But when I get to his shoulders, I slip up. They're just so tan. And strong. And without my permission, my thumbs start tracking between his shoulder blades. Declan hums in approval, and I move on to his neck. An area he could probably reach himself.

He turns his head, stopping short of looking over his shoulder. I withdraw my hands and step back.

"Um . . . all set." I dip my head and grab my towel, shaking it out.

Declan hasn't moved. I sit down and sink my feet back into the water. The combination of a gentle breeze and my wet skin makes the water feel slightly warmer. Declan finally walks over and sits next to me.

I glare at my hands. *Traitors.*

He finds a flat stone and skips it into the water. After five hops, it sinks. Declan brushes his palms together.

"Not bad," I say.

"Thanks." He clears his throat and nods toward Mackenzie

and Cory out in the water. "So what do you think, another week before Cory makes one too many physics jokes for her taste?"

"The crazy thing is, she eats them up. You were so right about them."

"What can I say, it's a gift."

"Oh, I totally forgot." I pivot toward him. "What's his big plan?"

"Uh-uh, I'm not telling. Just trust me; it'll be worth the wait."

And it is. A half hour later, we're all lying on the rocks again, Declan and I playing a game of I Spy, picking colors out of the forest around us and finding shapes in the clouds, while Gwen flips through one of Mackenzie's fashion magazines. Suddenly Cory is standing over us.

"I think we should skinny-dip."

My jaw drops. I turn to face Declan and he closes his eyes, nodding solemnly.

Gwen starts packing her stuff. "That's my cue."

Without waiting for any other response, Cory dives into the water. A moment later, he slaps his swim trunks onto the rock next to me.

I avert my eyes and lean away. I can't even.

Mackenzie stands up. She hesitates for just a second, then unties her top and shimmies out of her bottoms. She lets out a yell and jumps into the water.

I turn my wide-eyed stare to Declan. "That just happened."

"Indeed, it did."

Gwen shoves the rest of her stuff into a beach bag and gives us a wave. "See you guys later."

"Later, Gwen," Declan says.

I wave back and then shake my head, still in complete shock. "Wow. Okay, this may sound weird, but I'm kind of proud of Cory right now."

"I know what you mean. I wasn't sure he'd actually go through with it. And I *definitely* did not think it would work."

Their laughter carries over to us and I close my eyes. "Oh man, I can't watch this."

Declan's smile gets even bigger. "No, I think it's time we left these two alone."

I'm beyond relieved he doesn't want to join in. Not just because four seems like a bit of a crowd at the moment, but also because I'm clearly struggling with this whole platonic-friend thing. Pretty sure getting naked isn't going to help.

Still, there is serious potential in this situation that can't be overlooked.

"We're going to steal his clothes, though, right?"

Declan grins. "Oh, most definitely." He's already in motion, scooping up Cory's swim trunks and taking off down the shoreline.

Grabbing Cory's towel, I chase after him. We run past Gwen in the direction of the cars, the thick layer of pine needles

padding our bare feet. Mackenzie's laughter and Cory's desperate pleas fade behind us. For a moment I wonder if Declan will run all the way to our tree house.

Instead, we hide behind the side of his car, pressed against the front tire. I focus on the sky, the sun shining through branches of pine, and try really hard not to laugh. But every time I feel Declan shaking behind me, I erupt into giggles again.

I elbow him in the ribs, which only makes him laugh harder.

Needless to say, it's a matter of seconds before our hiding place is discovered.

Cory stops on the other side of the car, holding the T-shirt we left behind in front of him. I peer across the hood and lose my balance. I fall into Declan, who collapses all the way to the ground in hysterics.

"Very funny, guys. My shorts, if you please." Declan throws them at Cory's face and I hold up the towel. Cory rips it out of my hand and backs away. "You guys suck."

My abs start to hurt from laughing so uncontrollably, and I'm struggling to get enough air, which leads me to snort. Twice. My hand flies up to my nose in a desperate attempt to keep any other unbearable noises from coming out. Declan was just starting to recover, and he crumples over in another fit of laughter.

"You snorted!"

"I didn't." I shake my head slowly, but I can't seem to unscrew the smile from my jaw. "Nope."

Declan takes a long breath, avoiding eye contact with me until he pulls himself together. We're still sprawled out on the ground, and he props himself up on one elbow. He gestures to me.

"That's the smile."

I start giggling again. "What?"

His expression softens. He scratches above his eyebrow and shakes his head, suddenly looking almost bashful. "I've been waiting all summer to see that smile."

Twenty-Two

IT'S EASIER THAN EVER TO LIE TO MY PARENTS. DAD
is completely distracted most of the time, and Mom's got such
a bad case of chemo-brain, I could tell her just about anything
and she'd believe it.

Only, lying doesn't feel like getting away with something
anymore. And leaving the house every chance I get isn't the
escape it used to be. I just wind up feeling guilty. I love my
mom, and as helpless as seeing her sick makes me feel, I want
to support her. Which means showing up, being here for her
even if it's hard. Even if I'd rather be somewhere else.

Besides, nowadays Mom mostly asks about my friends. A
month ago I would have sooner had a root canal than will-
ingly spent the afternoon telling her about my social life.

Things have been different lately, though, and this past week I spent every day with Declan. Not that we've been alone, or done anything remotely *date*like, but even when we're with the whole group, he and I sort of gravitate to each other. Just like before.

But he's caddying this morning, so I'm home, snuggled up with Mom on her bed. I trace my finger over the paisley pattern of her bedspread while she clicks through some of the pictures on my laptop. She lingers over the picture I took of Declan during our first photography shoot.

"I feel like I've slept away the entire summer." She closes the laptop and stretches, flexing her feet under the wool blanket she has on even though it's more than ninety degrees out. "Tell me something new."

"I dunno. Class has been pretty interesting, actually. Mr. Harrison says I have potential," I say with a roll of my eyes. "And Mack and Gwen have become pretty good friends."

"And Declan?"

I smile in spite of myself. "And Declan."

She purses her lips. "You really care about him. Don't you?"

My smile fades. I nod.

That's been the only problem with this amazing week. It's great getting along with him again, but the friendlier Declan and I become, the harder it is to hide my true feelings. And sometimes, like the other day at the quarry, I get the impression it isn't just one-sided. But then he'll get closed off again, and I'll remember the way I felt after trying to kiss him earlier this summer.

Mom shakes her head. "I always knew it was just a matter of time for the two of you. Your father always thought you would end up with Cory, you know."

"Cory?" I laugh, then pause, thinking back over the last year and the way Dad always got a little grumpier when I said I was going to Cory's house. He trusts Cory, sure. But that doesn't mean he wants me to date him. "You know, that actually explains a lot. Don't get too carried away, though. Declan and I are just getting to know each other again, and he's leaving in two weeks."

"Why does that have to change anything?"

It's a pretty good question. Probably the biggest, most important question of all, actually. Last time Declan went away, I think some part of me had already resigned to losing him. But it doesn't have to be that way. Look at Gwen. Her boyfriend lives in a different state, and they obviously miss each other, but they make sacrifices and they make it work. Declan and I could do that. We may not be together anymore, but we can stay friends.

I'll make more of an effort to be open with him, and if things get shaky again, I won't run away from it. I'll be supportive. Stronger. This time will be different.

"It shouldn't. You're right. I just wish he didn't have to leave again. He wants to stay; he told me so. And I don't get why his dad keeps doing this to him. If it were Natalie, she would never ship him off."

Mom gives my hand a squeeze. "I know, honey. And I wish it could be different. But he's just doing what he thinks is best for Declan."

"Yeah, well. Maybe he could try listening to him instead."

Mom gives a sympathetic sigh and pats my hand once more. She seems to be at a loss for words. I scoot off the bed and reach for her mug.

"Your tea's gone cold," I tell her. "I'll make you some more."

With the kettle on the stove, I pull some of Mom's favorite ginger cookies out of the cupboard and shuffle through her file on the kitchen table, trying to figure out which pill she's supposed to take if the one she tried earlier doesn't help her nausea. She has a hard time keeping that stuff straight.

I pick up two pill bottles and look back and forth between them. Then back at the file. I have no idea. The kettle whistles, and I set the pills down and cross the kitchen.

Upstairs, something crashes in my parents' room. With my hand still on the gas range knob, I freeze. There's another thud above me.

I tear out of the kitchen, taking the stairs two at a time.

I find her lying on the bathroom floor, crammed between the bathtub and the toilet. She's cradling her stomach, and there is blood all over her pink pajamas. Why is there blood?

"Mom!"

I kneel down beside her and a sharp pain hits my knee.

I pull a small shard of glass out of my skin. Broken glass is scattered all over the floor from the vase she knocked off her sink.

"Mom, are you okay?" She nods weakly, but I can't tell what parts are bleeding. Her hands. But is that all? "Can you sit up?"

She rolls to the side and gets sick.

I jump up and feel my back pocket for my phone, but it isn't there. Grabbing the receiver off my mother's nightstand, I hesitate with my fingers over the keypad. Dad is at work and I don't have that number memorized, so I try his cell. It rings and rings and he isn't answering.

Hang up.

Call Graham.

But after one ring I remember Graham is visiting a friend out of town. And Bridget had a shift today so she's already at the hospital. I look at Mom and it seems like she's falling asleep, and that can't be good. My shaking fingers dial 911. I hear my voice ask for an ambulance.

"I don't know, I don't know what's wrong with her. I mean, she has breast cancer. But today, I don't know, she's just, she keeps getting sick and she cut herself on glass and I don't know how bad it is and I just think she should go to the hospital, only she can't walk."

"Okay," the too-calm woman on the other end of the line says. "I've sent an ambulance over; just stay with your mom and I'll remain on the line with you until they get there."

It takes them one hundred years to get here. Two medics and a fireman come into my house, and the medics strap Mom onto a gurney and wheel her out the door.

I jump into the ambulance and do my best to answer the series of questions they ask on the way to the hospital.

"What medications is she on?"

This is asked by the first medic, a petite woman who is taking Mom's vitals while I sit on my hands and stare at her. She's practically passed out. She can't keep her eyes open, anyway.

She was fine twenty-five minutes ago. How does this happen in twenty-five minutes?

"I don't know the names of any of them," I answer. "She's on treatment—chemo—and she takes some anti-nausea pills. She had one or two this morning."

So much noise inside the ambulance; I don't know how they can work with all this noise. The siren blares, echoing louder as we pass under a bridge, and everything around me rattles, as if all the gauze and equipment is as jumpy as I am, ready to be of service. Some chatter comes over the radio up front, and I barely hear the next question.

"What has she had to eat today?"

It comes from the second medic. He hooks her up to oxygen and speaks in a soothing voice, like this is the kind of thing he deals with every day. Which I guess it probably is.

"Half a yogurt and some tea."

Once we get to the hospital, they sweep her away to get

her hand stitched and I'm left all alone. I sit in an empty, fluorescent-lit waiting area for ten minutes before a nurse approaches me and asks if I need to call someone. I reach for my phone, but my back pocket is still empty. I left my cell on the kitchen counter.

I follow the nurse to a pay phone and dial Dad's number first. This time he answers after the first ring. He cuts me off, tells me he's on his way, and that he'll call Graham and let him know. I hang up and stare at the phone. I'm overwhelmed with a need to see Declan. To hear his voice tell me this will be okay, because he's the only person I know who has earned the right to say that. I need him to tell me how he kept breathing when his mother didn't.

I pick up the phone and dial his number.

I do a decent job of holding it together up until then. But the moment he answers the phone, a curious tone in his voice because it's a number he doesn't recognize, I just lose it. Lose everything—my sanity, anything resembling control, and certainly the tiny sum of strength I had left.

"It's Harper." I sniff and try not to sob into the receiver.

"Harper? What's wrong?"

"I'm at the hospital. Something's wrong with my mom."

"I'm on my way. Okay? I'll be right there."

I nod, as if he can see me. "Okay."

He makes it to me before Dad or Graham arrive. He rushes over, pulling me tight against his chest and not caring that I get

231

tears mixed with a good amount of snot all over the front of his shirt.

He strokes my hair and I work on slowing down my hiccup-breaths. We sit on aqua-colored vinyl seats, and Declan takes my hand. He doesn't let go for hours.

Dehydration was the biggest culprit. The cuts were mostly contained to her hands from when she fell onto broken glass on her way to the toilet. But they are keeping Mom overnight to run tests, so Dad sends Graham and me home.

Declan walks with us out to the parking lot.

"I know it's getting late," I say to him. "But would you maybe want to come over for a little while?"

He glances at Graham, who is a few car lengths ahead. "Sure."

"Okay. Um . . . I'm going to ride with my brother. I'll see you in a few minutes."

When we get in the house, Graham pulls me into a hug. "Thanks for handling this today. You did good."

"Thanks, Graham."

He nods. "I'll get out of your hair. Try to get some sleep, okay?"

"Sure."

He walks up to his room and I open the front door for Declan. He follows me to the kitchen and fixes a pot of coffee, knowing I won't want to sleep until Mom gets back. Then he grabs some bread and butter, and gets to work making me a grilled cheese.

"You don't have to do all this for me."

"It's no problem. Anyway, you need to eat."

He puts the plate down in front of me a couple minutes later and casts me a worried glance.

"Thanks," I say, even though I really don't want it.

He watches as I run my finger around the ridge of white glass. He shifts his weight and the wooden chair creaks.

"You have to eat something, Harper." His voice is quiet, almost nervous.

"I'm not hungry."

"Just a few bites." His hand floats an inch above my shoulder. Hesitantly, he traces a line of freckles. "Please?"

His eyes search mine and I crack. I take a bite, letting the melted cheese burn my tongue.

"Can you get me the ketchup?"

He smirks down at me before getting it out of the fridge.

Something close to a smile tugs at my lips. "I'll have you know, ketchup and grilled cheese is a completely normal and delicious combination." I shake the bottle and squirt some onto my plate.

"Just like bacon-wrapped pineapple?"

"Yup."

"And peanut butter and potato chip sandwiches?"

"Exactly." I take another bite and chew slowly, suddenly

worried that he'll leave as soon as I've finished. "Declan?"

"Hmm?"

"Is your dad home tonight?"

He shakes his head.

I pick at my crust. "So, you don't have to be home right away?"

"I'll stay as long as you'd like."

When I'm finished with my sandwich, we move to the living room. Declan sits on the couch and I grab the remote, flipping through channels until I find a comedy from a few years back. It's already almost an hour into the movie, but we've both seen it before.

"This okay?" I ask.

"Yeah, great."

I set the remote down on the coffee table and grab a blanket before sitting next to him.

"Mind if I turn the light off?" he asks. "There's a glare."

"That's fine."

The room goes dark, and I pull the blanket over my lap, shifting until I'm comfortable. But not relaxed. Because aside from the stress about Mom, I'm also fixating on the six inches of sofa separating Declan's leg from mine.

And I know it's completely inappropriate to be having these kinds of thoughts right now, but I can't help it. When was the last time we were alone in the dark?

I make it through ten more minutes of the movie before

sneaking a glance at him. He's slouched against the corner of the sofa, his eyes glued to the TV screen. I run my hand through my hair and turn away again.

"Harp?"

Crap. I'm caught. I keep my head turned toward the TV. "Yeah?"

"Did you mean what you said the other day? About wishing I could stay?"

"Of course."

His voice is husky. "And what happens after I leave?"

I stretch out the elastic on my wrist, then ease it back down. "What do you mean?"

His jaw shifts to the side. Then back again. "Do you think we'll still talk?"

I close my eyes for one slow breath. Then face him. "Declan . . . I know I messed up. I made a lot of really stupid choices this year. And shutting you out like I did, that was the worst one."

He watches me, his expression serious. Then he rubs his thumb over his mouth and pushes himself a couple inches up the couch. He cracks a smile. "So that's a yes, then?"

"That's a yes. Until you get sick of me calling, anyway."

The scenery on TV changes, casting a new, brighter light on him. His eyes flicker over my face. "You're tired. Sure you don't want me to go?"

I shake my head. "I won't be able to sleep."

"Okay." He rests his arm on the back of the couch and slouches until he's comfortable.

We both start watching the movie again, but if I hadn't seen it before, I would have no idea what was going on. This resolution between us is bittersweet. His friendship means everything to me, and I can't stand the thought of destroying it a second time. But the secrets I've kept are eroding my own happiness. Declan should have all the facts before deciding to have a relationship—any relationship—with me.

Another fifteen minutes go by, and I reach my limit. My pulse picks up. I open my mouth—nothing. I don't know how to start this conversation.

Declan's eyes are nearly shut, and his breathing is heavy. "Can't get comfortable?"

"No, I'm fine." I turn back to the screen.

"Here." He gestures for me to lean against him.

I scan the space left between us and hug the blanket to my chest. Pulling my hair over one shoulder, I scoot closer and settle against his side. My hands are in fists around the blanket.

"Um, can you . . ." Declan adjusts, gently moving my elbow so that it isn't digging into his rib cage.

"Oh, sorry." I turn a bit more so that I'm curved around him. Now one arm is tucked close to my side, but I don't know where to put my other hand. I settle on his chest and lean down so that my cheek is resting beside it. My head rises and falls with his breath. "Better?"

"Better," he says in a quiet voice.

Within minutes, his breathing slows down again. I glance up, and his eyes are completely closed. His lips are softly parted.

I listen to his heartbeat. It gets harder and harder to open my eyes each time I close them.

His fingers trace the back of my hand, pulling me awake.

"Harp?"

On an inhale, I lift my head. The movie is over. It's four in the morning.

"Sorry." Our legs are tangled together and his other hand is resting lightly over my hip bone. "Didn't mean to fall asleep."

He swallows. "That's okay. But I think your dad is home."

I hear it now too. The garage door. But my body isn't cooperating, and I'm still lying on top of Declan when Dad comes through the kitchen door.

He freezes when he sees us. Then straightens and clears his throat.

I push myself up, rubbing my eyes. "How's Mom? Is she okay?"

"She'll be fine," he says. "She's sleeping at the hospital tonight, but she'll be home after they run a few tests in the morning." His eyes shift to Declan. His mustache turns down. "Declan, I think it's time you went home too."

"Yes, sir." Declan's eyes flicker to mine, and he stands. I walk him to the front door. "Night, Harp."

"Good night."

He steps outside, and I catch his arm, pulling him into one last hug.

It's different from the frenzied embrace at the hospital. My arms wrap around his neck and his whole body is post-sleep warm against mine. One of his hands curves around the back of my head, the other is firm on the small of my back, pulling me closer.

"Thank you," I whisper.

He leans back, looking down at me. "Any time."

I let go and step back inside. He hops off the porch, and I start to close the door. But I can't take my eyes off him. He turns, walking backward down my driveway. Holding my gaze.

And even after everything that's happened today, I'm smiling.

Because it seems like maybe Declan can't take his eyes off me, either.

Twenty-Three

DAD IS STILL STANDING IN THE KITCHEN. THE
microwave dings and he takes a plate of leftovers out but sets it
on the counter and faces me.

"It's awfully late for Declan to be over, don't you think?"

I stretch and crack my spine. "His dad is out of town again.
And I wanted some company."

"Graham is home."

"Exactly." I will him to pick up a fork and drop the subject.
"So it's not a big deal."

His mustache twitches, but he nods and opens the silver-
ware drawer. His wiry hair is unkempt and greasy, like he's been
running his hand over it all night. His dress shirt is wrinkled,
and the knot of his tie hangs six inches below his collar.

He takes a bite and wipes his mouth on a napkin. "I'm going to take a quick nap and go back over there. Maybe you can run to the store later today."

"I'm coming with you."

He spears a potato wedge. "I don't think that's necessary. You should get some rest, your mother—"

"Why won't you let me help?"

He pauses midchew. Swallows. "That is helpful. All this stuff needs to get done."

"No, but . . . look, I don't mind going to the store. But I'm the one who was here this afternoon, I'm the one who called the ambulance and got her to the hospital and sat there for hours, waiting. I know I've let you guys down this past year, and that I haven't been around as much as I should have been lately, but I'm here now, and I'm coming with you."

Dad leans against the counter and crosses his arms. With his eyes closed, he takes a slow breath in and out. "Are you sure that's what you want to do? It could be a while before she's released."

"Yes, I'm sure. I want to be there for her."

"Okay." He gives me a tired smile and pulls his tie off. Then he rests one hand on my shoulder. "I don't think I've thanked you yet, for the way you handled things this afternoon. You kept your head, acted responsibly. I'm very proud of you."

"Thanks," I mumble.

An hour later we head back to the hospital for another long day of waiting.

Sadie paces around her room, gripping her phone against her ear.

". . . but you promised!" She twirls a pen with her free hand. "But . . . whatever. *I don't care.* Fine. Mmkay, bye." She hangs up and throws her phone onto her vanity. She looks over at me and smiles. "You're awake!"

"No, I'm not." I roll over and pull her pillow over my head.

She jumps onto the bed and snuggles up to my side, nudging her head under my arm like a puppy.

"Did you drink a Boomerang already?" I mumble from under the pillow. By some miracle, I managed to convince Sadie to stay in last night, which explains why she's already completely stir-crazy this morning. She bounces next to me on the mattress and yanks the pillow off my face. "Was that your mom?"

She rolls her eyes, looking totally over it. "Yeah. Bitch. Anyway, it's breaky time."

Mom didn't come home from the hospital until late yesterday afternoon, at which point Dad kicked me out so she could rest. And sure, I got Sadie to have a movie night, but that doesn't mean we went to bed early. I'm exhausted.

But Sadie looks like she will throw a complete shit-fit if I decline, so with one last groan, I drag myself out of her bed.

Breakfast is a relative term for Sadie, so we end up going to the Munchie Mart for coffee and cigarettes. On our way back to her car we pass Sadie's ex, Christopher. He's filling his car at pump number three. His new girlfriend is in the passenger's seat.

241

Sadie quickly straightens her posture and puts on a shy smile, which falls off her face as soon as they're behind her.

"I can't believe Chris is going out with a sophomore," she says as we reach her car. She yanks open the driver's-side door. "And she's in band. *Band*, I tell you."

I don't comment on the fact that just a few days ago, Sadie was showing interest in a sophomore herself. "What's wrong with band?"

Sadie doesn't have an actual answer to that, so she just shrugs and lights her cigarette. She holds out her pack to me.

I shake my head and take a sip of coffee. I'm done with cigarettes. "What I can't believe is that you broke up with him."

"You mean that I ever dated him in the first place? Me neither."

I bet his number is still in her phone right now. And those pictures, too. Every time I catch her looking at them, she reacts the same way. Always says something nasty about him, like it's a reflex she can't control.

"Right, I know. You don't care about him at all." I take another sip of scalding coffee and add, "That's why you still have his orchid."

She flicks some ash out of her open window. "You don't know what you're talking about."

"Oh. Okay, then." I wait, my eyes following the smoke that twists away from the end of her cigarette.

"He was going to break up with me anyway."

It's the first time Sadie has ever said anything like that, and she immediately starts moving, turning the car on and tearing out of our parking spot like she's trying to outrun what she just admitted.

"You don't know that," I say gently.

"Yes, I do. He never wanted to hang out anymore, never talked to me when we did. And it's not like I needed a boyfriend just to mess around, so . . ."

She banks a hard left out of downtown and speeds past our high school. I nearly spill hot coffee all over myself when she hits a pothole.

"Would you slow down? You're going to get pulled over."

"Want to do something later?" she asks, ignoring my irritation. "We could lay out at Mike's pool, or I heard some junior is having a party at his house this afternoon."

"I told you, I'm meeting Declan later." I check the center console for the time. Almost noon already. "Now, actually. Would you mind heading that way?"

"Fine." She turns right and circles back through town. "So what's the deal with you two, anyway?"

Her voice is just shy of a grumble, and I get the feeling that no answer will satisfy her.

"I don't know. We're hanging out."

She narrows her eyes. "Duh. I've barely seen you since you guys started *hanging out*. My point is, school starts in two weeks. Won't he be leaving soon?"

243

I flick my thumbnail against the lid of my coffee and set it down. I've been using brute strength to push the idea of him leaving out of my mind.

"I'm just looking out for you," she goes on. "I mean, how long did it take for everything to fall apart the last time he left town? You should think about that before you start something again." She pulls into my neighborhood, passes my elementary school, and comes to a stop in front of Declan's house. "It's not worth getting hurt, is it?"

She isn't looking at me when she says it, examining her nails as she rests them on her steering wheel.

Declan is perched on a ladder, painting the side of his house with Cory, Mack, and Gwen. Mackenzie flicks Cory with paint, and Declan breaks into laughter. He looks happy. And seeing that makes me happy.

"Declan would never hurt me."

"That's the funny thing about relationships, Harper." Sadie lights another cigarette and picks at the seam of the steering wheel as she exhales. "If you give someone the power to break your heart, you sure as hell won't see it coming when they do.

"I'm just looking out for you," she says again.

"Yeah. Thanks. I'll see you later," I say, grabbing my to-go cup and sending her a smile when really I want to tear her head off.

She saw how miserable I was without Declan in my life last year. And sure, I get that she wouldn't want me to go through that again, or have to put up with my moping again, for that matter. But I thought she would at least be happy for me now. Maybe not.

Maybe I don't care what she thinks anymore.

"Harper?" She stubs out her half-smoked cigarette. "If you're not too busy with your new friends, maybe you can come with me to a party Saturday night?"

"Yeah. Sure, Saturday." I smile and shut the car door behind me. Mack waves her paintbrush at me, spattering paint all over Cory. Again.

"Hey, guys," I say.

Declan steps down from his ladder and hooks his thumbs in his back pockets. "Hey."

I smile harder and hitch my bag higher on my shoulder.

"Here," he says, "you can put your stuff inside."

I follow him into the foyer and hang my bag up on a coat hook so Lula won't go sniffing around in it, then bend down to give her a few pets.

"Do you want to take your shirt off?"

I snap up. "What?"

Declan's eyebrows rise. "Oh, ha, no. I mean, I have a shirt you can borrow. So you don't get paint all over that one."

"Oh. Yeah, okay."

He gestures toward the stairs. We go up to his room, and I linger in the doorway while he sorts through his dresser.

It's a tidy space, with vacuum lines in the carpet and a perfectly made bed. The whole room is perfect, actually. Except for

245

a red stain on the carpet in front of his desk, put there when we were eleven and I made him laugh so hard, fruit punch came out of his nose.

Now a suitcase is tucked into the corner by his closet and there's a cardboard box resting on top of his desk. The sticker stars are still on his ceiling. It's his room, just a little too un-lived in.

He holds up a plain white undershirt. "This work for you?"

"Yeah, that's great. Thank you."

"No problem." He tosses me the shirt and taps his knuckles against the side of his dresser.

He steps to the side, like he's going to leave, and I pull his shirt on over mine. Then I thread the spaghetti straps of my tank top through the sleeves and push it down to my waist, over my hips, and step out of it.

Declan looks dazed. Like he's not quite sure what just happened.

Technically, I guess I just changed in front of him. I didn't even think before doing it; changing that way is second nature after a thousand swim practices.

I mean, okay, maybe I knew it was a little flirty. But it's not like I put on a striptease. It was the anti-striptease. Besides, he *has* seen the goods before.

I step back toward the door. "Ready?"

He nods and follows me downstairs. Declan sets me up with a paintbrush and nudges my shoulder.

"Watch out for Mackenzie," he says, loud enough for her to hear.

She points her brush at him. "Offensive. You better watch *yourself*, Declan."

He hides behind me, wrapping one arm across my collarbone like I'm his human shield. Without thinking, I sink back against his chest. He rests his chin on top of my head.

"Truce?"

Mack's lips twitch. "Fine."

He releases me and gives me a wink before climbing the ladder to help Cory with the second story.

Mackenzie gives me a playful tap on the arm. "*Aww*, he dominant-turtled you!"

I glance at Gwen, whose expression indicates she's as boggled as I am by the expression. I'm not sure I want to be dominated turtle-style.

"He what now?"

Mackenzie moves so that she's standing behind Gwen, lifting up onto her tiptoes so that Gwen's head is tucked underneath her chin. "Dominant turtle!" Gwen's eyes roll up and she crouches away in self-preservation, but Mackenzie keeps trying. "You know! It's how the male turtle shows his dominance. . . ."

"Kinky," Gwen says.

"*Soo?*" Mackenzie stomps her foot.

I blink. "So?"

She rolls her eyes at Gwen. "So, what's going on with you two? I caught that wink, too, by the way."

"All right, Nancy Drew." I dip my paintbrush into the can and shrug. And try really hard not to smile. And fail. "I don't know. We've been spending more time together. Things are good."

"How good?"

My smile gets bigger. "I don't know! And *shh*."

She sighs wistfully. Meanwhile, Gwen is still silently staring at me with pursed lips.

"What?" I ask.

"It's about damn time, is all."

I grimace. "Can we please talk about something else? You guys are making me nervous."

I start painting in broad strokes. Mackenzie tosses her brush down onto the tray between us. Paint splatters on my—Declan's—T-shirt and she is, of course, oblivious.

"I think I'm ready to sleep with Cory," she says.

"Gah!" I raise my hands to my ears. "New subject."

Gwen laughs beside me.

"Oh, come on," Mack says, putting her fists on her hips. "I need your advice!"

Licking my lips, I dip my brush into the paint again. "Um, actually . . . well. I've never—"

"Shut up. *Really?*" Gwen wrinkles her nose and leans closer. "You're a virgin?"

248

"Gwen!" Mackenzie takes a swat at her.

I glance up to the second story, but Cory and Declan are still absorbed in conversation while they paint.

"You don't have to sound so surprised."

"I think she just means, you know . . . !" Mackenzie jumps in, trying to cover for Gwen. "You're so pretty and popular! That's all."

Rolling my eyes, I focus very hard on the section of siding I'm working on. "Anyway," I tell her, "you're more experienced in that department than I am."

She's watching Cory. Analyzing him. She picks up her paintbrush and nods. "Yep, I'm ready. I think I'm in love with him."

"That's . . ." My jaw is working and I'm trying to say *great* but that's not what comes out. "Fast."

"Well, you know what they say about girls who drive sports cars. . . ." Gwen snickers and dodges Mack's brush.

Mackenzie shifts her gaze back to Cory. "He's just so *hot*, you know?"

I groan. I know too much.

"You've seen him in his Speedo," she says. "Don't tell me you haven't noticed."

"*Ew*, no!" I can't stop shaking my head. "No."

My brush moves over the same section I just finished because the idea of sex has now taken over my brain, and I've lost the capacity to paint efficiently.

"Well . . . good luck?" I say. "Or have fun? I don't know what to say to someone who's about to have sex."

"'Have fun' works," Gwen says with a smile.

Declan and Cory climb down off the roof and go inside to get a drink of water. They bring a pitcher and some cups out for the rest of us.

Declan fills a glass for me, and I take it without looking at him. Because suddenly I can't look at him.

Because sex. Is all I can think about.

"You okay?" he asks. "Everything still good with your mom?"

He has a crease between his eyebrows. I put it there. I hate that.

"Yeah," I say brightly. "When she was at the hospital they found out her white blood cell count was low, so she can't leave the house right now. But she needs the rest anyway, and she says she's feeling better already."

"Okay, good. What about you? You still look kind of tired. Did you sleep last night?"

"Not really. I spent the night at Sadie's. But I'm fine, I just zoned out for a sec."

I keep smiling until he nods and looks away. We trade our water glasses for paintbrushes and get back to work. But his frown is still there. Biting my lip, I try to think of a way to lighten the mood.

Then it hits me.

Declan's whole body freezes as I drag my paintbrush slowly

250

down from his temple to his jaw. When I finish, he turns toward me with pinched lips and raised eyebrows. He bobs his head, like he's agreeing to the terms of an after-school brawl. I grin and bop his nose with the end of the brush.

"Well then." He tosses his own brush down and lunges for me.

He traps me in his arms, nuzzling my face and neck and smearing the paint all over me. I let out a giddy squeal as he wrestles me back into the wet siding. He stops, his face inches from mine. Paint-coated eyelashes bat down at me, and we aren't laughing anymore. And six feet away from us, our friends are staring.

After another awkward beat of silence, I slide out from under him and playfully push his shoulder.

"Congratulations," I say, breathless. "You just ruined your own shirt."

He blushes. "Yeah, well. You started it."

We're both quite mature about the whole thing.

Gwen is biting her lip so hard, it looks like she might draw blood. Behind Declan's back, she starts making kissy faces. I send her a death glare and peel off some of the hair that's now stuck to my face.

Cory rubs his cheek and turns back to Mackenzie, who looks so pleased, she might burst.

"Well, we should probably go get cleaned up," he says. "That movie starts in an hour and a half."

251

"Yeah and I've got a Skype date with Jason." Gwen puts her brush away and pulls out her keys. "See you guys later."

"See you," I say. Then I turn to Declan. "I should probably check in at home, too."

With the back of his hand, he wipes some paint off his temple. "Yeah, okay."

"Harper, you want a ride?" Mackenzie unlocks her car and hangs on the open door.

"Yeah, thanks." I go inside to get my stuff, and stop beside Declan on my way to her car. "I'll wash your shirt and get it back to you tomorrow."

He waves his hand. "Don't worry about it."

"Okay."

He grins. "Okay."

I get in the backseat. To Mackenzie's credit, we make it all the way down Declan's driveway before she starts her giddy clapping.

"You guys are so cute!"

Cory shakes his head but wears a hint of a smile. "I'm staying out of this."

Twenty-Four

I'M ON THE ROOF WHEN DECLAN STARTS UP MY driveway. He spots me and nods a hello. I climb back through the window and down the stairs as quietly as possible. Mom is resting again.

He's waiting for me on the porch swing. I close the front door behind me and cross my arms. Uncross them. Shove my hands in my back pockets.

"Hey."

"Hey, you." He smiles shyly, then leans forward, grabbing a notebook out of his messenger bag. "I was wondering if I could borrow your photography notes from Friday. I was kind of out of it in class."

"Oh, sure. I don't know if mine will be any better, but you can take a look."

I go upstairs and snag my notebook off my desk, flipping through it quickly to make sure I didn't accidentally write anything humiliating in the margins, like *Remember to pick up tampons* or *Harper + Declan 4Ever.*

Which, to be clear, I totally stopped writing in my margins years ago. But better safe than sorry.

I come back outside and Declan sits up a little straighter, running his hands down his thighs.

Sitting beside him, I hand him the notebook.

"Great, thanks." He doesn't open it. Or even look at it. He looks at me.

My palms feel hot. And sweaty. And I can't stop thinking about yesterday, about his face against my neck, covering me in paint.

I resist the urge to sit on my hands. "No problem."

"So what do you do up there?" He gestures to the roof.

"Just think, mostly. Or try not to think, depending on my mood."

"What do you think about?"

"Oh, you know, fashion and makeup and whether or not I have split ends. Important stuff."

His lips twitch. "I'm serious."

I lean back and kick my toes off the ground, rocking the porch swing. "Lately I've been thinking a lot about my mom. And about going back to school; what that will be like now that I don't have swimming." I let the swing drift to a stop. "Sometimes I think about you."

He takes a measured breath. "Yeah?"

I pick at the wooden seat and nod. The top layer of dirt scrapes off, catching under my fingernail.

Declan lifts his hand and traces my fingers. His touch is featherlight, like he's trying to catch a soap bubble. His voice is low.

"Harp?"

I stare at our hands. "Yeah?"

"Why do you still wear my necklace?"

My heart speeds up. I lick my lips. Count to five. And finally look at him. "You know why."

His eyes drift down to my lips and he leans closer. Gently, he tucks a curl behind my ear, trailing his fingers down and across my jaw. My organs start nudging each other around and my breath hitches, becoming megaphone loud. This is it; another point of no return.

"Declan . . . there's something I need to tell you. About what happened. After you left."

His eyes don't leave mine. "Nothing I hear is going to change who you are to me. The only thing I need to know is how you feel about me now."

I mirror his last touch, tracing his cheekbone. He takes a sharp breath in, keeping completely still. "I'm wearing your necklace, aren't I?"

A smile comes and goes across his face in a wave. "Then I guess we can stop talking."

He leans in again. My eyes drift closed, and I wait.

The front door swings open. Declan and I jump apart, and I immediately cover my mouth and tug at my shirt, basically looking guilty as sin. Declan rubs the back of his neck and nods to Graham, who is giving him an arms-crossed, big-brotherly glare.

"Morning," Graham says.

I grit my teeth and smile. "Go back inside, please."

He frowns. "But it's so nice out. And I could use some vitamin D."

"So drink a glass of milk."

He wrinkles his nose and sits on the steps. "Nah. Where's the fun in that?"

Declan stands up. "Hey, I've actually got to head to work."

I stand too, tucking a stray lock behind my ears and trying desperately to think of a way to hit rewind. Declan's hands were in my hair and his mouth was so close, I could taste his breath. We were going to kiss.

But now he won't even look at me. He shoves his notebook into his bag and hands mine back to me. "I think I'll probably be fine without those. But thanks anyway."

"Oh . . . okay."

He steps around Graham. I follow after him, giving Graham a light kick on my way by. We stop at the end of my driveway.

"So, um, you're going to work?"

"Yeah, one of my last shifts."

"Oh, cool."

Declan shuffles his feet. "I'll be done around six. We could hang out then. If you're free tonight."

"Okay!" But then it hits me. "Wait, no. Sadie's been bugging me to go to this party with her. But I can get out of it."

"Nah, you don't have to do that."

Now I'm really confused. Does he want to hang out with me or not?

"Well, how about if I text you when we're on our way. You could come with us."

"I don't know. That's not really my scene."

"It might be fun," I say hopefully. "I just . . . I really want to see you."

He softens. His shoulders relax and his smile comes back. "I want to see you too."

"Great," I say. "So it's settled."

The minute we arrive Sadie pulls a pint of vodka out of her purse and takes a swig. Mike Wright saunters over and offers her a cup of beer. He's an ambassador, a scout for the rest of the guys sitting around a patio table calling her name. Apparently Sadie doesn't mind that he's clingy anymore. She passes me the bottle, promptly forgetting about it. And about me.

I'm alone, surrounded by people who aren't friends. Tightening the cap and tucking the bottle under my arm, I pull out my phone. Declan hasn't responded to the text I sent earlier tonight. But I figure he probably got home from work late. And then he would have had to eat dinner and shower and stuff. Right?

I text again. *Just got here. Let me know when you're on your way.*

I press send before I have the chance to second-guess it or add anything embarrassingly mushy.

Sadie is sitting in front of a bonfire across the yard. I wander over and sit in a lawn chair opposite her and Mike. I try to lose myself in the fire, but I'm acutely aware that twenty minutes have gone by, then forty, and Declan still hasn't texted back.

I try calling. After a dozen or so rings, it goes to voice mail. "Hey, it's me. I guess you got held up at work or something. . . ." I pause. Maybe he didn't get held up. Maybe I'm getting stood up. "Anyway, hope to see you soon!"

Ending the call, I spin the bottle of vodka around on my knee. Sadie laughs in high-pitched peals at something Mike said. I run my fingers through my hair, untangling the ends, and wipe lip gloss off the corners of my mouth. He could show up any minute.

Someone collapses into the chair next to mine. I glance over and do a mental groan. Kyle grins.

"All alone tonight, Harper?"

"I came with Sadie." I keep my eyes glued to the fire.

He looks over at Sadie, who is now sitting on Mike's lap, turned away from us.

"Right." Kyle pulls a glass pipe and bag of weed out of his pocket and packs a bowl. "Well, since she looks occupied at the moment . . ." He takes a pack of cigarettes out of his other pocket and extracts a lighter. ". . . and this is really more fun with someone else . . ."

He tilts his lighter to the bowl and takes a long inhale, holding the smoke in his lungs a few seconds before exhaling quickly. The smell is familiar to me now, despite my mom's best efforts to hide her habit. He holds the pipe out to me.

"No, thanks." I check my phone again. By now Declan has to have seen my messages.

My stomach twists painfully. In five days he's leaving for school. What if tonight is my last chance with him? Or if this afternoon was and now it's already gone?

I get up and pace a few yards away from the group. Gnawing on my upper lip, I dial his number again. With each ring, I repeat it in my head.

You and me. You and me. You and—

He answers.

"Hey," I say. "Where are you?"

"Still at home."

"Oh. . . . When do you think you'll head over?"

He hesitates. "I'm not sure I can make it."

My shoulders hunch. I kick my toe into the ground. "That's too bad."

I hear him moving around on the other end of the line.

"Yeah . . . listen, I'll try to stop by. I've just got some stuff to deal with here, and—"

"No, don't even worry about it. It's totally fine." My voice trembles. I close my eyes as my skin grows hot. "Anyway, I should get back."

"Okay. Hey, I'm sorry about this. I'd still like to talk later." *No hard feelings, okay?*

I don't trust my voice anymore. "Mm-hmm, sounds good."

"All right. Bye, Harp."

"Bye." My hands shake as I hang up.

I want to figure out when things changed. Because I thought after the hospital and the paint fight and the almost-whatever-that-was at my house this morning, I really started to think he still liked me.

I wanted so badly for him to like me.

I walk back to the bonfire and sit down next to Kyle. The flames dance in front of me, growing brighter as the sky dims. I hold up the bottle of vodka from Sadie and watch the fire through the glass.

Earlier tonight I was on my best behavior. While Sadie and I were getting ready, I didn't have a single drink. I didn't want to be drunk when I saw Declan. Didn't want to be the girl who needs a cocktail to have fun anymore. But I don't see what difference it will make now.

I don't have a chaser, so I take my first sip quickly. It burns, like the bonfire reached down my throat and up into my sinuses.

A few seconds later everything settles, and I take another sip. This time it's nice and warm, working its way to my stomach-knees-toes.

Kyle exhales another puff of smoke. "Mind if I have some of that?"

"Be my guest." I hand him the bottle, and he trades it for the pipe.

I've never smoked pot before. Drinking has always been my thing. But really, how bad could it be if even Mom smoked? It might be better than drinking. It might be exactly what I need.

"Change your mind?" Kyle sets the vodka on his armrest and holds out his lighter.

"Maybe." I look at the pipe again, then around at the party. It's just pot. People smoke it all the time. "Yeah. Why not?"

Bringing the pipe to my lips, I lean forward and Kyle lights it for me. Hot smoke fills my lungs, making them feel tight and itchy. I wrinkle my nose to put off coughing for as long as possible.

I hand the pipe back to Kyle while I get over my coughing fit, and sink back into the chair when it's over. He smiles at me and then it's my turn again. It's easier the second time. The smoke floats straight up to the crown of my head.

After my third hit I ask, "Do you smoke a lot, Pooh Bear?"

He ignores my nickname. "What's a lot?" He blows the ash out of the bowl and puts it back in his pocket. "Helps me sleep, though."

I wonder what he really knows about sleepless nights. About dreams and nightmares.

"I don't sleep much either," I tell him.

He looks at me and I look at him and his mouth twitches into a smile, and then we're both laughing uncontrollably over something that's actually quite sad.

"Shit, my dealer got me some good stuff this time," he finally says, running his hands over his face.

The vodka is still sitting between us. Suddenly I'm dying of thirst. I take a swig and pass it automatically to Kyle. Only an inch of liquid is left in the bottle, but I don't remember drinking that much and I wonder how much was gone when Sadie gave it to me.

Actually, I'm having a hard time thinking straight about a lot of things. Like why Kyle is leaning so close to me, and why his hand is resting on my thigh.

I sit up straighter, crossing my legs and angling them away from him.

"I miss hanging out with you," he says. His hand comes back, moving slowly but up, up more, on the inside of my leg now. Heat radiates from his skin onto mine. "Maybe we should go inside and catch up."

I push his hand away. "I'm waiting here for Declan." My voice sounds heavy in my head, and I'm not sure why I said that, anyway. I'm not waiting for Declan, because Declan isn't coming. "I have to go to the bathroom," I blurt out, pushing myself up and stumbling my way around the fire to Sadie.

Now that I'm standing, I feel the full effect of the past half hour and walking gives me trouble. Each step is like landing on sinking pavement. I lean close and whisper in Sadie's ear, hoping not to draw attention to my unraveling state.

"Sadie, can we leave? I really want to leave," I say quietly.

She pushes me away with one arm. "No way! This party is awesome; just go have fun."

"Sadie, please—"

"What, couldn't get ahold of Declan?"

"What?"

She glares at me. "Only time you come looking for me anymore is when he's too busy for you." She turns her attention back to Mike. "I'm not leaving."

Everything crashes down on me at once. All of the worry over Mom, the doubts about Declan, and the realization that it is always going to be like this, me trying to keep up with Sadie to hold on to her as a friend.

So what if I've been spending time with Declan? She's the one who cares more about her current hookup than her supposed best friend. And if she can't be here for me when I need her most, we have nothing left to argue about.

Suddenly tears spill from my eyes, and I hastily wipe them away. "Fine."

Pushing past everyone who's gathered in front of the door,

I stumble into the house. I find a bathroom and shut myself inside. Pulling out my phone, I scroll to Cory's number. They're best friends too. They talk all the time. Cory will know why this is happening.

Rocking back against the wall because my balance isn't so good anymore, I listen to it ring.

"Hey," he says when he answers.

"Did he say anything—" Someone knocks on the door. I run my hand over my forehead and squint at the phone. Cory. Why did I call Cory?

"Harper?"

"Yeah?"

"You okay?"

I remember. Declan. That's what I want to ask.

"Did he say anything about me?"

"Who?"

"Declan. I want to know what he said."

He pauses. "Are you drunk?"

Mackenzie's voice filters in from the background and I feel stupid because I probably interrupted their dinner. Or maybe they were about to have sex. I start laughing.

"Harper, where are you?"

"Just . . ." My hand latches on to the sink and I propel myself forward. "Never mind, 'kay?"

"Wait—"

"Just tell him it's fine. I get it."

I hang up. Then I rest my hands on either side of the sink and lean forward to look at myself in the mirror.

My hair is straight. Between that and the dark, smoky eye makeup Sadie applied, I look too much like the version of myself I'm trying not to be. I hate the girl who stares back at me.

I hate you.

Two poles pull me in opposite directions. There's the girl I've been lately, the things I've done. And there's the person I want to be. The girl Declan used to love. And right now I'm neither. I'm stuck, floating between the broken ends.

Someone knocks again, louder this time. I down the remaining vodka and throw the empty bottle in the trash bin, taking one last look at the girl I loathe before unlocking the door and spilling out into the hallway.

Kyle is waiting for me.

"Whoa, Sloan." He reaches his arm out to steady me. "You look like you need to sit down."

He takes my hand and leads me through the hall. I pinball against the walls behind him, and people are watching me, but I don't know who they are, they're just faces, and then we are up the stairs, standing in a room that's too dark.

Kyle fumbles around and turns the lights on. We both blink in the sudden brightness.

"Here, sit down," he says.

We sit on the end of the bed, and I curl forward, clutching

my head. This isn't what I wanted—I never meant to get this messed up.

"You don't have to stay here," I tell him.

Kyle shrugs. "It's a lame party anyway."

I sit up again, bracing my hands on either side of my hips. Kyle slides over, moving my hair off my neck. Then he's leaning close, skimming his nose across my jaw.

I shrug away, losing my balance. "Kyle, don't."

"What's the problem?"

His hand is on my waist, pulling me upright. My mind is working, but I can't keep up with how fast the room is spinning.

"Wait." I try to think faster. Kyle's hand slips under my shirt. "Stop. I love Declan."

His breath is hot on my neck. "It's okay, he never has to know."

I'm still working through this logic when his hand finds my leg again, squeezing the inside of my thigh. Kyle looks at me, same as he did all summer—like he wants me—and it's familiar and empty and Declan doesn't love me back.

I can't sit straight anymore and when I fall backward he comes with me and that's when the kissing starts. My limbs are made of lead and my eyes are watering and my lips are answering Kyle's.

The world spins further away and I feel nothing, nothing, nothing like what I had with Declan.

His hand reaches under my top, down my side, jumps

inside my thigh and presses up again, sliding under the waist of my jeans. Under everything.

This, finally, snaps me out of it.

I push his hand away, try to say no, but his mouth on mine keeps the words from coming out. But I can't do this anymore, and it doesn't really matter whether Declan loves me, because being with someone else won't make my feelings for him go away.

"Stop." I shove my hand against Kyle's shoulder. He's heavy on top of me and I can't breathe. "Kyle, stop!"

He lifts his head to look at me. His breath smells of stale beer and weed. "I remember what you like. It'll feel good, promise."

He leans down again and I turn away. His mouth lands on my neck and I gasp for air.

"Get the fuck off me!" It comes out piercing. Hysterical.

He lifts himself away with a scowl. "You used to be a lot more fun."

I curl to the side and roll out from under him, landing on my knees but then standing. The floor is too tilted and I crash against the door before walking through it, back into the hallway that's too loud but away from Kyle.

Hugging the wall, I move away from the bedroom and start down the stairs. I want to get back outside; I need fresh air. From the landing halfway down the staircase I see the sliding glass door to the backyard. Then, I see Declan.

He's standing just inside, and he sees me too. He weaves his way through a few people toward me, and I let myself breathe again because everything is better now. He came.

I sink against the railing, holding it with both hands.

"Declan."

"Hey." He smiles at me, like his night is better because I'm in it. "Sorry I'm so late. I got into this massive fight with my dad. But I have some good news—"

His eyes flicker over my shoulder and his spine straightens. I follow his gaze to the bedroom, to Kyle, who just emerged from it. Kyle brushes past me, past both of us, but Declan doesn't take his eyes off him until he's down the stairs and out the door. Then, slowly, he turns back to me. And I can see it. Suspicion. In the way the corners of his mouth turn down and his jaw works. His eyes skim over me, and all I can do is hope that my hair isn't too frazzled and that Kyle's cologne didn't rub off on me. Declan's eyes lock tightly on mine as though he's reading me. Deciding something.

I don't pass his test.

Declan huffs out a breath and his smile dims to nothing. He swallows and shakes his head and then he's backtracking, moving down the stairs faster than I can keep up.

"Declan, wait! Where are you going?"

I catch his sleeve when he gets to the door. He spins around. I shake my head, searching desperately for the words that will make him understand.

The words don't come.

Twenty-Five

THE WHOLE DRIVE HOME WITH GRAHAM, THE monster of guilt living inside of me keeps growing stronger, and my stomach starts to not feel very good. Every time he slows down for a red light a new wave of nausea rolls through me, and I clamp my hand over my mouth more than once to keep everything, including the truth about what happened, from tumbling out.

Graham leans back in his seat, pounding on the steering wheel with his fingers. "What I want to know is, how are Mom and Dad so freaking naive about your drinking? I got caught every time I sneezed in the wrong direction, but you . . ."

"Are you going to tell them?"

Graham stares out the windshield. "You're not giving me a lot of options here, Harper."

He steps away. "You haven't changed at all, have yo

I step closer and he matches me, backing up again.

"I have," I say in a small voice.

His hand tugs through his hair. "Just look at yo Harper."

My head is still swimming. I try to stand straighter, to swaying. "It's just . . . I didn't think you were coming."

It's the absolute worst thing to say. Declan grits his t and rocks onto his heels.

"Right. Real sorry to interfere with your plans." He tu and starts walking to his car. "Won't happen again."

I sink back against the door, pressing my forehead against the cool glass.

"Who were you even with tonight? What kind of friend gets so trashed they can't drive you home?"

"I went with Sadie. She didn't want to go home yet."

"Where was Declan?"

My eyes close, pushing a tear down my cheek. "He left."

"He left you there? Did he get you drunk? I swear to God—"

"It wasn't his fault. He wasn't even there while I was drinking." I hesitate. "Or smoking."

"Jesus, Harper, what the hell were you thinking, getting that wasted? Especially after what happened in the spring?"

Fresh tears well up in my eyes, and my brother shifts uncomfortably in his seat.

"This can't happen again. If Dad were the one to come get you, you'd be dead."

"I know."

"This is the last thing they need to deal with right now—"

"So don't tell."

I'm curled up, resting my head against the door, when we get to the house. Squinting through the window I see a light on upstairs. The clock in Graham's car reads 10:37, so yeah, my odds do not look great.

I'm falling asleep again.

"You need to get to bed, Harper. Are you ready to go inside?"

Weepiness saturates my voice. "I'm a bad person."

Graham sighs. "No, you're not. You're just a very drunk person."

He walks around to my side of the car, opening the door carefully. He guides me up to the front door and pauses.

"You're going to have to be super quiet, okay, Harper?"

I press my finger to my lips. Graham shakes his head, looking more than a little wary. He unlocks the door and we step into the foyer. No, he steps. I trip.

Just as he closes the door behind us, the downstairs light flicks on and I see my father standing at the base of the steps.

"What's going on?" he whispers through clenched teeth.

I lose my footing and stumble sideways into Graham, who catches me and pulls me upright. The nausea is coming back and I start to think maybe—no, definitely, I'm going to throw up.

"Shit," Graham says under his breath.

"Oh, *Harper*," Dad says in probably the most disappointed voice in the whole world.

Then I vomit on my shoes.

The next morning comes too quickly. I wake up all at once, feeling like I never slept. There's that moment, a fraction of a second, before I remember. Then that moment of blissful ignorance ends.

I groan and roll onto my side to push myself up. My head and stomach both feel kind of okay until the blood rushes back to my head, which starts pounding, and the nasty aftertaste of booze and . . . God, vomit, turn my stomach queasy.

After taking a sip of water and deciding that nope, I definitely do not want anything in my stomach, I drag myself into the bathroom and turn on the shower. I'm still wearing the same clothes from last night. Mascara is smudged under my eyes, blending into dark circles that stand out against my skin, which is paler than usual. I climb into the shower but don't have the energy to wash myself properly, so I just sit down in the tub, hugging my knees and letting the water cascade over me until it goes cold.

I shut off the shower and use the sides of the tub to help me stand. Before I wrap a towel around my waist, I stand and inspect my naked body clinically in the mirror. I look for a scar or a bruise, some kind of evidence of what happened last night blooming under my skin. But there's nothing.

He never has to know.

Please don't tell, I'll handle it.

The whispered words scream inside my head. I lean forward as bile inches its way up my throat, and spin around to heave the sick into the toilet. It takes me a few breaths to recover, and my mind is a loop of *What did I do, what have I done?*

I have to tell Declan everything. That I love him, that it was just a mistake. I have to tell him today.

I brush my teeth and wrap the towel around myself again, and for a few minutes I sit silently on my bed, my wet hair plastered to my face and neck, and put off the inevitable. Then I finish getting dressed and pause at the top of the stairs, taking in a deep breath before facing my parents.

Folding his paper, Dad looks up at me. "So. Would you like to tell me what happened last night?"

I lick my lips. They're dry and cracked under my tongue. "I had a drink. And it was stronger than I thought."

I cut a look over to my brother, who stares pointedly back at me, like he's keeping score of the number of lies I tell. Dad looks at him and nods toward the living room. Graham gets up from the table, taking his breakfast plate with him.

Dad rubs his face. "I just don't understand, Harper."

He doesn't say anything else. A minute drags by, and I can't stand the silence.

"I wasn't thinking. I'm really sorry."

"I don't want to hear that you're sorry. I want to know what happened to my smart, sensible daughter." He tosses his paper down and shakes his head. "How could you do this to your mother? Do you have any idea how much we worry about you? We gave you freedom this summer, started trusting you again, and you do this?"

My cheek twitches, and I pinch the skin inside my arm to keep from crying.

"You can trust me."

"I guess we'll see." He clears his throat. "You're grounded until I say otherwise."

"Dad, I'm sorry." It shreds my throat on the way out. I'm so tired of needing to say that word.

"Good. Now go up to your room."

I go upstairs, stopping outside my parents' bedroom. The door is cracked open, and I push it another inch, peeking in at my mother. She's resting on top of her comforter, her head wrapped in a blue silk scarf. She looks over and frowns.

"How are you feeling?" she asks.

I sink against the doorjamb as the first sob rakes out of me. She pats the bed. "Come here."

I crawl onto her bed, curling my knees into my chest, and cry. She reaches over, brushing the hair out of my face.

"I didn't mean to." A breath forces its way into my lungs. "I didn't mean for it to happen."

"Can't change what's already happened," she says. "You just have to learn from it. And you'll have plenty of time to think about it now."

I sit up, wiping my face. "My photography exhibit is tonight. I have to go."

She looks uncertain. "Did you ask your father?"

"I know I'm grounded, but this isn't going out. It's for class."

I hold my breath while she considers it. Finally, she sighs.

"I don't want you gone long. No more than a couple hours."

Two hours isn't much. But it might be enough for one last chance.

Twenty-Six

MR. HARRISON'S GALLERY IS IN A CONVERTED warehouse that from the outside looks a lot like the Bourbon Lounge. Judging from the number of occupied parking spaces, I'm one of the first people to arrive. The sky is overcast and gray, giving the afternoon a brittle feel that sends a chill down my spine as I cross the parking lot.

The interior of the gallery is divided into clean spaces with white walls housing various styles of art. Mr. Harrison's work has been cleared out and replaced with ours for our final class.

As I suspected, only a few of my classmates have arrived, and Mack and Gwen aren't among them. I head straight for the ladies' room and shut myself in a stall.

I tried calling Declan on my way here. I stopped by his house, too. But no one was home.

Or he just didn't answer the door.

I'm hyperventilating. I have to calm down before I see him. Closing my eyes and sinking back against the cool metal wall, I breathe in through my nose, out through my mouth.

He'll understand. He'll understand because . . . he has to.

I've got it all worked out. I'm going to get him away from here first. We'll go for a walk. And then I'll just tell him everything; tell him in a way that doesn't sound like an excuse for my bad decisions.

Exhaling another cleansing breath, I pull open the bathroom door and examine my reflection. I spent extra time on my hair tonight. It's curly, the way Declan likes it. But despite the cool air, I've sweat through my shirt. My hand clutches the fabric, wrinkling it.

"There you are!" Mack springs through the door and I quickly straighten my blouse.

Gwen walks in behind her wearing a tight black dress and an insanely bright pink headband. She notices me smirking at it and pushes it back a bit on her head. "Mackenzie," she says matter-of-factly.

"I figured as much."

Mack walks toward me and leans against the sink next to mine. "Are you feeling okay? You look kind of pale."

"Just the fluorescent lights, probably."

Her nose wrinkles. "Oh. I thought you might be a little . . . under the weather. After last night."

"What happened last night?" Gwen asks.

Mackenzie waits for me to answer, and when I don't she starts picking at her nail polish. "You know, I was hanging out with Cory when you called. He tried calling you back. . . . He said you sounded pretty upset about something."

Another girl from class comes in and shuts the stall door behind her. I turn on the faucet and wash my hands, grateful for the diversion. It doesn't last long enough. As soon as she's gone, Mackenzie corners me. All five feet four of her looks ready to Sherlock the answers out of me.

"So the rest of the night worked out okay, then?"

My stomach clenches because she isn't going to let this go. "Uh-huh."

Gwen holds up her hand. "Okay, both of you are acting so weird. Am I missing something?"

Picking at my lip, I back up against the sink. "You guys haven't talked to Declan?"

She tilts her head. "No. . . ."

Mack reaches for my hand. "Harper, you're shaking. Seriously, what's wrong?"

I throw my paper towel in the trash and my heart stutters after a skipped beat. I rub my sternum. "Um . . . something happened last night."

"Something. What kind of something?"

"There was this party. And Declan was supposed to meet me there, but he said he couldn't make it. So I started drinking, and then . . ."

He never has to know. I bring my fingers to my lips. Try to keep it in.

"And then . . . ," Gwen prompts.

"Kyle showed up. And he had some pot. . . ."

She winces. "Kyle?"

I clench my jaw and close my eyes, pushing the images out of my head. "I tried to leave with Sadie, but she wouldn't even talk to me. So I went inside to get away from him, but he followed me in. He brought me upstairs and then before I really realized what was even happening we were kissing, and he was trying to do other stuff—"

Mack's head whips up and she shifts toward me. "Whoa, wait a minute, what do you mean *before you realized it?* How drunk were you?"

"Three hits, half a pint of vodka. I was beyond drunk. Nothing ever would have happened otherwise."

"Right," Gwen says. "And when you say he was trying to 'do other stuff' . . . what exactly are you saying?"

Swallowing, I squeeze the pendant on my necklace. "I dunno, just that he wanted more, and I was so out of it . . . but when I realized what I was doing—look, we were both really wasted. And I stopped him before things went too far. It was stupid. A mistake."

Mack is still pacing. I don't like it. I want to tell her to quit it because now my knee is bouncing and I don't like that, either.

Laughter carries in from behind the bathroom door. Everyone outside is having fun and living their lives. I want that. I want to stop feeling Kyle's breath on my skin.

My fingers snap the elastic band on my wrist again again again.

Mack's hand covers mine. My leg is still trembling. I flatten my palm on my thigh, trying to force it to stop. "Anyway, when I came out of the room, Declan was there. He saw Kyle, and the look on his face . . ." I shake my head. "He didn't give me a chance to explain. I have to explain; it didn't mean anything."

They exchange a look. I don't trust it.

"You guys have to promise not to say anything. It was nothing; I'm not like that anymore." My voice is rising, becoming panicked.

Gwen holds up her hand. "Calm down, we would never tell people about this."

I'm watching Mack. She's pulling at the ends of her hair again. "Mackenzie?" She looks up. "You can't tell Cory. Promise me."

She drops her hair and crosses her arms. "Of course not."

I turn back to the sink and check my makeup one last time. I have bags under my eyes and I don't think I've been this pale before, ever.

With jittery hands I tuck my hair behind my ears and put on ChapStick. Ready as I'll ever be.

They follow me out the door. Cory is here to support Mack, and she runs over to him right away. But fifteen minutes later, Declan still hasn't shown.

I take a turn about the room, looking at everyone's pictures. I pause in front of Declan's nameplate. No picture.

"I was quite impressed with your submission," Mr. Harrison says behind me.

I turn around. He's actually talking to me. "Oh." I stand up a little straighter and let my necklace slip out of my hand. "Thank you."

He pushes his glasses up his nose and clears his throat, gesturing toward my picture a few feet over. "Okay, Miss Sloan," he says in his teacher voice. "What can you tell me about this shot?"

"Um . . ." I cross my arms and look at the picture. One I took at the cemetery, right before Declan found me. "Well, I like this shot because of the moment I experienced while taking it. It was a long night, and more than anything I just wanted to see a new day begin. I liked the contrast of people who are gone, people we miss, and the idea that we never really know what the future holds. I may not have captured all of that, but it's what I was thinking."

Gwen catches my eye from across the room and weaves her way over.

"I think you captured more than you realize," Mr. Harrison tells me. "You've shown a lot of progress this summer. I hope you'll continue your work."

"Thanks. I will." He moves on to the next shot and I turn my attention to Gwen.

"He's here."

I follow her gaze to the back corner of the room. "Okay."

Okay.

Declan is propped up against a wooden beam, staring at a black-and-white portrait of a mother holding a newborn baby. I try to get a better read on him as I make my way over. Something is off, but I can't quite figure it out. It's the way he's slouched against the boards, like he doesn't have the energy to stand up straight.

"Declan, I really need to talk to you."

His face is shut down, and above his eyebrow is an angry-looking cut.

"Oh my God, what happened to your face?" I touch his forehead and he jerks out of reach. I lower my fingers, unnerved by his appearance. I clear my throat and try again. "Did you have an accident at work or something?"

Finally, he looks at me. The bruise on his temple is worse than I thought. His jaw shifts to one side and he wears a smile that does not reach his eyes and seems more menacing than happy.

He shakes his head at the floor. "Something like that."

Before I can respond, he reaches into his pocket and pulls out a metal flask, waving it in my direction.

"Want some?" He holds the open flask under my nose. The

strong smell of whiskey burns in my nostrils and makes my stomach roll. I turn my head away. "Suit yourself."

Glancing over my shoulder, I make sure no one has noticed us and lean closer. "Dec, put that away."

He takes a long pull from it instead. He laughs, fumbling as he screws the cap back on. "What, did I bring the wrong liquor?"

The collar of his shirt is kinked up on one side and I want to fix it, but touching him again seems like a very bad idea. Declan is a tensed coil, and there is more belligerence in his eyes than I've ever seen before. I have no idea what his next move will be. Whether he will lash out or shatter.

He steps around me. Pauses. Snaps his fingers like he just remembered something. "Oh, and since you asked, I got fired this morning."

With that, he moves for the door, leaving me reeling from this new information and puzzled over what, exactly, his getting fired has to do with the way he just looked at me. Like I was someone he recognized but didn't really know.

He's already out the door when I start to chase after him.

"Declan, hold on!" He doesn't. "Will you please wait?"

My flip-flops slap loudly on the concrete sidewalk as I follow him all the way to the parking lot.

He spins around when he reaches my car, sliding onto the hood. Lifting the flask to his lips, he locks his eyes on mine and takes another shot. The taste doesn't seem to faze him.

"Listen, you have the wrong idea about last night."

He half smiles again, gesturing toward me with the flask gripped in his right hand. I notice for the first time that his knuckles are scraped and raw. My fingers tighten around the fabric of my shirt.

"Yeah? So what were you doing upstairs?"

I snap the elastic on my wrist and he notices. The corners of his mouth sink lower and his eyes narrow and it's awful.

"I went inside to use the bathroom," I say quietly.

Declan taps the flask against the hood.

Tap.

Tap.

Tap.

Tap.

I'm transfixed, flinching every time he makes contact. He breaks me.

"I was upset," I add. "I wanted to get away from the party. But then I kept running into people."

"Like who?"

The tapping stops. I can't get my voice to work.

"Who." He spits the word like it gives him a bad taste in his mouth.

Kyle's name comes out as a whisper, and although Declan begins to nod, his face remains the same: a carefully placed mask that has no dimples, no crooked smile. His eyes are as flat and gray as the sky above us. And I miss him; I miss my favorite Declan.

He slides off the car. "Couldn't even wait until I left town this time, huh?"

"No, that isn't—you don't understand."

He stares at the ground. "I got fired because I overheard Kyle telling all his preppy golf buddies—in a tremendous amount of detail, I might add—about how he hooked up with Harper Sloan at a party last night. He was saying things about you. . . ." Declan's jaw knots. "I confronted him. I got in his face and told him he needed to shut his mouth. I called him a liar."

I glance at his hand again and all the pieces come together. He takes a step toward me and the betrayal and hurt in his eyes rip through me and sever the last shred of self-respect I had left. His mouth barely moves when he speaks again.

"I've never been a very good judge of when I'm being lied to, though, have I?"

"You just have to let me explain."

"Explain what?"

My whole body is trembling. I pull my arms tighter across my stomach and dig my nails into my sides.

"What is it you want to tell me?"

He has a horrible, derisive smile on his face now, and my own mouth is closed with magnets. All of the words I chose before coming here are trapped beneath the lump in my throat. I can't get them out. Instead, I step closer to him, stopping short at his next words.

"Because, really, Kyle didn't leave much to the imagination."

"It's not what you think."

"No?" he asks in a tight voice.

Panic rises in my chest. I shake my head.

"Did something happen with him or not, Harper?"

My vision blurs and I dig my nails in harder, but I can barely feel it; my ribs are splintering.

"Yes," I breathe, my voice so soft it's a wonder he hears me.

But he hears me. His lips smash together and his breathing is heavy and he's blinking too fast. It hurts to look at; I have to make it stop.

"You don't understand," I rush to continue. My purse slips off my shoulder and crashes to the ground in my effort to get closer. I pull his arm as he turns away. "I was really messed up; it was a mistake!"

He hurls the flask across the parking lot and steps toward me with hair in his face. "Then I understand perfectly!"

His growl echoes across the half-empty lot and I keep repeating *I'm sorry, please, I'm so, so, sorry*. I keep reaching, too, trying always to get closer, close enough to rest my forehead against his, show him—*you and me*—but Declan won't let me touch him.

When he grows tired of pulling away, he turns and backs me into the side of my car. I can smell the whiskey and I do not like angry-drunk Declan.

He swallows. It makes his Adam's apple bob in his throat. He swallows again. "So did he get you off?" A whimper escapes my lips and I look away. He dips his head down so he's in my line of sight again. His eyes are wild. "You wanted to talk about it! Let's talk! Was he good?"

My hands are in my hair and I can't do this.

I stifle a sob and Declan pushes away from the car. "Whatever he said to you isn't the truth! He brought me upstairs and we sat on the bed and I told him—"

"Stop. I don't want to hear anything else." He steps back. "You think I'm gonna hold your hand when you're upset and then stand by while you screw around with another guy? And lie about it? I'm not a placeholder until you find someone you like better."

"No! I just—" Every time I try to speak my truth I feel it all over again: liquor burning in my stomach, the room spinning in my head, Kyle's body weighing me down—smothering me. I can taste him. "I lost control. And we were kissing, but it wasn't real; I didn't even want to do it."

He starts to pace and I follow him around my car, stumbling over a pothole as I try desperately to hold on to some part of him. Each time he slips through my fingers.

"I don't know how it happened; I'm so in love with you—"

"Bullshit!" He yanks his arm free again. "Don't say that to me now. Those are just words."

Any lingering hope I'd harbored flickers out. It's my fault, but I'm not sure how much anymore, and how can I say it any differently?

He laughs and covers his mouth. "I can't believe this. After everything I did this summer—working my ass off so that I could stay here with you—"

"What?" I'm in a vacuum of his words. "Are you . . . You're staying?"

He doesn't answer.

I reach for his hand again. "Declan, you are my best friend. You're everything." He tries to pull away and I don't let him. "It meant nothing!"

He knocks my hand away and pulls his fingers through his tangled hair, clutching at his scalp. "Just stop. Stop fucking with me, Harper. I'm so sick of your lies."

"I'm not lying, I'm trying to make you understand that what happened with Kyle . . . I didn't want it. I was confused, I thought—" I lick my lips but the rest won't come. "But I said no. It shouldn't have happened."

He glares at me. Deafened by his own anger. "It doesn't even matter. If it wasn't Kyle it just would have been someone else. Right, Sloan?"

"What?"

"I'm just saying, it's not like this is the first time we've been here." He holds my gaze, nodding slightly. "What happened in October?"

My forehead wrinkles. "You said it didn't matter."

He shrugs. "Changed my mind."

I step back. "You already know, don't you?"

"I want to hear you say it."

My throat is closing and my voice barely makes it through. "Please, don't do this."

He inches closer, close enough to kiss me, and the force of his hate makes me feel smaller and lesser than I have ever felt.

"*You* did this, Harper. And I am done with you."

My mouth tastes like metal. I'm biting my lip too hard, but I won't run away this time. I have to fix it. "It wasn't—I didn't want . . ."

"Go ahead. Enlighten me. I would love to know what it is that *you want*." His voice becomes harder. Crueler. "Because somehow, fucking idiot that I am, I actually started to believe you wanted to be with *me*. Turns out, all a guy has to do to get you into bed is pour you a shot of cold vodka."

In the sudden silence, his speech howls inside my head and hovers in the space between us. Attacking me over and over again until I go numb.

The air shatters, and the breath I finally draw in is filled with daggers. They scrape sharply against the backs of my lungs.

"That might be the meanest thing anyone has ever said to me," I whisper.

I fold forward, hugging my stomach.

His eyes squeeze shut and he pushes his fists into his temples. "Just tell me why."

He isn't even there anymore, the Declan who loved me. I lost him. It's done. There will be no redemption in his eyes. And all the man in front of me wants is to feel justified.

And I don't have anything left that isn't already broken.

So I tell him what he wants to hear.

"You know why." He stares at me like it's a trick. It isn't. "I'm a terrible fucking person. I'm selfish." My voice catches, but it doesn't stop me. "I'm a slut."

"Don't."

"Just say it."

I need to hear him say it. Need him to hurt me enough that he'll have to take some of the blame for us not being together. It's crushing me, the burden of our ruined relationship. I can't carry it all by myself anymore.

If he's going to hate me, if that's how all of this ends, then he is going to have to do much better. He has to hate me well enough for me to let him go.

We're almost there.

I push his shoulder and follow him as he jerks backward. "Come on, Dec. It's what you're thinking. Just say it!"

His head is hanging, and he lifts it to look at the sky before looking back down at me. His eyes fall on my necklace and he lets out an empty laugh that's actually closer to a grimace.

"That's how you want me to treat you?"

I don't respond. Don't move. Just hold my breath while the fragments of my heart ache inside my chest.

Then he lunges, roughly smashing his lips onto mine like he wants to throw all the pain I caused him back at me in one kiss. His tongue aggressively swirls the taste of whiskey into my mouth. His hand on my neck prevents me from pulling away, which I want to do because this is not how Declan kisses me, this is not how he treats me, and I miss his peppermint-laced kisses, and I was wrong.

I was wrong when I thought I could not be more broken.

My forearms are pinned between us, and it isn't until I stop struggling and start crying that Declan's lips soften. His hand slips down to my collarbone. His forehead rests against mine.

My arms are free and I hear the slap before I realize I've done it.

A sob works its way up and out and I cover my mouth. Try to wipe it all away. But I can still feel the pressure of his mouth on mine, and the sour taste of whiskey won't budge.

We stare into each other's eyes and I know I've gotten my wish, because his are filled with regret. So much hurt volleys between us, and he reaches out for me.

"Don't touch me." He takes another step and I shove him as hard as I can. "I hate you. You swore nothing you heard would change what you thought about me. You are just as much of a liar as I am."

His forehead wrinkles and he whispers he's sorry.

My head falls into my hands and I slump down to the pavement.

He's sorry.

And I'm sorry.

And it isn't enough to fix anything.

Twenty-Seven

I AM LOST IN THE UNSPOKEN BATTLE BETWEEN US, and I don't hear the footsteps or see Cory coming until he pulls Declan roughly away from me.

Cory doubles back for me and my eyes snap to Mackenzie, who is just catching up.

She told.

"Tell me what happened. Tell me what that son of a bitch did to you."

Declan lists forward. "I didn't mean to hurt her."

Cory ignores him, wants answers from me, and I look to Gwen, silently pleading with her to help me get out of this.

She steps between us. "Cory," she says firmly. "Back off. This isn't helping her."

Cory's eyes soften.

"You called me. I knew you were messed up but I didn't realize . . ." He runs his hand down the back of his neck. He shakes his head and I shake mine, because he can't possibly be blaming himself. "Are you okay?"

I look down at my hands, as if the answers are written on my palms.

Absurdly, Declan starts to laugh. "That's so perfect," he says, leveling a glare at Cory. "Hey, Mackenzie. How does it feel to have a boyfriend who's always coming to another girl's rescue?"

Cory's face turns crimson. His hand closes into a fist and for the first time in our lives, I really think he might hit Declan. But once again, Gwen intervenes.

"Shut up, Declan. You don't know what you're talking about."

He does shut up. He stumbles forward, looking at her—at each of us. He is drenched in wariness, like he's just stumbled upon a conspiracy against him.

"You tell me what's going on, then," he challenges her. "Why everyone's always defending her."

Gwen's eyes flick to me and he follows them. My hand involuntarily clutches my shirt. I can't do this all over again.

I slide past him to pick my purse up off the ground.

"You're truly amazing, you know that?" he spits from behind me. I find my keys and squeeze them to keep my hand from shaking. "How do you do it? Lie and treat people like they don't matter but still manage to keep our friends in your corner?"

Behind him, Mack is crying and Gwen is shaking her head and I am so empty inside.

"You still don't get it."

"No, I get it. I didn't want to believe it at first, but I get it now. Everything they say about you is true."

Cory grabs him, but he somehow manages to stand his ground.

"Then I guess your mind is already made up about me." I move to my car and Mackenzie is there. She takes the keys out of my trembling hand and guides me to the passenger's side. "But for the record, I didn't sleep with Kyle."

He strides forward, pointing his finger at me. "No, you—you're lying. You just said you did."

"I said something happened."

Declan's eyes are ticking back and forth, from me to Cory to Gwen. But still, he says nothing. And only one thing is left for me to say:

"There's a difference."

We sit on my porch in silence for a long time. Mackenzie rubs circles on my back, waiting. For me to be okay. For Cory to come home. For Declan to realize his mistake. Waiting.

Pretending is easy. I stand when Cory pulls into his driveway. Take a breath and thank Mackenzie for driving me home. Wipe my cheek and smile. Tell them I'm *finejustfine.*

They don't believe me.

But neither did Declan and now nothing matters.

Once I'm alone in my bedroom, I open my top dresser drawer. Reaching behind my neck, I unclasp his necklace. I grip the pendant tightly. And then I let go.

Twenty-Eight

FOR TWO DAYS I DON'T CHANGE OUT OF MY pajamas. I stay in bed until my bones ache and Mom yells at me to come down and eat something. Then I sit at the table and shred, shred, shred my food down because I can't eat, can't even think about having anything in my stomach. My stomach shrank at the same time my heart did, and there's no room.

On day three of being grounded, my phone dies. I don't recharge it. As far as I'm concerned, my parents can keep me locked in my room until I graduate. I don't even care anymore.

But Mom has never had much patience for moping. When I come downstairs for breakfast—a cup of coffee and four pretzels—she descends.

"Morning, honey!"

I grunt and shove another pretzel in my mouth, letting the salt dissolve on my tongue before chewing.

"So, I think we should leave in about twenty minutes. You better scoot if you want to wash your hair first."

I pause, midchew. Aside from the slight against my personal hygiene, I have no clue what she's talking about. "We're going somewhere?"

"Shopping! You need some back-to-school clothes, don't you?"

What is the deal with all this sunshine and happiness? Did she forget I'm being punished?

I swallow the pretzel-mush. "You want to buy me clothes?"

She smiles. "I think it will be nice to get out for a bit."

"You sure you're up for it?" I ask.

"Absolutely. It's a good day."

I open my mouth to protest some more, and Mom cuts me off.

"Look, sweetie, sometimes happiness is a choice. The cancer and the chemo are out of my hands, but I choose to have a life outside of my treatment. And I know you think my attitude is an act and that I'm being strong for you and your brother and father, but quite honestly, I just want to get out of this house for a little while." She smiles and gives me a side hug. "So, the mall opens in ten minutes."

And that about settles it. Because, okay, this may be the last thing I feel like doing. And I may be far from the perfect daughter. But I'm not going to say no to my sick mother when she's asking to buy me things.

"Okay . . . I'll just go shower, then."

"Great idea."

Twenty-five minutes later we're on our way, and Mom is singing along to the Top 40 station. She lowers the volume and glances my way.

"I noticed you're not wearing your necklace anymore."

My fingers curl around the collar of my shirt. For three days I've been trying not to think about him. Trying to forget the way he looked at me; the awful things he said.

And the worst part is, I still don't know whether he's staying or going.

No. The *worst* part is that even his cruelty the other night wasn't enough. I still love him.

"Did something happen with Declan?" she asks.

I bite the inside of my cheek. "It just doesn't fit anymore."

She pulls into the parking deck of the mall and finds a spot. Clicking off her seat belt, she turns to me. "Well, that does happen."

"Shall we?" I jump out of the car before she can ask a follow-up question.

Mom leads us straight to the activewear department.

"Look," she says. "Swimsuits are forty percent off! Why don't you try on a few—your old practice suit is getting a little ratty."

She looks down to sort through a rack of one-pieces, giving me a view of the top of her head. About a week ago she got tired of having random tufts of hair all over her scalp, and shaved the rest off. She doesn't like wearing the wigs on hot days, and the lavender scarf on her head is semisheer.

I'm almost used to seeing her without hair. And that scares me. Like, what if this is how I'll always see her now? Or what if she doesn't get the chance to grow it back?

But she will. The treatment has been going well—or according to plan, anyway. And her surgery is scheduled in another couple of months. She'll beat this. If Mom can believe in that, so can I.

"Here." She holds out a few hangers.

I take them into the dressing room and close the door behind me. Sitting on the plywood bench in the corner of the small space, I run my hands over the spandex fabric. They're not the same quality as my best training suits, but to get those I'd have to drive out to Raleigh or order online. Not that I really need a new suit in the first place. Mom still doesn't get that swimming is part of my old life.

Sometimes I do wonder whether I could get it back, though. I mean, Mom's right about one thing: I could try out again this fall. And sure, I wouldn't be captain anymore. But that was never really the point. The point was, I loved it.

I think of what Mom said about happiness being a choice.

Letting go of the things I can't control is never as easy as she makes it out to be, but maybe she does have the right idea. I mean, if she can manage to enjoy life despite having freaking cancer, then there's really no reason for me to wallow in my mistakes or let them dictate my whole future.

I strip down and put on one of the suits, then peek my head out the door. "Mom?"

"Right here." She steps around the corner and looks me over, nodding her approval. "That's darling. How does it feel?"

I turn back to the mirror. Looking at myself in this suit, I realize my mind is already made up.

"It feels good," I say.

It feels like change. And for once, I think it might be exactly the kind of change I need.

The next day is a Friday, the last one before school starts. And there's this energy in the air. Like everything is about to be different. Starting with Graham.

"All right," he says after loading his last bag into the back of his car. "Time to go."

He bends down to give Mom a gentle hug. She kisses his cheek and then holds his face between her palms. "No speeding, you hear me?"

"No speeding."

Dad claps him on the back. "You give your mother a call

sometime, okay? I don't want to go until Thanksgiving without hearing from you."

"I will. I might even come home for a weekend before that. We'll see how my schedule is."

I walk him around his car. "Finally have my bathroom to myself again."

He smirks. "I'll miss you too." He gives me a hug and gets in the car. He turns it on and rolls down the window. "Anytime you need help around here, with Mom or anything . . . I'm just a call away, okay?"

"I know. Thanks, Graham."

"Senior year." He puts on sunglasses and nods, like he's such a cool college kid, and smirks. "Be good."

"I'll do my best."

He backs out of the driveway, and I watch until he's all the way down the street. When I go back inside, the house feels emptier. Especially since Mom and Dad are on their way out too.

Mom's in the kitchen, packing her bag. She has another chemo session today.

"Honey, do you know where that gardening book is?" she asks Dad. "One of the nurses wanted to borrow it."

It's amazing that even at the hospital, where she goes specifically to get chemo, people still know Mom likes to garden and cook, and that she's more than just a cancer patient. Because she never lets the disease define her.

She finds the book and stuffs it in her bag. "We'll be back around dinnertime," she says to me. "And there's lunch meat in the fridge, okay?"

Dad grabs his keys off the counter. "Call if you need me."

"Of course. See you guys later."

Then they're out the door, and the house is entirely too quiet. I go up to my room and plug my phone in. It buzzes to life, and about a dozen messages from Mack and Gwen pop up. There are a few from Cory, too.

None from Declan.

I pace around my room for a few minutes, humming like a crazy person. But my phone finds its way back into my hands, and I type out a message.

Can we—

I hold down the delete button and toss my phone onto my bed. I start putting away clean laundry and take the tags off the clothes I got with Mom. The new bathing suit is at the bottom of the bag.

My thoughts shift to the swim team, to Jenny and that last day in the locker room. Jenny and I never talked about what happened with Jake. I never even apologized to her. And I can't help but wonder whether the past few months might have been different if I had. If I'd faced the fallout head-on instead of allowing her to hear a skewed version of the truth from someone else.

I'm tired of avoiding people. Tired of shouldering all the

blame. I don't want my senior year to be a blur of hiding in the library during lunch, or cringing every time I pass Jenny. I'm already ill at the thought of running into Kyle, and the list of people to steer clear of is getting laughably long for a place as small as Carson.

But maybe it isn't too late. Every attempt to talk in person has been a disaster, and I'm pretty sure it won't be any easier come school on Monday. I need to find a different way to reach out to her.

I leave the swimsuit where it is and scan my bedroom. My eyes sweep across my desk and land on my photography notebook. A letter. I grab the notebook and turn to a blank page. I fill it with writing, then two more pages after that. Then I carefully tear along the perforated edge and find Jenny's address in my old team directory. I write it neatly on an envelope and seal it, grabbing a stamp from the desk in my parents' room.

The mail already came this morning, and this letter can't hang around in my mailbox until tomorrow. I have to get it out of my hands right now. I grab my keys but stop at the top of the stairs.

I walk back into my room and stare at the shopping bag on my bed.

Technically, I am still extremely grounded. But Mom and Dad won't be home from the hospital for another three hours. And really, Mom is the one who kept pressuring me about the swim team. She's the one who told me I have to practice. I grab the swimsuit and head out the front door.

As soon as I drop the envelope into the blue postal box outside the community center, I feel the weight lift off my shoulders. I don't expect Jenny to forgive me, or even understand the mistakes I've made. But taking responsibility for it, acknowledging that I hurt her and let the team down and that I'm sorry—that's enough for now.

The familiar smell of chlorine hits me on my way to the locker room, and I inhale deeply. I change and stash my stuff and then I can't wait any longer. I need to be underwater.

When I dive into a lane, despite the months I've spent out of a pool, it feels safe. In the water, I focus only on my breathing. *Kick, three strokes, breathe.* Everything else falls away.

An hour later, arms burning and legs noodly, I finish my laps and head back to the locker room. Still wrapped up in a towel, I pull my phone out of my bag.

Can we talk?

I hesitate, staring at the blinking cursor. Declan said things that were meant to cut me in places he knew would hurt most. But I hurt him first, and I can't keep letting history repeat itself. I want to make things right, tell him the whole truth once and for all.

I press send and finish drying off. My shirt is halfway over my head when my phone buzzes with a new message. My heart starts to race before I can register who it's from. But it's Gwen again, checking in.

I try not to feel disappointed. Try to summon a smile as I dial Gwen's number.

She picks up almost immediately. "Well, it's about damn time."

"You can't be mad at me, I'm grounded."

She seems to consider this. "How grounded?"

I shrug the phone between my cheek and shoulder and grab the rest of my stuff out of my locker. I'm actually terrified of getting caught breaking the rules. I don't want to disappoint my parents, and I especially don't want to incur Dad's wrath if he finds out I snuck out. I have a long road ahead to gain their confidence again.

But the fact is, at this moment, I can't really get into any more trouble. And I'm probably not going to have another opportunity to see my friends for a long time.

"I have a bit of wiggle room."

I meet Gwen at Frank's to pick at pancakes and sip on coffee. She's trying so hard to make conversation, but every subject seems to be a sensitive one.

"So . . . Mack told me Declan is staying?"

I shrug and light up the screen of my phone. For the millionth time. "I'm not sure. It sounded like it, though."

She's itching to ask me how I feel about that, I just know. But what she says instead is, "Also heard you slapped him pretty good before we got out there."

"I was upset . . . but I shouldn't have done that."

"Sounds to me like he had it coming," she says quietly.

"Doesn't make it right."

A rambunctious group walks in and takes a booth behind us. I glance over my shoulder and snap back around. Stab my straw into the ice. Focus on the crunching.

"What?" Gwen looks over my shoulder. "What is it?"

My stomach has vanished. It's just a hollow space there now, leaving room for the rest of my organs to spin.

She sees him. "Oh my God. Is that Kyle?"

Her jaw drops. She's glaring at him, and then pulling her things together. She hesitates with one foot in the aisle, apparently torn between getting me to talk and getting me the hell out of here.

"It's okay," I say. I lick my lips and nod. "Really."

She has her purse in her hand. "Are you sure?"

"We go to the same school." I stab my straw into the ice again. "I can't avoid him forever."

As discreetly as possible, I peek again. His face is seriously fucked up. Black eye, busted lip. Cut across the bridge of his nose. A smile tugs at my lips but then it's gone, because picturing Declan doing that to him doesn't make me feel better. And imagining what Kyle must have said to make Declan snap *definitely* isn't helping.

Gwen wipes her mouth. "So, I guess your honor was sufficiently defended. . . ."

My phone buzzes on the table.

We both stare at it. With a shallow breath, I tilt the screen toward me.

I'd like that. Can you meet me? I'm at the quarry.

"He wants to meet."

She leans forward. "That's good, right?"

My heart is pounding. "Yeah. I'm just . . . I don't know what to say to him."

She smiles. "Say everything."

"Right. Okay, I have to go." I toss a few bills onto the table. Gwen stands and turns to go out the side door. "No. This way."

Kyle glares as I walk past. But I keep my head held high and I meet his stare. And I hold on to my truth.

With everything I have, I hold on.

Twenty-Nine

HE'S WAITING AT THE QUARRY'S EDGE, HUNCHED forward with his forearms resting on his thighs. He glances up when he hears my footsteps. Slowly, I walk the last couple of feet and sit next to him. We both stare at the water.

He lets out a broken breath. "Are you okay?"

"There's a difference," I whisper. "I was drunk. Kyle took advantage of that. And I know I shouldn't have put myself in that position, but I didn't want to be with Kyle. You need to understand that."

"I know." He looks up again, and my pain is his pain is my pain. "But you're okay?"

I hug my arms around myself and cave in. "I'm okay."

He stands and holds his hand out. "Let's take a walk."

"A walk?" The skepticism comes through in my voice.

"Not far. There's something I want to show you."

My palm slips into his and he helps me up. He holds my hand for a moment longer than he needs to, and then he lets go.

I follow him along the quarry. He veers into the forest, but I hesitate. I've figured out where he's taking me.

He looks over his shoulder. "Okay?"

The nerves about returning to our spot after all this time are overshadowed only by the dread that it won't be there at all. But I nod and keep moving. We walk the rest of the way in silence. Finally, we reach the tree house. I stop at the trunk and resist the urge to hug it. Looking up, I picture us the last time we were here. Me in my green dress and Declan in his button-down shirt. Racing up the ladder to escape the rain.

"Why did you bring me here?"

He takes a deep breath. "Do you remember what you said to me the night before I left?"

I reach for the necklace that isn't there anymore.

"You said it didn't matter that we'd be apart. Because we had forever. You said you'd wait. And then six weeks later, you were done waiting." He pauses. "I replayed our conversations over and over, trying to figure out what I'd done wrong."

"It wasn't that you did anything wrong."

"But I wasn't enough."

I blink against the burning in my eyes. "Don't say that."

He shifts, and it's excruciating, seeing it in his eyes. All the

309

damage I've done. "I've been so angry with you for so long, Harper. When I got back this summer, I figured I'd take the high road. Be there for you even though you weren't there for me. Because I wanted to prove you couldn't hurt me anymore."

The first tears spill over my lashes. I wipe my cheeks and cover my mouth.

"But then you kissed me at that party." He shakes his head. "And everything just came crashing down on me." He scratches his eyebrow and crosses his arms. "I wanted to kiss you back. And that made me angry all over again. But by the time I sorted things out and tried to talk to you, you'd already moved on."

I rock forward. "I was being so stupid. And I thought you were into Mackenzie. But I never cared about Kyle, you have to know that."

"How could I have known that? I mean, if that's true . . ."

It feels like getting punched in the stomach. "You still don't believe me about the other night, do you?"

He runs his hands down his face. "I . . ."

"Oh my God." I shrink back, tripping over a twig.

"Harper, wait." He strides forward, taking both my hands in his. "Of course I do. I believe you. And when I think about him putting his hands on you . . ." He grits his teeth and takes a long breath in and out. "But it was too easy for me to think it was happening all over again. That you were choosing someone else, rejecting me again. I was insanely jealous, and hurt—"

"But that's what I've been trying to tell you! I don't care about him, or anyone else. It's only ever been you."

His lips press together. "And that's why you kept my necklace?"

Relief washes over me. "Yes!"

"But you're not wearing it now."

I shift my gaze to the forest. "The other night, you were so . . ." I swallow. "You made me feel terrible about myself. I never thought you were capable of that."

His eyes close. He blinks them open and squeezes my hand. "There's no excuse for the things I said. The way I treated you . . ." He grimaces. "I am so sorry. You have no idea how sorry I am for hurting you."

But I do know. I know exactly how it feels to face someone after showing them the ugliest part of yourself.

Say everything.

"I'm sorry too. You deserved better from me. You deserved the truth."

"You tried to explain—"

"I'm not talking about the other night."

The contradiction slips off his face. "Oh."

I clasp my arms around myself. "What happened in October . . . I was terrified to tell you. I knew how you felt about my drinking, and I'd never been that wasted before. I blacked out. And the next day, when I realized what I'd done, I just . . . panicked. I didn't want to hurt you more than I already had, and I was sure I'd lose you anyway, so . . . I took the decision away from you. And I had no right to do that."

We're quiet for a moment, and I make a thousand wishes that we could go back. Change one thing, or change everything, and not have to do this. Not have to spend the next week or month or year making up for the fact that we hurt each other. That we are still hurting.

But we can't go back. The only way to change our past is by adding to it.

"Here," he says. "The thing I wanted to show you . . ."

He leads me around the tree and lets go of my hand, gesturing ahead of us. I stumble forward, not knowing what to look for. And then I spot the carving.

An infinity symbol, with our initials inside. I trace my fingers over the lopsided figure eight.

"When did you—"

"Last winter. When I was home for break. I got this idea in my head that you might see it. That it might make you change your mind."

I shut my eyes, sending a river down my cheek. I blink my vision clear and turn around.

"I have to leave again." He's staring at the ground between us. "My dad was going to let me stay, but then I got into that fight . . ." He cocks his head and smiles tightly. "He wasn't happy about it."

"So . . . what does that mean?" I don't say *for us*.

I hold my breath while he shuffles closer. "No matter what I said, or how I acted, I never gave up on our promise. I want to work this out, and I can wait. I'll wait as long as you need. I'll come home more often, holidays and weekends, I'll do whatever it takes. But after the way I treated you, if you can't . . ."

I focus on my hands. "I waited too, you know. I kept that promise."

He's searching my face. Then he's touching my cheek. "Harper . . . I'll understand if it's really over. I just need to know."

I lean into his touch, hungry for it even after everything that's happened. His eyes flicker back and forth between mine. The crease in his forehead stays put, but his lips soften. Slow as the tide, his mouth moves to the corner of mine, then ebbs. He's suspended millimeters above me, and then gently presses his lips against mine.

A residual sting runs down my sternum, and I pull back. Declan winces.

But this is not the same person who made me cry in an empty parking lot. This is my best friend. My favorite Declan.

Covering his hand with my own, I turn and brush my lips across his open palm. Then I tilt my chin up and our lips meet and it's sweeter than any touch we've ever had—our new best kiss.

Declan's thumb trails across my jaw while my hand curves around his neck, and I can feel Declan's smile and it is so contagious. He smiles harder, and then we're not even kissing anymore, just beaming at each other.

I try to forgive everything in that moment. Forgive Declan, for losing faith in me when I needed it most. For hurting me. And I try to forgive myself, too. For every epic mistake and for losing myself in them. It doesn't happen all at once, but I'll find that forgiveness, eventually.

Eventually, all of this will be behind us, only a small part of who we are. We may never reach a life entirely absent of regret, or forget the missteps we made along the way. All we can do is keep moving.

So I move closer. I slide my arms around his waist and rest my forehead against his.

"You and me, Declan . . . we'll never be over."

Acknowledgments

I'm incredibly fortunate to have met so many kind and talented members of the writing community on my road to publication, and I am forever grateful for all the support they have given me along the way.

My deepest gratitude goes to my agent, Lara Perkins, for all her guidance and for loving Harper and Declan as much as I do. Thank you for believing in me and for your thoughtful approach to everything you do. I am so lucky to have you in my corner.

Many heartfelt thanks to my incomparable editor, Sara Sargent. Thank you for swooning over Declan and, more importantly, for pushing me to do my best work, for challenging me and giving me room to grow. And for buying me my first butterbeer.

To the team at Simon Pulse, who have been amazing to work with and who took my cover thoughts and turned them into something truly beautiful. Endless thanks for all you've done to bring this book to life.

To my dear friend Olivia, for putting up with countless rambling calls/emails/texts about character arcs and for insisting Harper's story was worth telling, even after reading the terrible first draft—I love you more than sweet potato pancakes, and I couldn't have done this without you.

This story really grew its wings during a contest called Pitch Wars. To Evelyn Skye, for picking my manuscript to mentor and for killing so many of my darlings. Declan and I will always be indebted to you. And to Brenda Drake, for creating such a supportive and welcoming community, and for putting so much time and energy into helping other writers succeed. Thanks for being so awesome.

To my brilliant CP Laurie Elizabeth Flynn, thank you for your unwavering enthusiasm and encouragement through-out this crazy journey. I'm glad we got to share so many firsts together. (See what I did there?)

To my early readers, especially those who suffered through more than one draft: Jenna, Katie, Emily, and Lindsey—you guys are my heroes.

Thank you to my family, and especially my parents, for teaching me to follow my dreams, and for their patience, love, and support during all the years it took me to figure out what those dreams were.

Last but not least, my infinite thanks to Jim. Thank you for giving me the strength to keep going, even on the days I convinced myself I was wasting my time. Thank you for keeping me fed when inspiration struck and I couldn't tear myself away from this story, and for cleaning up after me when I was under deadline. I love you forever and always.